THE UNFORTUNATE IMPORTANCE OF

BEAUTY

THE UNFORTUNATE IMPORTANCE OF

a novel

AMANDA FILIPACCHI

W. W. NORTON & COMPANY
NEW YORK · LONDON

For information about permission to reproduce selections from this book,
write to Permissions, W. W. Norton & Company, Inc.,
500 Fifth Avenue, New York, NY 10110

For information about special discounts for bulk purchases, please contact
W. W. Norton Special Sales at specialsales@wwnorton.com or 800-233-4830

Manufacturing by R R Donnelley, Harrisonburg
Book design by Chris Welch Design
Production managers: Devon Zahn and Ruth Toda

Library of Congress Cataloging-in-Publication Data

Filipacchi, Amanda.
The unfortunate importance of beauty : a novel /
Amanda Filipacchi. — First edition.
pages ; cm
ISBN 978-0-393-24387-1 (hardcover)
I. Title.
PS3556.I428U54 2015
813'.54—dc23

2014037010

W. W. Norton & Company, Inc.
500 Fifth Avenue, New York, N.Y. 10110
www.wwnorton.com

W. W. Norton & Company Ltd.
Castle House, 75/76 Wells Street, London W1T 3QT

2 3 4 5 6 7 8 9 0

For Richard, and for my parents, Sondra Peterson and
Daniel Filipacchi

PART
ONE

Chapter One

Dr. Miriam Levy (Clinical Psychologist)

I'm waiting for my new patient to arrive, not suspecting that within the next hour she'll reveal herself to be the most interesting patient I've ever had.

Her name is Barb Colby. When we spoke on the phone, she claimed to be twenty-eight years old, but the woman who waddles into my office looks at least forty. She's quite overweight and tall, with glasses and frizzy gray hair. As I gaze at her face more closely, however, I notice that her skin isn't wrinkled. Perhaps she was telling the truth about her age.

She takes a seat.

"What brings you here?" I ask.

"It's my mother's dying wish that I see a therapist."

"Oh, I'm sorry. Your mother is dying?" I make a note of this in my pad.

"No. She's in great health, thankfully. But it's an early request. When she tried asking for it as her birthday present, I ignored it."

I cross out my note. "Why does your mother want you to see a therapist?"

"Because she doesn't like the way I look."

"The way you look . . . at life?" I say, not wishing to be pre-sumptuous a second time.

Barb seems confused. "Maybe that, but what I mean is she doesn't like my appearance."

"Ah. And she feels this issue would best be tackled psychologically?"

"Yes."

"As opposed to joining a gym or getting a makeover, for example?" I ask, just to be certain.

"That is correct."

"What does she dislike about the way you look?" The answer seems obvious, but again, it's best not to assume anything.

"She doesn't like my hair, my fat, my clothes, my glasses."

I keep making notes in my pad as she talks. I nod and say, "I see. I'm glad your mother convinced you to seek help. I think I can help you. In my work, I see a lot of women who suffer from low self-esteem. They think they're unattractive, but the way society today—"

"I don't think I'm unattractive," she says.

"That's good. That's great. It's not something women are always aware of on a conscious level, though. So, I would like you to be open-minded to the possibility that perhaps, deep down, you might be feeling unattractive without being aware of it. And if that's the case, you might feel there's no point in even *trying* to look better."

"Yeah but, no. I don't think I'm unattractive. And I don't think it subconsciously either."

I smile. "If it's subconscious, you wouldn't know it."

"Your comments are entirely influenced by the fact that *you* think I'm unattractive," she says. "If you thought I were beautiful, you wouldn't be suggesting I might subconsciously think I'm ugly."

"No need to get defensive. And anyway, what I think doesn't matter. It's what *you* think that matters. I want to try to help you to find yourself beautiful."

"I already do."

"That's good. And I'd like to get you to take baby steps toward making more effort with your appearance, if that's something you want."

"I make great effort with my appearance."

"I guess your mother doesn't agree, right? That's why you're here."

"Yes, she does. She wants me to make less effort with my appearance."

"Less effort? What effort would she like you to make less of?"

She doesn't reply.

"Can you give me an example?"

She remains silent.

"That shouldn't be too hard, right? To come up with just one example?" I say, clasping my hands (smugly, I must admit).

"No, it's not too hard," she replies.

"Okay, then, I'm all ears."

"It's not your ears you need. It's your eyes," she says, taking off her glasses and setting them on the little table next to her.

She reaches down into her bag and pulls out a small plastic container. She unscrews the lid. She sticks her fingers in each of her eyes and removes brown contact lenses, which she then drops into the plastic container.

She looks at me and her gaze is dazzling. The effect is that of light shining through aqua-colored glass.

She gets up, sinks her hands into her gray frizzy hair and pulls it off, revealing an incredible head of long, silky blond hair. She tosses the wig on a chair.

I'm trying to gather my thoughts, think of something to say, when she starts unbuttoning her shirt. She takes it off. Underneath is a thick jacket which she unzips and peels off as well. She's wearing a little white tank top. Her torso is slender, her breasts full, her arms toned.

Not taking her piercing aqua gaze off me, she unzips her jeans, takes them off. She then unzips the fake-fat pants she's wearing underneath and slides her long slender legs out of each thick leg tube. She tosses these pants on top of her other clothes on a chair in the corner. The whole pile jiggles like a mountain of Jell-O.

Barb pulls fake teeth out of her mouth and places them next to her contacts on the little table. I hadn't noticed her teeth being particularly unattractive, and yet, somehow, the removal of this fake set tremendously improves the shape of her mouth. Her real teeth are lovely. Framed by her beautiful hair and punctuated by her real teeth, her face is now noticeably exquisite.

I need time, a few days, maybe, to think. I feel put on the spot.

My new patient is standing in my office in her underwear—

majestic. She's probably the most beautiful woman I've ever seen. She reminds me of one of those superheroes after removing their ordinary clothes. She is now ready for action. I almost expect her to open the window and fly out of my office.

The effect is muted somewhat when she scratches her arm self-consciously, though that's an understandable display of discomfort, considering that her therapist is gawking at her.

"Do you understand, now?" she asks.

I look down at the note I wrote in my pad, which reads: "Mother wants her to make more effort with her appearance."

I cross out the word "more" and replace it with "less."

"Yes, I see," I say. "How often do you wear this disguise?"

"All the time, pretty much."

"Why?"

"I find my real appearance impractical."

"But isn't your disguise even more impractical? Isn't it heavy?"

"Yes, it's a bit heavy. But I feel much lighter in it. Being dowdy is liberating."

"Liberating in what way?"

She shrugs. "I'm left in peace."

"Peace from what?"

She doesn't answer.

"From men? Model scouts? Love at first sight?"

She says nothing.

"When did you start wearing it?"

"Almost two years ago," she says.

"Did something happen?"

She doesn't answer.

I repeat, "Did something happen, almost two years ago, that made you start wearing this costume?"

She looks suddenly weak, visibly upset. She sits down, drapes her shirt over herself, no longer resembling a superhero so much as a lost girl from a fairy tale. She doesn't say anything.

"Tell me what happened," I urge softly, suspecting abuse, sexual harassment, possibly rape.

I can tell she's having trouble. She doesn't want to cry, but if she attempts to speak, she will.

I try a different approach. "People must find it surprising that you go around looking like this. Do you get a sense of what they think?"

"Sure, they think I'm fat and ugly."

"No, I mean the people who've known you longer than two years?"

"They think I *got* fat and ugly."

"Really? Is there anyone, other than your mother, who knows that this is just a disguise and not the way you really look now?"

"Only my four closest friends."

"If I were to ask your mother or your closest friends why you disguise yourself this way, what would they tell me?"

She shrinks a little further into her chair, and again can't answer.

"What would they tell me?" I repeat.

BARB

As soon as my therapy session is over, I rush home, slip some evening wear over my bloat wear, and find my friend Georgia already waiting for me in a cab in front of my building. I scoot in beside her. She shifts along the seat to give me the room I need.

A bouquet of sunflowers rests on her lap.

"For Lily?" I ask.

She nods.

The driver carries us away. We tell him to go as fast as he can because we're late for Lily's concert. Or rather, we're late for a mission she's sent us on before the concert. At twenty-five, Lily is the youngest of our group of five friends, and the most talented. She asked us to get to the concert hall early so that we tell her whether Strad, the jerk she's in love with, shows up.

As the cab driver zigzags through traffic, I look at Georgia and say, "Don't you wish we could go to Strad's store and just shake him and say, 'Are you blind? Don't you see how extraordinary Lily is?'"

"That's the problem. He's not blind."

"Georgia, please."

The driver makes a sharp left and Georgia gets knocked against her door. "Ow!" she yelps, rubbing her right shoulder.

I myself have toppled onto the space between us.

"Hey, watch it!" Georgia yells at me when she sees I'm lying on her laptop.

"Why'd you bring that?" I ask. "Are you planning to write *during* the concert?"

Before she can answer, the driver makes a sharp right, and it's Georgia's turn to land on her laptop and mine to bang against my door, though I suffer no injury due to my fake fat, which bounces me right back into place.

"Maybe," Georgia answers. "I like writing to Lily's music."

Georgia Latch is a successful novelist. The five novels she published were critically acclaimed, translated into two dozen languages and taught in universities. The second one, *The Liquid Angel,* was made into a film. She thinks her career would be even more successful if she were more prolific, but her writing process is slow. So she's always struggling to find ways to write more. Her recent method has been to take her laptop wherever she goes, in hopes of getting work done.

The traffic slows and the driver can't weave anymore. We are at a standstill.

We finally arrive, late, at Zankel Hall, a concert venue at Carnegie Hall. Anxious about our tardiness and not wishing to waste a moment, we pay and open the cab doors before the driver comes to a full stop. A pedestrian on a cell phone dives in as soon as we've burst out.

Midway to the concert hall's entrance, Georgia stops in her tracks. "My laptop!"

We spin around. The taxi's gone.

"No, no, no, no, no," she says and drops the sunflowers.

Neither of us took a receipt, so we don't have the taxi's medallion number.

Georgia is bent over, hands on knees, repeating, "Oh my God."

She has often told me she thinks the novel she's been working on for the past few years will be her breakthrough, the one that will win the most awards, the one that will garner the best reviews, the one that will sell the most copies—the very same one that is now taking a ride in a vanished taxicab somewhere in New York City. Georgia hasn't backed up her work in three and a half years, ever since her external hard drive broke while she was completing her last novel. She never got around to buying a new one.

"Have you e-mailed a copy to anyone? Or even to yourself?" I ask her. "Is it printed out?"

"No, no, and no. I never showed it to anyone."

I pick up the bouquet of sunflowers and put my arm around Georgia, holding her up. "I'll call the taxi company," I tell her. "I'll keep calling, until someone turns it in."

I lead her inside the building. We sit on a bench in the entrance hall. Georgia cries, her face in her hands. After ten minutes of unsuccessful phone calls which begin with directory assistance, move on to the Taxi and Limousine Commission, and end up with the Central Park Precinct, I'm told by the precinct that no laptop has yet been reported found, and that I should call later to check if that status has changed.

Georgia is staring at me with watery eyes. Her face is red and puffy. Strands of her short dark hair are stuck to the tears on her cheeks.

Our friend Jack Felsenfeld comes out from inside the theater. Though he's only twenty-nine, he walks with a limp and a cane.

"What are you guys doing?" he asks. "Penelope and I have been here for half an hour already."

I tell him what happened.

He leans his cane against the bench and squats in front of Georgia. He holds her hands, looks up at me, and asks, "Did you call the Central Park Precinct?" Being an ex-cop, Jack knows these things. He could have saved me time.

"Yeah," I say.

"You have to keep calling. It might get turned in."

Not forgetting about why we're here, I tell him, "Let me go backstage and say hi to Lily. Is Strad here?"

"No sighting yet."

I ENTER LILY'S small dressing room right as the *Rolling Stone* magazine journalist who's been interviewing her is making his exit.

I close the dressing room door behind me.

It's just me and Lily. And the mirror.

Mirrors take on a whole new meaning when Lily's in the room. They become a loaded silence.

"How are you holding up?" I ask her.

"Fine." She's standing at the sink, soaking her hands in hot water, which she always does before a performance.

"Will you be okay if Strad doesn't show? Or if he does show?"

"I'll try to be."

I know if Strad doesn't show up she'll be devastated.

"These are from Georgia," I say, giving her the sunflowers.

"That's sweet." She puts the flowers in a vase of water.

I decide not to tell her about Georgia's lost laptop in case it disrupts her preparation. "Just remember, you are fantastic. You'll be great. You'll knock 'em dead," I say, staring earnestly into her eyes. I hug her.

The sad thing is, now that I've known Lily for eight years, I find her nothing but beautiful. My perception has been skewed by affection. I know what she looks like to others because I remember what she looked like to me when I first met her. My breath was taken away, repeatedly, by the ugliness of her features and their arrangement. I found myself hoping she'd change expressions, but every time she did, the new configuration was worse than the last.

Lily is not disfigured. Her face is not deformed or medically abnormal. It is simply extremely ugly—the kind of ugliness that is inoperable. Any attempt at improvement would be fatal. Changing the distance between one's eyes is not surgically possible. In fact, it is one of the few facial characteristics that cannot be altered. But Lily's eyes being far, far too close together is only one of her multitude of flaws. She does have one attractive feature, though. Ironically: her eyes. But only when looked at one at a time, in isolation.

As for her body, it's fine but irrelevant because people always focus on her face.

Despite the fact that Lily takes some getting used to visually, in every other way she is pure loveliness.

When I get back to our seats, Jack and Georgia are chatting quietly. Our friend Penelope, looking sumptuous and beautifully dressed as usual, is pacing the aisle at the other end of the theater, keeping an eye out for Strad.

He never shows. Lily plays magnificently, but through the whole concert all I can think about is how upsetting it is that someone as talented as she is suffering so much over someone like him.

AT THE END of this strange, upsetting day, when I return to my building, the doorman mutters to me, "You fucking bitch."

His insults are nothing new. They began gradually, about three months ago. I accept his claim that I haven't done anything to provoke him because I can't think of anything I did. I'm concerned that he must be suffering from some sort of mental illness. Tourette's syndrome, perhaps. That makes me feel protective of him.

I don't think his insults could be related to my disguise, mostly because I was wearing it long before I moved to this building a year ago. None of the doormen has ever seen my true appearance. They have no clue this is not it.

I'm not in the mood to acknowledge his insult tonight. One day, though, I should encourage him to seek professional help for his possible disorder. Which reminds me of a phone call I need to make.

Chapter Two

As soon as I step into my apartment I call my mother. "Your ridiculously early dying wish has been fulfilled."

She gasps. "Thank you. How did it go?"

"Okay, I guess."

"Do you think you'll get rid of the padding?"

"It's not that easy to lose weight."

"But it's not attached!" She always harps back on this point.

"Just because it's not attached to me doesn't mean I'm not attached to it. It's attached to my soul."

"Do you think you'll try another session?" my mom asks, full of hope.

Since I'm not sure, and I don't want my mom badgering me about it, I will nip this nagging in the bud by claiming I will never go back. Even though the therapist seemed fine, she did say one ridiculous thing, and that is the thing I relay to my mom so that she will leave me in peace on the topic forever.

"No, I'm not going back," I state. "She's stupid."

Pause. "Oh? What makes you say that?"

"She told me I should go to a support group for fat people."

Another pause. "That seems reasonable to me," my mom says, and adds, "You're fat."

"No, I'm not. And you know it and she knows it. I stripped for her."

"In the eyes of the world you're fat."

"Whatever."

"Please promise me you'll go to a support group for fat people. At least once."

"That's crazy."

"No. Wearing fake fat is crazy."

Whenever my mom dwells on her favorite topic—my fake fat—I try to change the subject with her second favorite topic: her upcoming trip to Australia in March.

"Hey, by the way, have you figured out what hotels you'll be staying at in Australia?" I ask.

"No, not yet," she says. "I can't concentrate on that and I won't feel at peace until you promise me you'll meet with a group of fat people."

"You said I didn't have to go to more than one meeting with a therapist."

"And you don't. This is different. It's a support group. Give it a chance, please. I don't often ask things of you, do I?"

I don't answer.

"Barb, I beg you, do it for me."

"Okay, fine," I answer.

We say good night and hang up. I take a deep breath. I wish my mom could be patient. I *will* take off my disguise, in time, when the disguise of old age takes hold of me.

I adore my mother. We get along very well. Our only point of tension is my appearance. I inherited her looks. She used to be a top model, appeared on dozens of *Vogue* covers, as well as all the other major fashion magazines. Despite her disapproval of my appearance, she is not a shallow person. Unlike many ex-models, she is not obsessed with beauty. She's not particularly interested in clothes or fashion. But even she has her limits. And I surpass them.

She grew up in Des Moines, Iowa, and moved to New York to become a model. The first year she was here, she met my father, a professor, at the New York Public Library when she wanted to escape the unbearable summer heat and spend a relaxing hour in one of the beautiful, cool, quiet rooms. They immediately fell in love and married soon after. She continued to work as a model until she had me.

Eventually, my dad started having affairs with younger, beautiful women, often his former students. My mother was devastated. She tried leaving him a few times, but he always persuaded her to stay, promised her that things would be different. But they never really were. Even when they were for a short while, he resented her for it, and then things went back to being the same. His affairs were making her life too miserable, so she finally did leave him, after having been with him for thirty-five years.

She bought a house in Connecticut, an hour and a half away, in the woods.

Far from being devastated by the split, I was relieved. I'd seen her so unhappy, and now she would start a new life. She was fifty-six and still looked great.

A few months after the separation, she tried dating a man,

briefly. But her heart wasn't in it. After him, I heard of no one else. She would come to the city sometimes, and we'd have lunch or dinner.

It was Georgia who noticed that my increasing lack of interest in my appearance coincided with my mother's suddenly finding herself alone. Without really realizing it, I guess, I started dressing more casually and stopped wearing makeup. I took things even further, of course, after my close friend Gabriel died, almost two years ago.

A year after Gabriel's death, I moved into this beautiful apartment which I love and which I thought would distract me. It has a ballet bar anchored to the floor, because the woman who owned the apartment before me was a dancer with American Ballet Theatre. I'm not a dancer, but I still find the ballet bar beautiful and handy. I'm a costume designer. All around the edges of the room are mannequins wearing some of my most extravagant, historical, fairy tale-like creations. These mannequins—many of which are fur-covered animals with upright human bodies— are all wearing fanciful masks I designed. Atmospheric stage lighting adds to the effect, making the room look like some kind of enchanted forest.

But my beautiful living room can't distract me from thoughts of Gabriel, and neither can my ugly disguise shield me from them.

Gabriel, who was my best friend, made it perfectly clear in his suicide note that he was killing himself because he was in love with me. Until that note, I had no idea he had romantic feelings for me (or perhaps I chose not to know it). He never told me. He knew I didn't feel the same way and never would, and he was right.

Why didn't I fall in love with Gabriel? He was quite handsome, had an amazing voice—deep and smooth—and had so many other qualities. I don't exactly know why I didn't develop those kinds of feelings for him. I suspect the reason was something intangible.

His suicide was a complete shock, and yet, looking back, he often seemed a bit melancholy. I noticed it especially when I was alone with him.

In some ways he was the most talented of our group, because he was the most versatile, intelligent, and funny. He was a renowned chef who owned one of the best restaurants in New York City. But unlike Georgia, Lily, or me, who are creative only in our specific fields, Gabriel was creative in all areas. When any of us encountered a bump in our work, he seemed always to come up with some suggestion, some little idea that made all the difference. We were in complete admiration. No one could talk to Georgia about her novels the way Gabriel could. He was the only one she actually discussed her ideas with as she was writing them.

He was a private person, never granting interviews or posing for photographs. Even with us he was a bit reserved and mysterious. Whenever we asked him if there was anyone he was romantically interested in, he just brushed the topic aside good-humoredly. Yet there were plenty of people interested in him. When I walked down the street with him, I noticed women and men eyeing him. And they flirted with him when he stood in lines. He could have had his pick. But he never seemed interested in anyone. I had no idea it was me he was in love with.

I do remember one evening when he was supposed to drop off some food. I was wearing a dress I'd just finished making for a period movie and I was eager to get his reaction to it. I loved showing him my costumes because his face was expressive and gave away his opinion even before he spoke.

When he arrived and I opened the door for him, I said, "Tell me what you think of this dress."

He didn't look as pleased as I'd hoped. He stared at me and said, "I can't."

"Why not?"

"It's physically painful to look at you, you're so beautiful."

I smiled broadly. "I knew you'd like it! I think it might be my best one yet." I twirled.

"It's not the dress. Your beauty interferes with my ability to judge the dress." He looked away.

My whole life, people have given me compliments on my looks, so this compliment didn't particularly stand out. I felt my face drooping. "So you don't like it that much?"

"I'd have an easier time judging it on a hanger." He seemed pained as he went to the kitchen and put the food in the fridge.

After that, there was a period when I hardly saw Gabriel. He threw himself into his work and began dating obsessively. Eventually, that tapered off and he spent more time with us again, until one day, after I had a pleasant and uneventful visit with him at his apartment, I exited his building, and he caught up with me by taking the most direct route.

Falling at me from the twenty-eighth floor, he shattered himself at my feet. I don't think he intended to traumatize me for life—though he has.

I REFUSED TO leave my apartment for weeks after Gabriel died, except to attend his funeral. I was devastated by the destructive effect I'd had on him without realizing it. I wondered if I might be harming others as well. I moped around, feeling dreadful, feeling like a wreck. My face felt shrunken and shriveled, ravaged by sadness, as though it must have aged twenty years, but each time I gazed in the mirror, hoping I looked as bad as I felt, I never did.

I found it unbearable. It didn't have to be that way. There could be ways to solve this problem. And if anyone had the skills to solve it, I did.

I began by trying on a frizzy gray wig. It helped a little, but I still looked very good. So I experimented with some imperfect fake teeth that changed the shape of my mouth in a slightly unflattering way. I toned down the brilliance of my aqua eyes with brown contact lenses. And I put some glasses on top.

There was still the problematic body to deal with. I knew how to create a simple-but-convincing jiggling fat suit. I'd made several for body doubles in movies.

I had the materials delivered, and constructed the suit. It was easy to put on, weighed about ten pounds, and made me look eighty pounds heavier. It helped tremendously.

I finally agreed to see Georgia, who had been trying unsuccessfully for weeks to get me out of the apartment. I was wearing the full disguise when I opened the door for her. She seemed startled and said, "Oh, hi. I'm a friend of Barb's. Is she here?"

"It's me," I said.

She was speechless. She squeezed my arm, to feel the consistency of my bulk, perhaps wondering if I'd genuinely gained all that weight in a few weeks.

When she had assured herself that my fat was fake, she said, "Is this one of your new costumes? I'm glad you're working, at least."

"No. This is how I should have looked. Then Gabriel would still be alive."

After a pause, she said, "Yes, he probably would be."

She walked around me, examining me from every angle.

"From now on," I said, "I think I should wear this costume. I don't want to hurt anyone anymore. My looks are to blame for his death."

She looked stunned for a moment, but then said, "Absolutely."

I knew that tone of hers. She was humoring me, to be shocking.

So I reminded her, "His suicide note said he killed himself over me and that my appearance was causing him pain."

"I think this costume is an excellent idea," she said. "Your beauty is a deadly weapon. Wielding it recklessly is irresponsible. You must treat it like a personal handgun—keep it hidden, handle it with care, and *never* point it at people, not even in jest, unless you intend to use it."

I detected a note of anger in her voice, and I was no longer sure if she was humoring me or blaming me for Gabriel's death.

"I wasn't exactly flaunting my looks, you know," I said.

"If you think your meager attempts to hide your beauty were successful, you're deluded. Is a gun in a holster hidden?"

"You're talking to me like I'm a five-year-old who accidentally shot my best friend to death."

"That wasn't my intention. Despite what his suicide note said, it's not your fault he died. Your beauty is not you. But it is in your possession and you should control it."

"Stop comparing my appearance to a weapon. I didn't kill him."

"Exactly. I rest my case," she said, giving me a small smile.

Through her usual psychological manipulation, she got me to say the exact opposite of what I was saying at first.

"So you *don't* think my disguise is a good idea?" I asked.

"Of course not. And I hope you don't either."

"Yes, I do."

"It's not your fault Gabriel died. And if you believe it is, you're wrong. And if you still believe it is, forgive yourself for his death. And if you can't, so be it, but you can't be serious about wearing this disguise."

"I am."

She stared at me and finally gave up. "Fine. Anything that helps you get out of the house is fine."

I liked the disguise. It felt like a punishment and a protection all at once, both of which I'd been craving without realizing it.

Breaking the news to my mother about my new appearance was not a fun prospect. I made an effort to dress well for the occasion—not in my usual sweatpants, sneakers, and ponytail. Instead, I wore an enormous pair of tailored fancy pants over my fat suit, and dressy black pumps, even with a slight heel. A very large silk shirt over my fake-fat jacket. I wore my well-combed gray frizzy wig, my subtly ugly fake teeth. For the first time since my parents had split up, I even put on a little makeup.

I wobbled toward the car, my huge thighs rubbing against each other. I opened the passenger door and said, "Hi Mom!" I plopped down in the seat next to her with a huff. It was strenuous carrying all that weight around.

She didn't say anything at first, just stared, looking aghast. And then she asked, "What is this about?"

"This is how I have been looking for a while. And my life has been better. I've been happier." My words were reminding me of people who break the news to their parents that they're gay. "I like looking ugly," I added bluntly.

Over dinner, we were silent for long stretches. She hardly looked at me. I, on the other hand, observed her carefully. She was now sixty and still hadn't been with anyone since her brief attempt at dating after she left my dad.

"Why are you doing this?" she finally asked.

"It helps me cope with Gabriel's suicide."

"You weren't responsible for his death, regardless of what his note said."

I nodded, looking down at my food, my eyes filling with tears, inevitably.

"Is that really the only reason you're doing this?" she asked.

"No."

"Why else?"

I cleared my throat. "This is how I'm going to find the man of my dreams."

She took this in. "Really. That's an interesting method. Not exactly tried and true. Good luck with that," she said, irritated.

"This is how I'm going to find my soul mate," I repeated, "someone who doesn't care much about beauty, who values other things about me—someone able to fall in love with me even if I don't look good."

My mother was gazing at me.

Gently, I added, "Someone whose interest in me won't fade as soon as my looks do."

My mother looked down. "So this is about your father and me."

Unfortunately, my disguise put the idea in my mother's head that I should go and see a therapist—a request she began frequently badgering me about and which I didn't give in to until today: almost two years later, two years of wearing the disguise every day, making small improvements to it along the way.

THINKING ABOUT GABRIEL always makes me want to read some of his letters again—something I do often. So, after calling my mother I go and fetch two of them and sit on the couch. With great care, I unfold his suicide note. His handwriting is beautiful and interesting, like he was.

Clenching my lips, I read it once more. I know it practically by heart.

> *Beloved Barb,*
>
> *I'm so sorry I have to say goodbye to you and to life.*
> *You didn't know. I never made a declaration of love,*
> *nor even a declaration of desire. I was very careful*
> *not to send you signals revealing my feelings because I*
> *knew they were not reciprocated. And worse, I knew it*
> *would change our relationship and make you uncom-*

fortable. You would never be the same with me again, never be yourself.

You often mused to me about your future, wondering what your life would be like, whether you'd have children and how many, where you would live, who you would end up with. But you never saw me that way.

You made a drawing of me, once, with that talent of yours which matches your beauty—that beauty that has grown so painful for me to behold. In the drawing, I felt you had captured my soul. You made me more attractive, more appealing than I am. If that's how you saw me, why couldn't you love me?

Meeting you meant I was doomed. It has sapped me of my ability to derive pleasure from anything but you. Everything is ruined for me because nothing can match you, nothing can compare. I've never been as happy as when I'm with you. And I've never been as miserable. Sometimes those two feelings are separated by only a moment.

My work, my success, people's praise—all those things that mattered to me—mean nothing to me now. My professional ambition has deserted me because I know it will not get me your love.

Beloved Barb, I adored you from the moment I met you. You have touched my soul in ways you will never know.

Goodbye, sweet heart.

More later,

Gabriel

Reading this letter always leaves me devastated, even after all this time.

Those two words, "More later," which under any other circumstance would seem very banal, baffled my friends and me for a while. That is, until I began receiving more letters from Gabriel—letters he'd prepared before his death and had arranged to be sent to me on specific dates when he knew he would be dead.

The second letter resting on my lap is one of those—Gabriel's latest, and by far strangest, one. I received it two days ago and have discussed it with my friends at length. We have no idea what he's talking about. It reads:

> *Dear Barb, Georgia, Lily, Penelope, and Jack,*
> *One of you confessed to me that you did something*
> *very bad. I don't want to reveal what it is until it's absolutely necessary. And it will be necessary soon.*
> *Love,*
> *Gabriel*

Chapter Three

After folding the two letters and putting them away, I turn off the living room lights.

I'm tired. I go to the other room, which is not only my bedroom but my office. There's a desk in the middle of this large room and a couch in a corner. The bed is simply a mattress on the floor because it satisfies my bohemian taste. I've lined the room with floor-to-ceiling storage space. I have built-in drawers that hold supplies for masks, sketches, fabrics for costumes, sewing equipment, etc. I also have a big closet where I keep dozens of costumes I've made or am in the process of making. My own clothes take up only a tiny portion of the closet because I have little interest in my appearance other than to make sure it's bad.

I'm in the midst of getting ready for bed, taking off my fat, when Georgia calls in tears. She can't sleep; she's devastated about her lost novel in her lost laptop. I tell her to take a sleeping aid, and we'll try calling the police again tomorrow. She says she already took one and it's not working. I tell her to come over and sleep on my couch if she wants.

A half hour later, Georgia is sitting curled up on my couch, sipping a cup of hot chocolate.

I first met Georgia five years ago when I was the costume designer for the movie based on her novel *The Liquid Angel*. It was my first job in costume design, and it basically made my career, earning me a Satellite Award and an Oscar nomination. (I chose Gabriel as my escort to the Academy Awards, and we had a memorable time even though I didn't win.) Job offers poured in after that and I dropped out of Tisch's MFA program to devote myself full time to freelance costume designing. I haven't since been nominated for another major award, though my designs continue to get positive reviews that praise their originality, freshness, and psychological insight.

Georgia and I became good friends right away and we often turn to each other during difficult times, such as now.

"I don't see how I can write again, now that I've lost my best work," she cries, putting down her cup of hot chocolate.

"You're a great writer. You'll write it again and even better."

"I've lost work before. I don't write it better. I write it worse."

AFTER SHE LEAVES, I work all morning on a series of masks and costumes I've been hired to design for a TV movie.

I would happily keep working till dinnertime without taking a break, if only I hadn't promised our friend Penelope I'd have lunch with her and her parents. I always try to do whatever I can to help Penelope. She's a dear friend who's had a tough life. Or rather, she had a tough three days, six years ago. She was kidnapped and kept in a coffin for sixty-nine hours. She doesn't often ask for favors, so when she begged me because she didn't want to see her parents alone and she claimed they had always wanted to meet me, etc., I couldn't refuse.

Penelope doesn't want to see them alone because of the ongoing tense exchange she has with her wealthy father over the issue of her not yet making a living at the age of twenty-eight. He pressures Penelope to get a job, or to make money some other way, any other way. Instead, Penelope decided to take a pottery class. She discovered she had no talent for making attractive pots. Impressed with her classmates' pots, which were merely ugly, not hideous like her own, she decided to open a store and sell their ugly pots. Her father disapproves of her business venture. He thinks the pots are ugly and her idea stupid. Worse, the pots aren't selling and the store is losing money. And he's the one who pays the rent on her store and on her apartment. He hasn't given her a trust fund, just a monthly allowance for food, bills, clothes. If he wants to, he can stop supporting her at any time, and she would have nothing, not even a place to live.

It seems obvious to me that Penelope is tortured by her lack of achievement. She would give anything, I think, to possess a special gift, an ability; even the smallest, most modest skill.

She did make efforts to please her father over the years, she did try a few jobs, but hated them and left each one within a couple of months. The pottery class, however, she enjoyed greatly and she continues to take at least two ceramics classes every semester: Wheel Throwing and Handbuilding.

Penelope told me that each time she sees her father, which is every two weeks, he bitterly asks her how sales are going. She never lies, always says, "Terrible." She's becoming increasingly stressed by his questions.

——————

PENELOPE AND HER parents are already seated when I arrive at Cipriani Downtown. They shake my hand warmly. They don't know I'm wearing a disguise. Penelope assured me she never told them. In their eyes, I must make a striking contrast to their daughter, who's sitting there all prim and ladylike in her cream cashmere sweater set and her immaculately applied makeup.

The waiter takes our order. After telling him I want to start with the steamed broccoli and then have the grilled sole, no sauce, Penelope's very skinny mother leans over to me and says, "I admire your discipline. My willpower leaves much to be desired." She rubs her stomach, as though it were convex instead of concave.

"It's not discipline," I say. "I just don't like fatty foods." It's ironic that I, of all people, possess the rare trait of not enjoying the things that destroy one's beauty. "Fat and sugar make me want to throw up," I explain.

"Really? Then how do you maintain your . . ." She seems unsure how to finish.

"Girth?" I offer.

She nods sheepishly.

"It's actually not that easy to get rid of, you know. For emotional reasons, I guess."

"I sure know what you mean," she says, squeezing her bony upper arms critically, as though they were covered in a layer of thick flesh caused by years of compulsive eating due to emotional torment. "I don't know how Penelope does it, with what she went through six years ago . . ."

I nod politely.

Not for a moment did Penelope's father hesitate to pay the exorbitant ransom when his daughter was abducted. He got it ready as soon as the kidnappers told him the amount, but before he had a chance to deliver the money, the police found the criminals and freed Penelope. The kidnappers had kept her in a coffin so that she'd sound all the more distraught when her father asked to speak to her. They held up the phone to the coffin and instructed her to talk to him through its walls and describe her situation. She was crying and had to shout to be heard.

"Barb!" her father booms at me. It's the first time he's spoken since I sat down. "You make a living designing costumes, right?"

"Yes," I say, hoping he hasn't figured out I'm wearing one.

"You make a good living at it, from what I gather from the magazines." Penelope must have shown her parents the few articles that have been written about me during the past couple of years.

"It's okay," I say softly, sorry that my presence didn't protect Penelope from her dad's obsession.

"I wish my daughter would follow your example. She has so many advantages and opportunities."

No one responds.

Penelope's father turns to her. "How's your store going?"

"Quite well, thank you," she says. I look at her, startled.

Her father does an auditory double take. "What do you mean, 'quite well'?"

"Selling vigorously," she articulates. "Compared to before."

"Are you putting me on?"

"No."

"Are you selling new merchandise?"

"No."

"I can't believe those pots are selling."

"I'll show you the sales records next time I see you."

"No need. I can look at them today when we go to your store."

"But we're not going to my store."

"Yes we are. I want to see the records. After lunch, we're going back to your store with you."

"Today's not a good day. I'm not in the mood."

"Nonsense. Your reticence is very suspicious, I hope you realize."

When lunch is over I try to take my leave, but Penelope grabs my arm so tightly it hurts, even through the padding, and in a low voice says to me, "Please come with us."

"I really need to get back to my work."

"I beg you with every shred of my being. For moral support," she says.

In the store, Penelope's father examines her recent sales records. Appearing impressed and amused, he says, "It looks like you've indeed been selling these pots. Didn't I say customers can be endlessly surprising?"

He gets up and gazes at the merchandise. "It's beyond my comprehension why anyone would buy any of this pottery. It's abominable."

Penelope says, "That makes it art, more than craft."

Her father reaches for a big, misshapen brown mug. To my

surprise, the handle comes off in his hand while the rest of the mug stays on the shelf. Startled, he turns to his daughter, holding the handle.

"You broke the mug!" Penelope says. "That was my best piece."

He picks up the rest of the mug and attempts to put mug and handle back together. "I'm sorry. The handle just lifted right off."

"It was a fragile, delicate piece. Very refined and elegant."

He looks down at the two pieces of mug in his hand. "You grew up in a house filled with refinement and delicacy. This mug is a big clunky chunk of mud, the farthest thing from elegant."

"Absolutely, according to your narrow-minded and unsophisticated definition of elegance."

Looking irritated, he puts the pieces back on the shelf and reaches for another item—a bowl. It breaks in two as soon as he's touched it.

He looks at Penelope. "This bowl was broken," he says.

He picks up a plate, but only half of it goes with him. "What's going on? All these items are broken," he says.

"I can see that. It's a shame you broke them," she says.

"Stop it."

Penelope blushes fiercely.

"Stop the bullshit. I want an explanation," he says.

In a voice that sounds so strangled I myself can barely breathe, Penelope says, "Customers have to pay for what they break."

A chuckle escapes me. She has gall. She may not be a creative genius like Lily or Georgia, but nature was a genius in making her.

After a moment's reflection, her father's eyes open wide.

"*That's* how you've been selling your merchandise? You make people believe they broke a piece of crap, and you make them pay for it?"

"I was *kidnapped*," Penelope says.

"Ah, here we go again."

"I was kept in a coffin for three days."

"*SO?*" he screams. "Why do you always bring that up to defend your inadequacies?"

"Please don't be so harsh," Penelope's mother finally says.

His tone softens. "Don't you feel ashamed to do business this way?"

"It's a selling technique," Penelope says.

Feeling sorry for her, I jump in. "Positioning the broken pieces in such a way as to make them appear unbroken requires great skill. I wouldn't be surprised if, in the long run, the art of the deception becomes the true art of the piece." I reach for an ugly mug that looks in perfect condition. The moment I raise it from the shelf, a piece of the rim falls inside the mug. "Wow," I gasp. "It looked so undamaged. Your technique is remarkable, Penelope. Achieving this effect of false wholeness, this illusion of integrity, must take a lot of work. It's a tough balancing act."

"Yes," she says.

Her father is not satisfied. "But don't customers object to paying for something they didn't break? How did you manage to get so many people to pay for the pieces?"

"I cry," Penelope says.

"You *cry* to sell your broken merchandise?" her father screams.

"Yes, it helps! And I'm thinking of branching out and selling glassware, too."

"I'm embarrassed by you."

"I was *kidnapped!*" she exclaims again. "And don't pretend you don't see how that could possibly affect the rest of my life. I was kept in a *coffin* for three *days* and three *nights.* No food. No water. No physical movement. Hardly any air to breathe. No toilet. I should be *dead* right now." She gives her father a searing look.

Her father turns to me. "You seem well balanced. Do you have a good therapist you could recommend?"

I stammer, "I have one... since yesterday... uh, I don't know how good she is."

Penelope says, "I didn't go to a therapist when I came out of the coffin—I don't see why I should go to one now."

Her father takes her by the shoulders and stares deep into her eyes. "You're the one who keeps using the coffin excuse to defend every poor choice you make and to justify your lack of... achievements—which I don't say is invalid, but it tells me you might want to deal with your coffin issue. Face it, you never really got out of that coffin. Let a therapist free you."

Seeing no reaction from her and unwilling to wait more than two seconds for one, he adds, "And anyway, if you don't start contributing to your living in a legitimate way very soon, I'm going to stop supporting you. Then you'll have no choice but to make money, honey."

THE TENSION OF the last couple of hours has exhausted me. I decide to go straight home instead of buying some more materials for my masks, as I'd intended.

By the time I arrive at my building, I have a blasting headache.

The doorman opens the door, saying, "Here you go, cunt."

I cringe because I'm afraid he'll be overheard by the other two doormen at the front desk. There are other staff members as well in this large lobby: porters, handymen, the super, one of the employees from the management office. What worries me is that he'll get fired, end up homeless, kill himself, and it will be my fault because something about me—my kindness, my compassion, who knows—made him feel safe enough to drop his inhibitions and allow his mental problem to surface in my presence.

"Having a bad day, huh, Adam?"

"Yeah."

"Me too. Hope it gets better," I say cheerfully, trying to make my tone raise his spirits. And I go up to my apartment.

Chapter Four

That evening, Lily, Georgia, Jack, Penelope, and I go to a bar to blow off steam. We're all upset. Lily's shown us a post-card Strad sent her:

Hey Lily, Sorry I can't make it to your concert. Hope it goes/went well. Last month I read that great article in Time Out about your new music's powers. Congratulations on your success! Strad

When we meet up, Penelope gives me a gift to thank me for helping her deal with her parents at her store of ugly ceramic items. The gift is an ugly ceramic item: a hideous box with a beautiful metal clasp encrusted with a small green stone. But at least the gift is not broken.

"Sorry I didn't wrap it," she says. "I made it. Except for the clasp. Someone in the metal department at school created it for me in exchange for two pots."

"Thank you!" I say, kissing her on the cheek. "I'm so touched. It's wonderful. It has such character."

We all make a show of admiring the box, though secretly we're just admiring the clasp.

Penelope tells the others about the fight with her dad in her shop of broken pots and his threat to stop supporting her if she didn't start contributing to her living in a way that wasn't against the law. They're astounded to hear about her selling technique.

I'm sad for Penelope, after the fight with her father, and I'm sad for Georgia over her lost novel. Mostly, though, I'm angry on Lily's behalf. So I scan the bar, as has become my habit, for a possible scapegoat, for a shallow man to represent all shallow men.

At the same time, I'm also searching for an exception, for a man capable of falling in love with a woman for reasons other than her looks. That's the only kind of man I could ever fall in love with.

While my friends huddle on a banquette and order drinks and snacks, I spot a man reading a stack of handsome books at the bar. He's a bohemian type. Chin-length hair.

I approach him. The books are small, old editions with lovely bindings. The man himself is attractive, too—not that that matters. As I near, I glance at the spines of his volumes: *Cinderella, The Sleeping Beauty, Little Red Riding Hood, Rumpelstiltskin, Tom Thumb, The Princess in Disguise, Hansel and Gretel, Rapunzel,* and *Snow White.*

Maybe this isn't an occasion for my usual bar ritual. The presence of the books gives me hope that perhaps this guy isn't as shallow as all the other strangers I've approached.

I stand behind him and look over his shoulder. The page he's looking at has a beautiful illustration of Sleeping Beauty, with a few lines of text.

"This is the first time I've ever seen a man reading fairy tales in a bar," I tell him.

He looks me over and tersely replies, "I'm doing it for work."

"Now I'm dying to know: what kind of work?" I sit down on the barstool next to him.

He closes his eyes wearily and says, "I'm a kindergarten teacher. I really have to focus right now."

He has to focus, and yet I can't help noticing him turning his head to look at several attractive women who have entered the room.

"Bringing fairy tales to a bar must be a great way to meet women, though I don't think classic fairy tales are the best things to read to children," I say.

"*Excuse me?*" he says, in a tone that conveys annoyance, not only at what I'm saying, but at the fact that I'm still talking.

I'm fully aware that I'm very annoying during my bar ritual. That's the point.

"Haven't you noticed how the heroines are always beautiful?" I say. "There are no ugly heroines, no ugly girls that are worthy to be loved. There are poor heroines, dirty heroines, like Cinderella, but never ugly heroines. That sends out a terrible message to kids."

"I can see how that could make certain ugly women angry," he says, not looking up from *The Sleeping Beauty.*

I glance at my friends and hold my nose to indicate that this is a real stinker. Georgia mimes stabbing gestures toward the man, which startles me. That seems a bit excessive, even for her.

As for Penelope, she has been trying to gently break her empty water glass in such a way that it can be reassembled and held together with nothing but the glue of gravity. She told us it's practice, for when she will make good on her promise to her dad to branch out into glassware.

I say to the kindergarten teacher, "Actually, you'd be surprised at how little it has to do with being ugly. I have plenty of female friends who look just like those beautiful heroines. They have hair that looks like this," I say, taking off my wig. "They have the same kind of body, typically considered to be beautiful in our culture. Very similar to this," I say, taking off my fake-fat jacket. "Some of them look remarkably like Cinderella, Sleeping Beauty, and that whole classic bunch, and yet they still feel angry about the kind of message the fairy tales communicate to children."

Out of the corner of my eye, I can see Georgia's whole body gesticulating. She invariably gets wired when I begin taking off my wig in front of a guy.

As for Lily, I always worry it might pain her to watch a man's transformation from jerk to gentleman as I go through my own transformation from unattractive to attractive. The difference between how men treat an ugly woman, like herself, and one who is beautiful is not something she needs her face rubbed in, but my compulsion to go through the ritual overpowers my need to spare her the sad spectacle. If she is hurt, she never shows it.

The kindergarten teacher looks at me as I take out my fake teeth. To my amazement, he appears angry. I'm pleasantly surprised. It's refreshing to meet a man who doesn't become sweet and gooey when I unveil my looks. I'm about to compliment him on his consistency, when he says, "I feel robbed and violated."

"What do you mean?" I ask.

"You deceived me. You stole . . ." he trails off.

"What did I steal?"

"My opportunity to make a good first impression."

"I didn't prevent you."

"Yes you did, by misleading me into thinking you were—" He cuts himself off, but I know what he was about to say. I misled him into thinking I was ugly and fat, and thus not worth his time and attention.

"Ah, I think I get it," I answer. "When you say I stole from you the opportunity to make a good first impression, you mean that in the same way as how you stole from every ugly woman you've ever laid eyes on the opportunity to impress you with something other than her looks."

"You're crazy, you know that?" He sweeps his fairy tales into his big bag and leaves the bar.

I go to the restroom, change back into my disguise, and rejoin my friends.

I scoot into their booth. The glass Penelope broke is now sitting in front of her, reassembled and looking intact except for the break lines running across it like scars. She is holding the postcard Strad sent to Lily, gazing at it grimly.

"May I?" I ask, taking it from her. As I look at it again, the slight relief my ritual gave me wears off. This postcard is soul-crushing. No one would understand why it's soul-crushing unless they knew Lily's story. And we know it well.

Lily met Strad—a name he'd given himself in honor of his

favorite violin-maker, Stradivarius—three years ago at the musical instruments store where they both worked when she was in her second year of graduate studies at the Manhattan School of Music. She developed a crush immediately. Strad Ellison did not reciprocate her interest—was perhaps not even aware of it. He had a very active dating life. He said he had high standards and that he was very idealistic and romantic and was looking for a great love. The reality is that Strad is a superficial guy, only interested in dating beautiful women.

And yet Lily had not aimed too high. Strad was not "out of her league," as the expression goes—certainly not mentally, and not even physically, that much. He wasn't particularly good-looking, but in Lily's eyes he had enormous charm. I met him a few times at the store where they worked and noticed he did manage to be dashing, occasionally, but never for more than five minutes at a time.

One day, Lily invited Strad to watch a studio recital in which she was going to play two of her compositions on the piano. She was hoping to impress him.

But when they went for coffee after the recital, he merely told her politely she'd been good. On the other hand, he raved about Derek Pearce, one of the other composers who'd performed. He particularly praised one of Derek's pieces, saying, "That's the kind of music that is more than just beautiful. It beautifies the world around it. You want it never to end."

Lily said, "At home I have recordings of some of his other compositions, in case you want to come over and hear them."

"Why not?" Strad said, and they left the coffee shop and went to her apartment.

Strad lay on her floor. It was better for his back than sitting on the couch, he said. She put on a recording of Derek's music.

"Why don't you turn out the lights and light some candles? I love listening to music in the dark," he said.

Understandably, Lily was hopeful.

Strad asked if he could smoke. Even though Lily hates smoke, she said okay and gave him a plate as an ashtray.

She lay next to him, resting on her elbow, and feasted her eyes on his profile which was glowing dimly in the candlelight.

The lines of his face mesmerized her. They had character, were so lived in. His features were weathered yet humorous, connected by tremendous laugh lines, and encircled by silly curly hair. He had an ugly kind of beauty or beautiful kind of ugliness which was why, in her secret heart, she hoped that her own ugliness could appeal to him the same way his appealed to her. Unfortunately, his particular brand of ugliness appealed to a lot of women, she noticed.

His physical appearance was not what she had first fallen in love with. She'd first fallen in love with everything else about him. His considerate nature. His love of his dog. His way of laughing at things she said when she had no idea why.

That night, as Strad was lying on the floor of her apartment, listening to Derek's music, he began commenting, "He's good. Not as good as he was tonight—he's gotten better. Music like his, music that has the power to make things around it beautiful—that's great music. Music that improves people's perception of reality. That's music's highest power, most noble ability. Making the world more appealing."

Strad took a drag on his cigarette and after blowing the

smoke toward the ceiling he said something that changed Lily's life. He said, "I would fall in love with—and marry—any woman who could create music like that. If Derek was a chick, I'd ask her out." He flicked his ashes onto the plate.

And then he talked of all the various women he had recently dated, was presently dating, and was thinking of dating.

Lily made a decision right then in the dark: to attempt the impossible. She knew she couldn't win Strad with her looks. Her strength lay in her talent. She would win him through her music. She would impress him so deeply that he would have no choice but to fall in love with her. She would try to create music that beautified the world.

Lily quit her job the next day, wanting to set to work immediately on her project. But beautifying the world with her music was not an easy task. It took her eight months of the most intense dedication. It required an extraordinary amount of perseverance.

After many failed attempts, she decided that perhaps she was aiming too high. So she tried beautifying merely her neighborhood instead of the world.

But she still couldn't manage it.

She scaled down, focusing on her street.

But still, she didn't pull it off.

So she went to the supermarket and picked out a single item at random: a banana. She brought it home, put it on her piano, and stared at it for a while, rotating it, trying to see the unique beauty in the banana. She then imagined having a craving for it. And slowly, slowly, a melody came to her.

She was excited. She found other objects in her apartment,

spread them out on her piano, and studied them while trying to compose flattering pieces for them.

She called us, told us she'd succeeded and wanted to test her music on us. We gathered at my apartment.

"The piece of music I'm going to test is the one I composed for junk mail," she told us. "But before I begin, I want to make sure you all dislike junk mail."

We confirmed we not only disliked it, but hated it.

She went to my week-old pile of mail near the front door, pulled out all the junk mail, and plopped it on the ottoman cube in front of us.

"You haven't changed your minds yet, right? You still hate junk mail?"

"Right!" we all exclaimed.

"As I play the piece, pay close attention to your feelings and let me know if you detect any change in your perception of the junk mail. Let me know if you start finding it more beautiful and desirable."

She sat at the piano and played her junk mail melody while we gazed at the pile of junk mail.

When Lily was done playing her piece, Penelope said, "I'm sorry, Lily, but this was not a valid test."

"Why not?" Lily asked, rising from her piano bench.

"Did you take a look at this junk mail before you set it down? It's not normal junk mail!" Penelope said, kneeling at the foot of the ottoman cube and looking through the envelopes and leaflets. "In fact, technically, I don't think this is junk mail at all. I mean, look at it; it must have cost a fortune to print. The quality, the colors, the sheen, are all exceptional."

"She's right," Jack said, pulling the ottoman cube closer to him. "And not just the colors, but the words. There's humor!"

"And there's irony, too," I said, skimming some of the text. "And depth. And double meanings."

"And cliff-hangers!" Georgia exclaimed, dropping to her knees next to Penelope and zeroing in on a leaflet of junk mail. "It's actually gripping! Listen to the suspense in this line: 'Who dry cleans better than us?' They don't answer the question! They just leave it hanging like that, torturing us. It's a great hook and extremely thought-provoking."

Lily just watched us.

Since the music had ceased a minute ago, its effect was now wearing off. Our interest in the junk mail was starting to fade, but not before we reiterated that this had not been a good test because the pile of junk mail was better than average.

Lily sat at her piano and played the same piece over again, which caused us to fight over who would get to keep the junk mail, even though it was mine. We ended up Xeroxing it on the machine in my living room closet, so that everyone could get a copy, and I kept the originals. When I mentioned that I might bind mine, not only did they not think it weird, they decided they might bind theirs as well. That is, until Lily stopped playing, and the pile gradually appeared for what it was: junk.

This was five months ago. Things progressed quickly after that. Lily's career took off and she now gets highly paid by stores like Barnes & Noble, Tiffany, Bloomingdale's, Crate & Barrel, and others, to compose music that will beautify their merchandise. Her music is played while customers shop, and soon these customers get an urge to buy more books, more toothpaste, more jewelry, or more of whatever Lily was assigned to enhance musically. Recently Barnes & Noble told her, off the record, that its sales had almost doubled since it started playing her book music.

The critics have been impressive in their ability to look past her music's commercial use (one pundit even called it "crass usage"), appreciating its genius. The reviews have been glowing.

Lily wanted Strad to find out about her achievement on his own, without her having to brag about it. Considering how many articles have been written on her in the last few months, it was a reasonable hope. She assumed he would contact her as soon as he heard she had accomplished what he said should be the ultimate goal of music: to beautify the world.

And yet she heard nothing from him.

"He probably doesn't read, the idiot," Georgia said.

"I don't know about that," Lily replied. "As I've already told you, when I gave him one of your novels, he not only read it and loved it, he immediately bought your other four books and read and loved those too. It's funny you're so down on him. He's a huge fan of yours. He said one of his greatest joys in life would be to meet you."

"Well, then, it will be one of my greatest joys never to meet him," she said simply, and smiled.

Eventually, Lily sent Strad an invitation to last night's concert, thinking that if he didn't know about her success yet, he would now. The beautiful printed invite included a bio, which described the particular musical powers she'd recently developed. (The invitation also reassured any nervous guests that none of her "influential" music would be played that evening, and it wasn't.)

During our dinner after the concert, Lily told us, "I'm worried I didn't exactly achieve what Strad was talking about. He spoke of music that beautifies the world, not music that beautifies consumer products."

"Consumer products are part of the world," was Georgia's response.

Lily shook her head. "Strad probably doesn't see it that way. He's an idealist."

"You've achieved so much more than what he was talking about. You've achieved actual magic."

"Magic is not necessarily more important than poetry. I think he was talking about poetry."

Penelope finally stepped in with, "Lily, you've achieved something extraordinary, that's never been done before. If Strad hasn't contacted you, it's because he doesn't know about it yet, not because he's not impressed. He probably didn't bother reading your bio in the invite, nor did he see any of the articles about your music."

We all hoped Penelope was right and we were disappointed today when the arrival of this postcard proved her wrong. Lily's not getting what she wants out of her inspired musical accomplishments, not a speck of the affection she craves. In his message, Strad doesn't suggest they see each other. There is no: "Stop by the store and say hi one of these days. I'll give you a good price on a flute. ☺"

"Are you all right, Barb?" Jack asks me.

I'm suddenly aware of the grim expression on my face. "He's not worthy of you," I tell Lily. "Do you think you can forget about him now?"

"No," she replies. "Actually, I'm going to call him tomorrow and suggest we have coffee."

Soft sounds of concern and disapproval escape us.

She explains, "If I've failed to create the kind of music he was talking about—and I guess I have, judging from his postcard—I want to know how I can do better."

Doing better is not the issue. Looking better is. That's what she doesn't understand. At least that's my bleak take. I would love to be wrong.

As we're chatting, we're oblivious to the waitress who is refilling Penelope's water glass. Before the water reaches the top, the glass falls apart and the water spills all over the table.

"Oh! Shit! I'm sorry!" Penelope exclaims, as the water slides onto her lap.

"What on earth?" the waitress says, staring at the broken pieces of glass.

"The glass was broken and I reassembled it, stupidly. I'm sorry," Penelope says, mopping up the water with her napkin.

"You reassembled it? Why?"

"To see if it could look intact."

"It's very dangerous," the waitress says.

"I know. I'm so sorry, I forgot about it, I didn't intend to leave it that way."

We call it a night.

I walk home. Adam the doorman greets me with: "I hope your evening was as dreadful as you are."

"Not quite."

"Wait a minute," he says, closing his eyes and pressing his thumb and forefinger against his forehead. "I'm trying to imagine you with a personality." Opening his eyes and shaking his head slowly in bewilderment, he says, "No luck. If I throw a stick, will you go away?"

I say goodnight and oblige.

Upstairs, I receive a call from my mom saying that she researched support groups for fat people and found Overeaters Anonymous, Food Addicts Anonymous, and Eating Disorders Anonymous.

"The problem is," I tell her, "I don't overeat, I'm not addicted to food, and I don't have an eating disorder of any kind."

"Listen, I'm not an idiot. I can see there's a slight discrepancy. But I couldn't find a group called Fat People's Support Group, otherwise I'd say go to that. You've got to make do with what's out there, sweetie."

After we say good night and hang up, I brush my teeth, take off my fat, and carefully hang it up. I love the sensual protectiveness of my disguise. It's like being a turtle or a snail: you can go out and wander around, yet still have the benefits of staying at home. No one bugs you.

I haven't had sex in two years. I haven't even gone on a date since Gabriel died and I donned my padding. It's not that I'm not open to it, as evidenced by my bar ritual. If some man were open-minded enough not to shut me out the second he sees me in my ugly disguise, I'd consider going out with him. But I haven't found such a man. So I spend a lot of time with my friends, who happen to all be single at the moment as well.

Peter Marrick

Friday, 13 October

Something has happened to me. I finally got around to looking in the laptop I found in the taxi three days ago, and I think my life may never again be the same. While searching inside the computer for its owner's contact info, I stumbled upon a diary. I know I shouldn't have looked, but I did. I only meant to glance at it quickly, to see what an average person concerns himself with. Turns out this journal was not written by an average person. It belongs to the novelist Georgia Latch. I haven't read her books, but over the years I've thought I should. Their concepts intrigue me.

Her friends, though, intrigue me even more. I found it painful to read her descriptions of these artistic people. It reminded me once again that I'm not living my life how I want.

I must meet them. And there's one I'm completely enthralled by: Barb. First of all, there's the simple fact that I've never seen anyone as beautiful as her. In the laptop there are photos of how she really looks— incredible—and how she makes herself look each day—unrecognizable. The mere fact that she wears this disguise is just . . . so eccentric, in a good way. I read in

Georgia Latch's diary about Barb's routine in bars, how she takes off her disguise in the middle of conversations with men who show no interest in her. And then she walks away. It's very spunky and sexy. The way Georgia writes about her, she sounds incredibly interesting.

I'll return the laptop tomorrow. I'm tempted to make a copy of the photos of Barb—especially the gorgeous ones—but I know I shouldn't. Still, they seem too beautiful to part with.

These people must never know I'm the one who found the laptop. First: they'd be angry I took so long to return it, especially poor Georgia. And secondly and more importantly: according to the journal, Barb will never date a man who has already seen her physical beauty.

I have to think of the best way to meet them. There is an obvious way, but as I've learned detrimentally late in life, the obvious path is not always the best one.

I'm glad I'm writing down my thoughts. Despite my many attempts to keep a journal, I've never been able to stick to one for long. Life gets in the way.

Chapter Five

Before meeting Strad for coffee, Lily makes very little extra effort with her appearance because there is not much that can be done. In fact, Lily has often noticed—and others have agreed with her—that in her case, the less done the better. Lipstick only emphasizes the ugliness of her lips. Mascara does the same disservice to her eyes, drawing attention to their unfortunate proximity to each other.

She feels that her best hope today with Strad is her talent, her music.

They meet at The Coffee Shop in Union Square (she tells me all about it later). They sit at a table in the back. They make small talk. He congratulates her again on her success without lingering on the topic.

So she decides to probe. She says to him, "I was very influenced by your words a while back when you said that music's most noble ability is to beautify the world."

He looks at her blankly, nodding vaguely. Then he talks about other things—movies he's seen.

She persists. "The kind of music I've developed, does it approach in any way what you were talking about?"

"When?"

"When you said that beauty—I mean music's—highest purpose is to beautify the world."

"Hmm, I don't remember that conversation."

She blinks, confused. She doesn't understand how he cannot remember. Or is he lying, out of discomfort? Yes, perhaps he remembers it perfectly and feels embarrassed about having said he'd marry any woman who could create that kind of music. Maybe he doesn't want to be held to that statement.

In an anxious attempt to understand his feelings, she murmurs, "You said that one should strive to create music that alters people's perception of reality, music that beautifies reality. I always kept that in mind."

He shakes his head. "Doesn't ring a bell. I mean, I'm glad you were inspired by what I said." He laughs and bites into his toast.

Lily stares at him, her heart sinking. She can tell with absolute certainty that he's not pretending. He genuinely doesn't remember. That's how unimportant that conversation was to him. And here she's been worrying that perhaps she hasn't created exactly the kind of music he had in mind, that perhaps she hasn't executed his vision in quite the right way to please his discriminating sensibility.

But maybe there's still hope, she thinks. Just because he doesn't remember uttering those words doesn't mean they might not be true.

Gently, she says, "It's funny that you don't remember,

because you seemed to feel pretty strongly about it at the time. You even said you'd fall in love with—and marry—any woman who could create that kind of music."

"Did I say that? Is that why you composed your recent music?" he asks, and immediately bursts out laughing. He puts his hand on her wrist. "I'm kidding; I flatter myself. But seriously, I can't believe I said that music's highest purpose is to beautify the world, and much less that I would marry . . . whatever. I mean, I do believe you, that I said it, because I know what asinine things I'm capable of saying, but you should know me well enough by now not to listen to half the stuff I say."

While she tries not to cry, something in her dies.

But she doesn't want to give up just yet. She's not even sure he actually heard her music. Perhaps he only read about it. Perhaps if he hears it, he'll be won over. The entire last year of her life was built on the statement he made in the dark. She refuses to believe it was utterly meaningless and her efforts were pointless.

"Have you heard any of my music?" she asks softly.

"No, I haven't had the pleasure yet. I don't go to stores much. Except the one I work in. Been so busy. But some friends of mine have heard it. Get this," he says, leaning forward on his elbows. "One of them heard the piece that's at the florist. He ended up shelling out $100 he hadn't intended to spend. Oh, and I have a client—remember Mrs. Lockford?—well, she bought thirty tubes of lip balm at Walgreens." He slaps the table and thrusts himself back in his chair, as though to say, "Case closed."

Lily smiles, nodding sadly. She has indeed composed music

for Astor Flowers and Nivea lip balm. She sometimes gets hired to compose music for entire stores and sometimes for specific products in stores.

Strad grins and sweeps the hair out of his face. "I love the little signs the stores are forced to put on their doors by law. What's the wording again? It kills me." He pauses and thinks. "'Warning: Your tastes may be temporarily compromised by the ambiance in this store.' And then, then, my favorite part is something like, 'Be aware that you will be buying under the influence. You are advised to familiarize yourself with the return policy of this establishment prior to making any purchase.' Ha!" He slaps the table again, startling the cutlery.

Lily smiles and nods. She's always been charmed by Strad's bursts of enthusiasm.

But she's not going to let them distract her now. Focus and perseverance—one might even say fixation—have always been among her greatest strengths, as well as greatest sources of misery. She may be sweet and fragile, but she's like a missile. When she has a mission, nothing can distract her, and as long as there's a shred of hope, she doesn't give up. Now her last shred of hope rests in playing him her music.

"Could you do me a big favor?" she says. "I'd really like to play something for you, to get your opinion on it. Do you have a few minutes? We could stop at the Building of Piano Rooms."

Strad hesitates only a moment, and then says, "Sure. I have a few minutes."

Lily pays the bill and they walk to the Building of Piano Rooms two blocks away.

They rent a small room. She feels a little uncomfortable, as though they're booking a hotel room for sex, which of course she would much prefer.

The room contains nothing but a piano and two chairs. In her state of mind, it feels grim and seedy. The piano is giving off the vibe of a bed. She knows that's just her perception, skewed by years of longing and frustration. In actuality, the space looks like a miniature classroom.

Strad sits on a white plastic chair near her.

She will play exquisitely. She wants him to be in awe. She's not sure this is the most effective path to love, but she knows of no other way. If she can incite in him a very intense degree of admiration, perhaps the leap to adoration will be possible.

"What do you want me to beautify?" she asks.

He looks confused. "I thought there was a piece you wanted to play for me, to get my opinion."

"Right." She forgot. "But I need you to pick something randomly for me to beautify. I need to know how well I perform when I'm not prepared. That's what I need your opinion on."

"Okay. How about a pen or something?" he says, tapping his pockets. "Do you have one?"

She takes a ballpoint pen out of her purse and places it on the music stand. "Before we start, pay attention to your feelings toward the pen. Form an opinion of it. On a scale of zero to ten, how impressed are you with the pen right now?"

"I guess . . . zero. No offense, I hope."

"No, of course not."

She focuses on the pen.

This is more important to her than any concert she has ever played. She takes a deep breath and begins a piece for the pen.

After a minute, the pen starts looking poetic. As Lily keeps playing, the pen acquires depth. Gradually, it comes to represent the epitome of human thought, of human invention.

"Hey, that's wild! It really does look better," Strad says. "It's like looking at a pen in a movie. A dramatic movie with beautiful sets and costumes. It's like the pen suddenly has a story, or a history. How'd you do that?" He looks at Lily ardently, and before she can answer, he says, "I'm sure you'll understand when I say I need to get to a stationery store urgently." He laughs. Putting on his coat, he adds, "That is so impressive, that you were able to develop this skill. You could have a lot of fun with it. You're very talented."

She gives him a sad smile and mumbles thanks.

"No, thank *you* for playing me your stuff. It was a blast!" he says. "I love it."

Sure, he loves it. But he doesn't love her.

Outside the Building of Piano Rooms, they say goodbye and each go their own way.

She walks in the cold, briskly at first. Sniffling, she tilts her head back and looks up, helping gravity sink the tears back into her lovely but unfortunately positioned eyes.

Lily heads back to Union Square. She walks through the park, slowly, looking down, gazing at the leaves in her path— golden, crispy leaves, now transformed into a rotting mush. She listens to the cars rolling through puddles. She feels lonely. She sees homeless people. She sits on a bench, holding onto its cold arm.

She remains sitting there for quite a while, and then calls me to meet her.

As I'm walking toward her, seeing her looking so lost in the surrounding grayness, I can't help but think of Gabriel.

"I gave him my best performance," she says.

I nod.

"Why did I think Strad would be any different?" she goes on. "It's not as if I ever see any interest in the eyes of any man I ever meet. Ever."

That's when she tells me about her meeting with Strad, about how he was being his usual self: casual, detached, full of fun, without the slightest romantic or sexual interest in her. She says that even in her easily deluded state, in which his smallest gesture can seem loaded with imaginary meaning and promise, there was no room for hope. She now realizes it wouldn't make any difference how extraordinary she became musically, magically, or otherwise—except visually.

Imagining her in that piano room with its undoubtedly merciless fluorescent lighting, and the letdown she must be feeling now, is tough. As she talks, she looks beaten. I wish I could protect her from ever sustaining another blow. I'm afraid that in life, every hit we take chips away at us. How many more hits can she take before she breaks completely?

"I think you should forget him," I tell her.

"Oh, I'm not giving up quite yet."

"You're not?" I ask, with a weird mixture of alarm and relief.

She shakes her head. "No. I've thought of another project I'm going to start working on. And if I succeed, there's a good chance Strad's feelings for me will turn into love."

———

MY MOM CALLS again. She asks if I've picked a meeting of fat people to go to yet.

"Yes," I say.

"Which one?"

"Excess Weight Disorders Support Group."

"That's not one of the ones I told you about."

"This one sounds better for my fat problem. I Googled to find a group whose very name doesn't make me feel like a fraud."

"When are you going?"

"Next Friday."

"Why not today? Today's a Friday."

"I can't. My friends are coming over."

"Every day, every hour that you wear your disguise is an hour when you could be meeting a nice guy you could love spending the rest of your life with, but he won't notice you because you're hidden within that mountain of horror."

"If he doesn't notice me, he's not a nice guy."

I WASN'T LYING. My friends are in fact coming over for a Night of Creation.

Our Nights of Creation take place in the evenings, not at night, but Georgia's publicist didn't care about this inaccuracy when she dubbed them that and each of us a "Knight of Creation." Her goal is fame for her authors at any cost.

These creative evenings of ours started four years ago when Georgia and I decided to throw a party as a way of meeting each other's friends. Lily and Gabriel were among the friends I brought. Penelope and Jack were among the friends she brought. Georgia had met them a couple of years earlier when she interviewed them for a magazine article she was writing about Penelope's kidnapping and her deliverance from the coffin by Jack, who was the cop who had rescued her.

The party Georgia and I threw was successful. People stayed late. But the six of us stayed the latest. We were engrossed in conversation. We talked about our lives and ambitions. We confided in each other. Most of us were in the creative fields and we lamented the loneliness of the artist's life. Georgia said she found the isolation so unbearable that she often went to coffee shops to write. She liked the noise and bustle. It helped her concentrate. But she said it had gotten more difficult each year as she'd grown to dislike the feeling of anyone looking at her screen or reading over her shoulder. As she was telling us this, she suddenly had an idea: she suggested we try getting together to work on our separate arts in one another's company.

It probably wouldn't have worked for most people. For some reason, though, for us it did. Everyone being industrious was inspiring. We felt like family—which for some of us was very appealing, our real families leaving much to be desired. Georgia's embarrassment over the name made the rest of us even more eager to embrace it facetiously. Over time, of course, it stuck.

Our Nights of Creation take place once or twice a week in my large living/dining room. Lily plays and perfects her compositions at a piano she keeps at my apartment for this purpose. A few feet away, at one end of my dining table, Penelope makes hideous little ceramic sculptures. At the other end of that same table, I design and construct my masks and costumes. Sitting between us, at the long side of the table, Georgia types her novel on her laptop (or at least she did, before she lost it). Gabriel would cook up delectable creations in my kitchen and bring them quietly to each of us while we toiled.

Jack doesn't do anything creative. If he's not lounging on the couch, reading psychology magazines, he's lifting weights, enjoying himself watching us work. Some of the injuries he sustained while freeing Penelope from the coffin were permanent and serious enough to prevent him from ever returning to the police force. Even though he's an invalid, he's more athletic and stronger than any of us. He walks with a limp and can't run, but there are plenty of things he can still do that we can't, such as walk on his hands and do back handsprings (as long as he lands on his good leg). Financially, he's okay, thanks to a huge anonymous gift of money he received after the rescue—perhaps from Penelope's father, no one knows. He makes extra with a part-time job at a senior center, which leaves him with plenty of free time—much of which he spends with us.

Even though it was wonderful working to the scent of Gabriel's culinary inventions and our evenings have never been the same since he died, we still enjoy working in one another's company. We cherish that sense of camaraderie and companionship. Everyone's art mixes with and affects everyone else's.

Tonight, as usual, Lily, Georgia, Penelope, Jack, and I busy ourselves with various activities. I'm working on a pair of fantasy pants for a play. Georgia is mourning the loss of her novel by slowly flipping through the pages of her last novel. Penelope, hammer in hand, is finding new and delicate ways to break pots and balance their pieces back on one another in a deceptive appearance of wholeness. Jack is browsing through psychology magazines. And Lily is throbbing away at the piano, but today, instead of looking at her hands or at nothing in particular, her gaze is fixed on Jack, which I find peculiar. Jack notices it and starts making faces at her in an attempt to snap her out of her hypnotized stare.

"Don't mind me. It's my new project," Lily tells him, interrupting neither her playing nor her gazing.

"Does your new project involve me, somehow?"

"Yeah, I'm just practicing on you. I'm trying to beautify you."

He blinks quickly as he processes this information. "You don't find me good-looking enough?"

"Of course I do. I'm just trying to make you even better-looking. So get back to your reading and let me work."

Lily continues her playing and staring.

After another half hour, Jack says, "It's starting to hurt."

Lily stops playing. "You're kidding!"

"No."

"What hurts?"

"My ego."

"Oh." She instantly resumes playing.

He adds, "To watch you trying to beautify me while wearing that frustrated expression makes me feel self-conscious and unattractive."

I KNOW I'M acting like a mother hen, but I call Lily before going to bed to make sure she's okay. I keep thinking of Gabriel.

"How are you holding up?" I ask.

After a pause, she says, "Okay."

Her tone is odd. I don't buy her reply. "How are you doing?" I ask, more slowly. "Really."

She's silent, and then says, "Oh, I'm sure it's nothing. It's just..."

"What?"

"My hands... They've been strange today."

"Strange? How?"

"You're going to think I'm crazy."

"That's okay." I add, "No, I won't."

"Okay... After I saw you in the park this afternoon, I came home and I started playing the piano. As you know, I was really depressed. Well, I gave in to that feeling, I sank into it. And something scary happened."

"What?"

"My hands started changing," she says.

"They did?"

"Yes. They became gray and shiny. And they felt different. Sort of empty. Or hollow."

Now I'm the one who's silent. I finally say, "Gray and shiny?"

"Yeah... Kind of like silver."

"Are you exaggerating?"

"Do I ever exaggerate?"

I think about it. "No."

"I'm actually understating it," she says. "Because then my hands became worse. They got shinier, until they were very reflective, like mirrors." She is silent, as though waiting for me to react. But I don't know what to say, so finally she asks, "You do believe me?"

"Yes," I say, not technically lying. Sure, I believe that her hands were reflective—reflective of her mental state, a mental state which concerns me greatly. "And do you have any idea what triggered this?" I ask.

"I think my mood."

"What was your mood, exactly?"

"I told you. Extremely sad."

"Do you know what the reflectiveness was?"

"It felt like death. As though it was trying to take hold of me. And the worst part was, I was tempted to let it, because it was a welcome relief. But then I resisted it and it went away."

THAT MAKES ME think of Gabriel, of course. I'm still thinking about him the next day when I check the mail and, to my surprise, I have another letter from him:

> *Dear Barb, Georgia, Lily, Penelope, and Jack,*
> *One of you, in addition to Barb, was my very close friend. Our friendship was deeper than the rest of you suspected, even deeper than my friendship with you, Barb. This person knew about my love for you, Barb, and kept my secret, and for that, I'm grateful. During times when I was depressed over my unrequited love, this human being was my only source of comfort and knew that sometimes I wanted to end my life and that one day I might.*
>
> *I will refer to this special friend as "KAY." Eventually, I will tell you what this acronym stands for, but for now let me simply say that just because KAY is more popular as a girl's name than a boy's, do not assume KAY is female. Do not assume anything.*

My closer level of friendship with KAY started one day when we were alone and confided in each other more deeply than we had with the rest of the group. We began meeting one on one without telling the group. We confessed more about our lives, our feelings, our opinions, our dreams.

We'd meet for walks. For coffees. It was strangely like having an affair, except that it was not sexual—just a very caring intimacy.

One day, KAY did something very bad and told me about it two weeks later and made the decision to do something very bad again, but not immediately; instead, KAY would do it exactly two years from then— which is now just a couple of weeks away.

You'll have to prepare yourselves for the date (Friday, October 27), hopefully get through it, and then put it behind you, and try to forget.

In all honesty, you will never be able to forget. But with a little luck and my postmortem guidance, your group might be able to return to some semblance of what it is today. I know it's asking a lot, but I hope you will see your way to forgiving KAY her/his folly.

Love,

Gabriel

I call Georgia.

"Hello?" she answers, sounding loud and excited and out of breath.

"I just got another letter from Gabriel."

"Oh yeah? It's so nice of him to stay in touch, isn't it?"

I'm not in the mood. "Not funny."

"Sorry. What does he say?"

I read her the letter.

She greets it with stunned silence, which jibes with my mood much better.

"How weird," she finally says.

"Are you KAY?" I ask.

"Oh, I am more than okay."

"Not O-KAY. KAY!"

"No."

"You're not making much effort to deny it."

"If I don't sound fully engaged, it's because I was just about to call you with some news. I GOT MY LAPTOP BACK! Someone dropped it off at my building with a note that said, 'Sorry for the delay. Been busy.'" She laughs.

"I'm so happy for you. That makes up a little for Gabriel's letter."

Her tone sobers up. "Oh, yeah. What a disturbing letter. He's even weirder in death than in life."

I decide I want to read the letter to the others in person when I see them tomorrow, in case their expressions reveal which one of them is KAY.

Peter Marrick

Sunday, 15 October
I had the intern return the laptop. That's one thing off my plate.

I've been spending a lot of time trying to think of ways to meet Barb and her friends, other than the obvious way. I haven't been able to come up with any ideas due to my damned lack of imagination—ironic and rather tragic in view of how much I crave to be creative. Which is one of many reasons why I need to meet these people.

I got a complaint at work that I look distracted.

I can't obsess about this anymore. I will meet them the obvious way.

Chapter Six

On Sunday, I invite my friends over and read Gabriel's letter out loud to them. They act surprised in appropriate ways (except for Georgia, who's heard it already), and I can't decipher which of them might be KAY.

While we work, Lily continues trying to beautify Jack through her piano playing, but without success. Upset and frustrated, she leaves abruptly.

Georgia says she doesn't like her novel anymore, that it's not as great as she thought it was when she believed it was lost forever. She says the memory of it took on monumental proportions, and now the reality of it is just a bit of a letdown. She attributes this to absence making the heart grow fonder, and it makes her sick.

Penelope says Georgia is probably simply suffering from some sort of post-traumatic reverse syndrome of taking something for granted as soon as she gets it back.

And I remind Georgia that she's always told me this was her best novel yet, so it probably is.

———

LILY DOES NOT call that night even though I asked her to when she stormed out of my apartment earlier. I'm concerned about her. I know she's upset that she hasn't been able to beautify Jack through her music. I restrain myself from calling her, not wanting to be overly protective.

What dramatically increases my concern is that, at two o'clock in the afternoon the next day, movers show up at my apartment to take away Lily's piano. They tell me those are her instructions. They show me a form she filled out requesting its removal. While they carry out the upright piano, I'm anxiously trying to reach Lily by phone. She's not picking up. I curse myself for not calling her last night.

As I run out of my building to look for Lily, I pass Adam the doorman who says to me, "One day you'll find yourself, and wish you hadn't."

I'm a bit unsettled by that comment as I jog the few blocks to Lily's apartment, trying to refrain from holding my bouncing fake fat.

I ring Lily's downstairs buzzer. There's no answer. A tenant on his way out lets me in. I knock on Lily's apartment door. No answer. I can't stop my worry from mounting, though I know it may be irrational. I call Jack, Georgia, and Penelope. Within minutes, they have joined me. Jack gets the super to open her door. Lily's not in her apartment.

We go to my place. We keep calling her.

At five p.m. we're sitting on my couch, trying to reassure ourselves that she's okay, but not doing a very good job of it. I mention to my friends that three days ago she seemed delusional, claiming her hands had turned to mirrors and that it felt like death was trying to take hold of her, but that she fought it and it went away.

"Yeah, she told me that too. Not reassuring." Georgia pauses and takes a deep breath before adding, "But let's be optimistic. I'm sure she is fine, and will be fine, and in fact will probably make all her dreams come true. I've noticed that in life there are three ingredients that, when present simultaneously, create a potent combination: talent, love, and lack of beauty. One's love for someone, unrequited due to one's insufficient beauty, can motivate one to do great things to win that love, if one has the talent. Just look at what Lily's achieved so far. And I bet it's not stopping."

Twenty minutes later, the doorman buzzes me. We brighten, gripped by hope.

But when I answer my doorman intercom, I hear Adam's voice say softly in my ear, "Hi, piece of shit. There are some deliverymen here for you."

My heart sinks. I was so hoping for Lily.

"What do they want?" I ask him.

"To deliver something, moron."

"Deliver what?"

"I've only got one nerve left, and you're getting on it."

Ignoring him, I repeat, "Deliver what?"

"A piano."

A piano is not as good as Lily herself, but it's the next best thing. "Thanks, Adam. Send them up."

We're surprised that the upright piano the deliverymen carry into my apartment is made of mirror. We admire it, while they place it in the spot I indicate by the window.

Forty-five minutes later, Lily strolls into my apartment.

When she sees her new instrument, she says, "Ah. Good. It's here."

"We were worried to death!" I scream at her.

"I'm sorry. I was busy."

"With what?"

"Same project. But I'll be practicing on myself now instead of on Jack." She sits at the piano and starts hitting single keys, listening to the sound quality. "I bought this piano thinking it might inspire me. My project is so insanely difficult. Impossible, probably. But I'll work on it until I croak, if that's what it takes."

"Why don't you just give up?" Penelope says.

"Because then life might not seem worth living."

"See, *that's* the project you should be working on—making life worth living for reasons other than Strad," Jack says.

"I can't. I need love." Lily starts playing scales very rapidly, testing the piano. She stops, says, "Sounds good."

We're all standing around the musical instrument, our scowling expressions reflected back at us.

BEFORE BED, I call Lily at home to get a better sense of how she's doing and ask if she's had any more trouble with things like her hands becoming reflective.

"Yes. Yesterday I was in the pits of depression and then the hand thing happened again a couple of times while I was playing the piano. I stopped it each time from spreading, but I was so tempted not to."

"It spreads?"

"Yes. Up my wrists and arms."

"How do you stop it?"

"I will it to stop. I refuse to let it overtake me—out of fear, I guess. Even though it feels good. I mean, it feels good because it feels like nothing, which is good compared to how I feel, which is terrible. Death is the ultimate painkiller. When I will it to stop, it recedes, and the pain comes flooding back."

"I'm glad," I say quietly. "That you make it stop. And since yesterday, it hasn't happened again?"

"No. So far it's only happened when I hit bottom. But today I'm okay. Buying the mirrored piano cheered me up a bit."

On Friday is the meeting of the Excess Weight Disorders Support Group, which I promised my mother I'd attend and have been dreading.

When I arrive I see there are about twenty people in the group, all overweight or obese, mostly women. And there is a leader, fitting the same description.

The meeting begins. A woman shares her story. A few people make comments. Another woman shares. More comments. I wait for an opening to tell them the truth about myself. I'm nervous.

For a long time, I see no opportunity until finally a woman says, "Ever since my first child was born I've been struggling with my weight. I gained a lot and then lost some and then gained back more than I lost, and then lost some again, but whenever I lose any weight, I gain back all of it and more."

Another woman jumps in with: "I'm a total yo-yo dieter, too! I take the weight off in the summer and fill my closet with skinny clothes, and then I put all the weight back on in the winter."

Heart pounding, I say, "Same here. I take the weight off at night and hang it in my closet and put it back on in the morning."

No one seems to hear me.

Someone else says, "I guess I have a really slow metabolism. I gain weight so easily. And it gets worse as I get older. Anything I eat goes directly from my lips to my hips."

"I totally know what you mean," I say. "For me it's even more direct. It bypasses the lips altogether."

A couple of chuckles and puzzled looks, but the group doesn't pause, keeps on talking. I'm not sure my mom would be satisfied with my efforts.

I finally see my opportunity when a woman says, "I mean, I know I'm thin on the inside."

"Me too! See?" I spring up and flash the assembly. Everyone stares inside my fat jacket, gaping at my thin torso and shoulders.

"What are you doing? Why did you come here?" the leader asks, not looking happy.

"My therapist says I have a serious weight issue, like the rest of you, and that just because my way of getting fat is unusual doesn't mean the source of the problem isn't very typical."

"You don't belong here," another woman says.

"But I'm fat."

"Yours is removable."

"So is yours. It just takes longer."

"You're a thin person."

"So are you, on the inside. Like me."

"I assume you don't even have an eating disorder, right?"

"No, but I've got a weight disorder," I insist. "I engage in unhealthy, compulsive behavior like everyone here. When you guys go to the store to buy your fatty things, I go to a store and buy a different kind of fatty thing. And then I go home, and instead of eating mine, I put it on my body. My brain and emotions have the same need as yours to be fat, but my body is unable to manufacture that fat for reasons of taste. I hate the taste of fattening foods. I hate overeating. And I hate being inactive. But that doesn't mean I don't have a very serious weight problem. I can't stop putting on the weight. When I take it off, I can't keep it off. Either your way or my way, the fat ends up visible to everyone, and the result is the same in the eyes of the world."

"Okay," says the group leader. "Let's move on ... Sally? Would you like to share?"

I sit in silence for forty more minutes until the meeting finally ends.

GEORGIA TELLS US her agent wants to know if our whole group would be willing to appear on TV, on *News with Peter Marrick,* to be interviewed about our Nights of Creation and our creativity in general.

"They want us on Wednesday night at six," Georgia explains. "They're doing a segment on creativity. They read about our Nights of Creation in that *Observer* article last year."

We agree to do it. We're particularly excited that the great

Peter Marrick himself, America's favorite local news anchor, will be conducting the interview. Even if he weren't so charismatic and charming on camera, the incident a few years ago when he ran into a burning building and saved three children would make him America's sweetheart. His cameraman captured the spectacle of Peter running out of the burning house, his hair on fire, carrying a baby in one arm and dragging two small children in his other hand. The only injury he sustained was to his hair follicles. His decision to continue anchoring the news with singed hair and then with a shaved head drew even more viewers. And when his hair grew back nicer and more unusual than before, that didn't hurt the ratings either. He looked angelic—almost ethereal with his hair floating around his head, light and airy, like a halo.

"You should all go on the show without me," Georgia says. "I've got nothing to say about creativity anymore. When you lose your faith in your work, what have you got left as an artist? Nothing much."

"Haven't you done any writing in the last week since you got your laptop back?" Jack asks.

"I tried."

"And?"

"I've become an expert at backing up my laptop. I've set up three different backup systems. The first is manual. The second is automatic, hourly, wireless, in the apartment. And the third is automatic, daily, in the cloud, which means that all of America could blow up and I could still retrieve a backup from the Internet in Europe, assuming I wasn't *in* America when it blew up."

Chapter Seven

I discover a new letter from Gabriel waiting for me in my mailbox.

That letter shocks me so deeply that I'm not able to call my friends right away to tell them about it. I do research online for about an hour. Then I think. I spend the entire night thinking. I don't even try to sleep.

IN THE MORNING, I call my friends. I tell them to come to my apartment at three. This way, I'll still have a few hours to think more about the letter.

MY FRIENDS ARRIVE promptly. We settle ourselves on the couch.

Not beating around the bush, I unfold the letter.

I take a deep breath and begin reading—

Dear Barb, Georgia, Lily, Penelope, and Jack,
This is my final letter to you before October 27th. I
didn't want to upset you sooner than necessary, but
now I must tell you the terrible thing one of you did,

and I must issue an urgent warning that I hope is no longer necessary, but if it is, you must heed it.

On Lily's birthday, we were all out at a bar. It was a great evening. We were in high spirits, having a wonderful time, laughing a lot. Lily was turning twenty-three, and we were teasing her about her youth, which we secretly envied but also cherished. She seemed to find it very amusing. Then she and Barb went to the restroom, and just when they had rejoined our table, we heard a guy a few feet away make a despicable and ludicrous comment about them to his buddy. We never talked about it, but we all heard it.

If you do not remember what the man said, I've written it down in the small envelope I've enclosed in this letter.

I stop reading and hold up, for my friends to see, a tiny, pale blue envelope on which are scribbled the words "Offensive Comment." (I opened it last night, not because I didn't remember the comment, but to check if Gabriel's recollection matched mine. It did.)

My friends look uncomfortable, staring at the blue envelope. I'm waiting to see if any of them want to read it.

Blushing painfully, Lily says, "Okay, first of all, guys, this walking on eggshells is not necessary. The man's comment was something like, 'Look at that hideous chick and her gorgeous friend. Isn't it amazing how her ugliness brings out the other's beauty, and vice versa? It would ruin my evening, having to look at a dog like that, not to mention if I had to be seen with one.'"

Lily waits for our reaction to her recollection. After a moment of stunned silence, we mutter our grim indignation at the man's comment.

I don't read the next two sentences of the letter. I recite them, my gaze locked on my friends' faces so as not to miss the slightest quivering of an eyelash: *"The man who made the comment was murdered that night, in his apartment, by one of you."*

I note a few sharp intakes of breath and a couple of frowns. Penelope's hand flies to her mouth.

I continue: *"The killer among you (K.A.Y.) confessed it to me two weeks later. Please take a moment now to look at the article I've enclosed about the man's murder."*

My friends look at each other and at me in shock. Lily looks particularly distressed, which I can well understand. Even if she's not the killer, she might nevertheless feel indirectly responsible for the man's death.

I hand them the *New York Times* article.

They crowd around it, looking at the man's photo under the headline "Murder Strikes Home In Tribeca Neighborhood." They try to read bits of the article over one another's shoulders, while appearing uneasy about possibly huddling too close to a murderer.

"Read it out loud," Jack finally instructs Georgia, who's holding it.

She reads:

Tribeca residents were stunned yesterday to learn that a local resident, 33-year-old Lawrence Finn, has been found murdered in the kitchen of his Vestry Street home.

Mr. Finn was discovered yesterday morning in his apartment on the third floor of his elevator building by his housekeeper who alerted authorities. It is believed that Mr. Finn was killed by a single knife wound to the throat, but police are not releasing specific details of the crime. It is not known if a weapon has been recovered.

"This was a senseless and bloody act," said Detective Vince Monticelli of the First Precinct. "We are appealing to anyone who may have seen anything suspicious in the Vestry Street area between the hours of midnight and 3 a.m. to come forward. The motive for this crime does not appear to have been robbery. It is possible Mr. Finn knew his attacker and allowed him or her entry into the apartment."

Mr. Finn was an employee of Morrison & Partners, a New York-based hedge fund company. "Larry was a nice guy," said Anthony Morrison, chief executive officer of Morrison & Partners. "I know of no one who wished him any harm."

Police are investigating the recent trading activity in which Mr. Finn was engaged for clues to a possible motive. The often secretive trading practices of the unregulated hedge fund industry frequently result in large gains and losses for investors. Companies targeted by hedge fund traders are also known to resent the impact such trading has on their market valuations.

A friend of Mr. Finn's, Mark Stanley, was the last known person to see him alive. Mr. Stanley and Mr. Finn were together on Tuesday evening at the Saratoga Lounge on East 16th Street. According to Mr. Stanley, he left Mr. Finn at the bar at approximately 11:45 p.m. "I can't believe this," said a stunned Mr. Stanley. "Larry always liked to party hard. We were having a great time." Mr. Stanley was interviewed by the police but is not considered a suspect. Detectives have questioned employees at the Saratoga Lounge and are trying to ascertain at what time Mr. Finn left the bar, and if he was alone at that time. They are asking anybody who was in the Saratoga Lounge on Tuesday evening after 8 p.m. to come forward with any information they may have.

When Georgia finishes reading the article, she gazes at Lily. We all do.

Slowly and quietly, Lily says, "I'm horrified by what you've just read. How do we know this letter is really from Gabriel or if it is, that Gabriel is telling the truth?"

Georgia turns to me. "Barb, have you looked into the case?"

I inform them that I researched it online last night and that the murder has never been solved. The police believe it was an isolated, spontaneous act. It didn't appear to be related to any other crimes that had taken place in the city.

"As for the authenticity of the letter," I add, "I can't imagine what motive anyone could have for forging Gabriel's handwriting and making all this up. I think our safest bet is to assume the letter's real and that Gabriel is telling the truth. It would be risky not to take it seriously."

Jack nods. "Still, I'd like to get the opinion of a forensic handwriting expert to make sure this letter really is from Gabriel."

"Good idea," Georgia says.

"But what if Jack is the killer and has a motive for creating a false report?" Penelope says. "You would trust his 'expert'?"

"We can get a second opinion, if you want," Georgia tells her. "Why don't you find us a second expert and ask him or her as well?"

"Okay, I will," Penelope says.

"I doubt the letter's forged," Georgia says. "I think what's more important is figuring out who KAY is."

I continue reading the letter from where I left off: *"A few weeks after confessing this crime to me, KAY said, 'I don't want you to think this will be a recurring thing I do, but there's someone else I've decided to put an end to. I'm going to kill Strad.'"*

"Wha—?" Lily gasps. I carefully observe her reaction.

I continue reading:

KAY said to me, "I've made up my mind that in two years' time, if Lily still loves him and he still doesn't love her, I will try to kill him. But I will leave it partly in the hands of fate. What I mean by that is that in two years, on the evening of October 27th, sometime between the hours of 8 p.m. and midnight, I will kill him if I get a chance. I may even plan it in advance. I will put a fairly serious amount of effort into it. But if I don't succeed during those four hours—like let's say there are constant obstacles—I will take it as a sign from fate that Strad should not be killed, and I will not continue trying. See, I'm easygoing and flexible."

I did my best to dissuade KAY from this plan, but nothing worked. I even threatened KAY, said I would call the police and tell them about the first murder.

KAY said that was my right, and that I should do it if I wanted to.

My dear friends, I'm sorry to be keeping KAY's identity from you, but I'm afraid that if I don't, you'll turn KAY in to the police. You may judge me harshly, but I care too deeply for KAY to send him/her to prison.

I need to take a break from my reading because Lily is crying. "Are you okay?" I give her a sympathetic look and hand her tissues.

"Please finish the letter," she says, wiping her nose.

I continue reading:

I'm sorry to be leaving you with this burden, but your job now is to protect Strad on October 27th (next Friday), between the hours of 8 p.m. and midnight. If you succeed in keeping him alive during that time, KAY will never again try to harm Strad or anyone else. KAY promised. And I believe KAY.

Just because Georgia may be the likeliest candidate, don't assume it's her. Or that it's not. Just because Lily may be the least likely one, don't assume it's not her. Or that it is. Any of you might be the killer, except you, Barb. I'm exempting Barb because all of you will have an easier time protecting Strad if at least one of you has been cleared of suspicion.

You should know that KAY loves you all and would never harm any of you. In addition, KAY promised never again to kill anyone, other than Strad. This

was a solemn promise. You may wonder why I choose
to believe a homicidal maniac. I don't have an easy
answer. I'm sure you know, though, that I would not
leave you in the hands of anyone I thought would ever
harm you.

"Oh my God, he's insane," Georgia says. "How can he trust a
psycho? I think we're in grave danger."
Jack looks at her and nods grimly.
I continue reading the letter:

If, on the day you read this letter, Lily is no longer in
love with Strad, or if she is and he loves her back, then
you can disregard this letter.
There are some rules you need to be aware of:
1) KAY will not hesitate to kill Strad in front of any
of you. If the attempt is successful, KAY will leave it up
to you to decide if you want to help KAY hide/dispose of
the body or turn KAY in to the police. KAY trusts that
you will make the right decision.

"Oh, how horrible," Georgia groans. "How could you put us
in that position, whoever you are?" she says, looking at Jack,
Penelope, and Lily.
After duly noting her reaction, I resume reading the letter:

2) KAY will not go so far as to kill Strad in front of
anyone other than you guys because KAY would then
without question get turned in.

3) KAY has agreed not to set up a lethal situation that would kill Strad outside of those four hours. For example, KAY can't give Strad a package between the hours of 8 p.m. and midnight that will explode after midnight.

I don't want to explain to you in great depth KAY's motives for wanting to kill Strad, mostly for fear of inadvertently revealing KAY's identity. So I will limit myself to saying that KAY feels that Strad's existence is ruining Lily's life. I assume you will try to present arguments to change KAY's mind, and perhaps you'll have better luck than I did, but don't count on it.

I told KAY that I would warn you of KAY's murderous plan before it's meant to happen. So don't think that my letters to you are much of a surprise to KAY. I told KAY I would instruct you all to do everything in your power to protect Strad during the four dangerous hours. KAY accepted this, said your success or lack of it would be part of what KAY will interpret as destiny's will.

In case you're wondering why I revealed to KAY that I would alert you, I had no choice. I was afraid that if KAY felt betrayed by my letters, KAY would decide to change the rules and would make an attempt on Strad's life at another time, on another day, when Strad wasn't protected.

If you ever find out who KAY is, I hope you will be compassionate and able to forgive her/him.

*I wish I could say "My thoughts will be with you," but
I will have no thoughts. And that's what I'm looking for-
ward to. Please be happy for me and love one another as
I love each of you.*

*You will never hear from me again. Barb, this is my
final letter.*

Much love,
Gabriel

I fold the letter, my eyes moist despite my anger at Gabriel.

Lily is the first to speak. "If one of you kills Strad and if the cops don't get you, I will hunt you down myself and kill you and then kill myself." She pauses. "Is that clear?"

"What a charming day," Jack says.

Georgia says, "I think we have to settle one question: Do we want one of us, a friend, to go to prison? I mean, Gabriel was afraid we would, which is why he didn't want to tell us who it is. But is he right?"

We all look at one another.

"Maybe it depends on who it is," Georgia adds.

"Oh?" says Jack. "And which of us would you feel good about sending to prison?"

"No one. I'm just throwing the question out there. Maybe some of you would feel okay about sending someone like . . . oh, I don't know . . . *me*, for instance, to jail, and not someone like, um . . . Lily. Or Penelope."

A little impatiently, I say, "Please, Georgia, we don't have time for your insecurities and paranoia right now. Of course we don't want to see you go to prison, what's wrong with you? Especially if you're not the killer. Now, let's focus! The 27th is only five days from now."

The truth is, I would sooner die than see Georgia go to prison.

But I can tell she's offended by my tone. I brace myself for her favorite retaliation technique: gently demonstrating to everyone that her intelligence is superior to the offender's (we all know she can dwarf us intellectually without effort, and it baffles me that she still feels the need to prove it).

On this occasion, she goes about it in the following insidious fashion. Adopting an innocuous tone, she says: "It was smart of you, Barb, not to read us the letter as soon as you got it. Did you use that valuable time to try and test us to figure out who the killer is?"

"No," I reply, truthfully.

And the reason I didn't is because even though I spent most of my time since yesterday afternoon trying to come up with ideas of how to test my friends, I failed to come up with any good ones (except for one little test I intend to try later, but which I doubt will work).

"Oh, that's too bad," she says. "The best time to figure out which of us is the killer would have been between the time you received the letter and the time you read it to us—when only *you* knew the situation. It's a shame not to have made some use of that precious window of opportunity."

"No, it's not a shame, because there's really nothing I could have done," I say, with some confidence considering the nearly twelve hours I spent thinking about it. I feel pretty sure that even Georgia, with her superior intelligence, could not have thought of how to uncover the killer's identity.

"Oh, I don't think that's true," she says. "I've no doubt there's something one might have thought of."

"Like what?"

"I'd have to think about it."

"Why don't you. And let me know how you make out."

"Okay." A split second later she says, "Oh, I just thought of one."

"What is it?"

"Not worth mentioning now. The opportunity's gone." She shoos the idea away with her hand.

"But please do. I would be very interested."

"It's really nothing special. I'm sure you would have thought of it yourself if you had spent even just twenty minutes trying to come up with something. And plus, as you so rightly pointed out, don't we have more important things to talk about?"

I have an impulse to slug her. "Just tell me what you thought of."

"All right. Here it is. You could have sent a letter to each of us, pretending to be Gabriel."

I look at her sternly, waiting for her to elaborate. She doesn't. I cave in: "Elaborate."

"Each letter would have to appear to be a single, unique, confidential letter. The letters could say something like, 'As you may or may not already know, I have sent a letter to Barb announcing your plan to kill Strad. In it, I do not reveal that you are the killer. I'm protecting your identity. But let me entreat you now, one last time, not to kill Strad.' Blah, blah. End of letter. It's obvious what would happen next. The three of us who are not the killer would be utterly baffled and freaked out by the letter. We'd be calling you up, shrieking: 'Oh my God, Barb, I just received this crazy letter from Gabriel saying I have a plan to kill Strad, but I don't!' The killer would be the only one who wouldn't call. Simple."

I could indeed have done that, I realize sadly. It would have been brilliant. I'm deeply demoralized by this huge missed opportunity. I feel as though I've let Lily down (assuming she's not the killer). Georgia is a worthier friend than I am (also assuming she's not the killer). She's a smarter friend.

"Barb, you can't compare yourself to the queen of convoluted thinking. None of us can," Jack says, as though he's read my mind.

Georgia, too, has sensed my distress. She backpedals, her entire tone softening: "Jack's right. And anyway, I wouldn't wish this ability on anyone. It makes my life wretched, feeds my paranoia, makes me overly complicated, irritating to others, including to myself, but on some rare occasions, such as this one, it comes in handy."

I gaze at my friends. "There's something I'd like to say to whichever one of you is the killer." My tone is chilling. I have their full attention. "If you, KAY, were so close to Gabriel and were his confidant to the degree that he even told you of his suicidal thoughts, why didn't you prevent his death?" I start shouting at them, shooting them furious glances. "You could have sought out help! You should have told us. At least you should have told me of his love for me. I would have done something, acted differently, been more attuned to the situation. But most of all, *you* could have stopped him from killing himself. How could you let him die? Are you so incompetent, so lame, so self-ish, what? Didn't you care enough about him to save his life? You certainly *are* a murderer."

I haven't taken my eyes off of them for a second. My words were painful. Yet they had to be said—because they were the test I came up with last night. I wasn't very optimistic that it would succeed in its purpose of provoking the killer into betraying him/herself. And I think I was right. The only purpose it seems to have served is to make us feel really awful.

I scrutinize my friends' faces to try to catch any trace of emotion, any quivering lip, any distress, because I know the killer cared deeply for Gabriel and I'm certain my words must have inflicted particularly acute pain on him or her.

But as I contemplate these people, no single reaction stands out. They all display attitudes that could be used against them. Jack sighs and looks down. I ask him what's up. He says he agrees with me, that the killer should have prevented Gabriel's death, but that it can be hard to prevent such things.

Georgia also looks suspicious because she's staring at me fixedly, her jaw clenched.

"Why are you looking at me like that?" I ask.

"Because I agree with you, too. You would think the murderer could have stopped this suicide if he cared about Gabriel." But she says this a bit stiffly, which makes me narrow my eyes. Yet I move on.

Penelope acts perfectly normal, which is questionable in itself.

And Lily is wiping tears from her face, which is either shady or completely understandable.

We discuss whether or not we should request the help of the police.

"We can't tell the police," Georgia says. "KAY is sick and needs to be protected by us. I know you may take offense at this, Lily, and I'm sorry about it, but I care much more about KAY not rotting in prison than Strad staying alive."

"You're right, I do take offense at that," Lily says softly.

Jack, who—perhaps because he's a cop—has been looking especially glum since hearing me read the letter, says, "Telling the police would be one easy way to find out which of you is the killer. Unless the killer took extreme precautions, all the police would have to do is match each one of you against the forensics from that crime scene two years ago. But the price of finding out would be high—not only for KAY, who'd end up in prison, but for the rest of us, who'd lose her. I can't see myself sending one of you to prison for life."

Georgia exhales loudly with relief and clasps her hands. "You feel as I do, sweet Jack!"

"What kind of cop are you, to think this way?" Lily says to him.

"A cop who's very fond of every single one of you," he replies, gazing at her steadily.

Penelope asks him: "Aren't you afraid that the killer, who must be a psycho, could be dangerous not only to Strad but to anyone, including us? Personally, I'm going to be afraid now of being alone with any single one of you." She pauses thoughtfully. "That's not to say I'd be capable of turning any of you in. I wouldn't be."

Jack says, "Keeping the killer among us is a risk, but I don't see what other option we have. We just have to hope she cares as much about us as we care about her."

"I feel very differently from you all," Lily says. "I would rather see one of you go to prison than see the man I love get killed."

"The man you love," Georgia scoffs, rolling her eyes. "Has the man you love been wonderful to you the way we have been? Have you developed a close, loving relationship with the man you love the way you have with each of us? Would the man you love do anything for you the way we would? Does he love you at all, even just as a friend?"

Lily's hard expression softens with this reminder of our devotion to her.

"And yet you want to take this to the police?" Georgia asks her.

"Yes, I want to. But obviously I can't."

Now it's Georgia's turn to soften. She smiles and puts her hand on Lily's arm affectionately. "Aw, so you *do* feel the same way we do."

"No." Lily removes her arm. "I have another reason. If we bring the police into this, it'll ruin my chances with Strad. The police will reveal everything to him. They'll tell him that for years I've been so in love with him that one of my friends is ready to kill him to bring me peace and free me of my obsession. I'd be so embarrassed if Strad knew any of this. I could never face him again. And he'd be so horrified, he'd never want to face me again either, I'm sure."

In the end, we are unanimous: we will not take this to the police. We will protect Strad ourselves on the evening of his possible murder. The only thing left to do is figure out how to go about doing this.

We're aware the killer can kill Strad without physically being with him. KAY can have Strad killed by a hired gun. Or plant a bomb that will be scheduled to explode during the four-hour window. Or countless other more ingenious ideas.

So it quickly becomes clear to us, for all sorts of reasons, that on the evening of the 27th, making sure that no one from our group will be with him won't be enough protection. Strad must not be left alone. He must be actively protected.

My friends say we should all be with him. That's the part I find weird.

"I understand why we can't leave Strad alone that evening," I tell them, "but I still don't understand why I can't protect him by myself. Gabriel made it clear I'm the only one of our group you can all trust. Strad and I could be alone in this apartment, and I wouldn't let anyone in, and no one would have access to him."

"I don't feel good about you being alone on that occasion," Jack says. "I'd want to be there to protect you. You never know what the killer cooked up. I understand you can't be sure that I'm not the killer so you'll want either all of us there or none of us there. So it has to be all. We can control whichever one of us is the killer, if she tries anything."

Georgia says, "And the other problem is that Strad isn't likely to want to spend an evening alone with you, Barb, in your apartment, unless it's a date. And wouldn't it be weird vis-à-vis Lily if you were to have a so-called date with Strad? And would Strad even want to go on a date with you? No offense, but your disguise may not be the kind of look he's into. He thinks it's your real appearance."

Penelope says, "And another good reason for having us all there is that if an attempt is made on Strad's life, we'll get to see who among us is the killer, which we'd like to know anyway."

I finally reluctantly relent. We will all protect Strad. The location we pick for the evening with Strad is my apartment, which I will make killer-proof for the occasion.

Before everybody goes home, I make one final request. "I want to know if the killer among you has changed his or her mind about murdering Strad. After you leave here today, I'd like you, KAY, to call me and press any digit on your phone one time if you no longer intend to kill Strad, and three times if you still do. You don't have to speak to me or reveal who you are. Just beeps. One beep is no. Three is yes."

"You do realize we should protect Strad regardless of the answer you're given," Jack says. "Gabriel said that KAY would put considerable effort into killing Strad on the 27th. Such effort could include encouraging us to let down our guards by pretending she no longer intends to kill him."

"Yes, I know."

Chapter Eight

The next day, Monday, we're gathered at Lily's apartment for lunch, which we ordered from L'Express.

Lily tells us that when she invited Strad to have dinner with us this coming Friday, the 27th, his reaction was, "You're kidding me! The Creators? The Knights of Creation will be there?" Strad had read one of the silly articles about us that explained no one gets to pierce our "holy circle." The word choice was unfortunate, though the gist of it was true.

"Is there any chance we could do it on a different night?" he asked Lily. "I already have plans for dinner that night and I'm attending a party afterward."

"No, see, that's the thing, it can only be on that night," she said.

"Okay, consider me there. But, just curious . . . why only that night?"

"Oh, it's Georgia. Who knows. She gets these ideas in her head, and it has to be that night, no other night."

"Yes, of course. She's an artist, quirky. Wonderful. I've been wanting to meet her for ages."

Upon hearing Lily's account, Georgia grimaces with disgust.

During dessert, we discuss the planning of the evening with Strad.

Georgia's fear is that it will be tedious. "What will we do to kill time while we protect him?"

"You could ask him to play the violin for you," Lily answers.

"Is he any good?"

"Not really. I think that's why he recently decided to pursue acting."

"Don't make me listen to him perform a soliloquy. It will kill me."

My cell phone rings. I answer it. I hear three beeps and then a hang-up. I stop breathing as a wave of nausea sweeps over me.

I look at my friends. "I got three beeps."

"Oh my God," Penelope gasps.

"Asshole!" Lily exclaims, slapping the table.

I call back the number, which has no name attached. It rings a long time, and then someone, to my surprise, picks up.

"Hello?" a man says.

"Did you just call me?"

"No."

"Who are you?" I ask.

"Someone who answered a pay phone."

"Where?"

"Uh ... Forty-Seventh Street and Second Avenue. In Manhattan."

"Outdoors? On the street?"

"Yes."

"Did you see who just called me a minute ago?"

"No."

"Is there anyone unusual standing around? Or anyone looking at you?"

"Uh . . . no, not really."

"What corner of the intersection is the phone on?" Not that it matters. Not that there would be any point in rushing over there right now. I'm just being thorough because you never know in life what details will come in handy.

"Uh . . . Northeast corner."

"Thank you."

We hang up.

My friends all glance at one another, undoubtedly trying, as I am, to decipher who among them is the killer.

I look at Jack, yearning for his help, but uncertain he's innocent.

I say, "I guess one of you asked someone—or hired someone—to make this phone call?"

I find the concept of someone being hired to make this phone call terrifying. It makes the whole thing seem like a bigger, more serious production: there's personnel involved—staff! Who knows, maybe the killer has hired an assassin as well, or many, to do the dirty work. And to think that all this is being orchestrated by someone in this room, someone who is looking at me right now with affectionate eyes and a familiar face—a beloved friend. Unimaginable.

"Probably," Jack says.

Georgia nods.

"I don't appreciate what you're doing," I say to the mystery killer among us. "Don't you care that you're making our lives miserable, devastating our group, probably even destroying it? And don't you care about how much you would hurt Lily, perhaps even ruin her life, if you killed Strad? Assuming she's not the killer."

I doubt my words are persuasive. I'm sure the killer was aware of these risks when he/she made the decision to kill Strad, and yet must have concluded Lily would still be better off if Strad were dead.

LUNCH IS OVER and we each go home. When I arrive at my building, Adam the doorman has his hands in his pockets. When he sees me, he opens his jacket and flashes me his white T-shirt on which is written "Bitch" in big red letters.

I look around. Lucky for him, no one saw him.

I spend the afternoon making preparations for the evening of Strad's possible death, four days away. ("Evening of Strad's death" is what we got into the habit of calling it. This isn't a sign of resignation—it's simply shorter than including the word "attempted," or "possible," but now that I think about it, calling it "Friday" would have been even shorter.) I start making things safe.

I must anticipate every trick the killer might pull.

My apartment, since yesterday, has been off limits to my friends.

This morning I placed an ad on the NYU website, looking to hire a few students to help me search my apartment for any weapons the killer might have already planted there.

I will, of course, frisk my friends when they arrive on the night of the dinner.

My brain is so muddled from stress that I haven't been able to focus on anything except getting things safe for the dinner. My work has suffered. I'm supposed to be creating a hat that goes with the quirky green velvet outfit I finished two days ago. Ordinarily, I'd be able to come up with an original hat concept in less than twenty minutes. But now my mind has deteriorated almost to the point of asking myself, "What's a hat?"

I take a walk down Fifth Avenue to Washington Square Park, trying to imagine every weapon the killer might think of using, and I dismiss the ones I assume I don't need to worry about, such as a gun—which frisking would detect—and a vial of poison —which I plan to guard against by keeping my friends away from the food until it's served. A wire to strangle Strad would be easy to smuggle in but does not worry me because getting strangled takes a couple of minutes and we'd have more than enough time to pull the killer off Strad. More dangerous are the weapons that can be used in a split second, such as blades, especially razor blades. They're simple to sneak in and they're quick. But perhaps most importantly, a blade was the killer's weapon of choice the first time around.

AT NIGHT, I wake up in cold sweats. My friends are not the types to do anything very bad, much less kill someone, but I'm aware we don't always know people as well as we think we do, and Gabriel is not the type to lie. So I try to figure out, yet again, which of my friends murdered the man from the bar.

Jack is, of course, the most obvious, mainly because he has killed before. He killed two men in the shootout with Penelope's kidnappers, the same shootout that left him limping. In addition, he's still very strong despite his injuries. He would certainly be capable of slitting a man's throat if he wanted, probably far more easily than Georgia, Penelope, or Lily, at least on a physical level. On a psychological, emotional, and moral level, that's another matter. I think back on when he first got his part-time job at the senior center, which he took soon after rescuing Penelope, when he realized he'd never be able to get back on the police force due to his limp.

After a few weeks of serving meals and asking after grandchildren at the senior center, he was feeling depressed, missing the kind of work he'd done as a police officer. That was when the seniors started getting into frequent fights—a couple of them a week. Jack broke up the fights. He thought it was strange that the fights were so numerous, but the truth was, he didn't mind. He felt more useful and less depressed this way.

Jack had broken up six fights in the three weeks since the fights had begun. He decided to ask the director of the senior center what was going on.

"Thank you for keeping the peace and breaking up the fights," the director said to him.

"No problem."

"The fact that the fights are fake should not in any way diminish your sense of accomplishment."

"The fights are fake?"

"Yes. The seniors were excited to have a hero such as yourself working here, but they were worried you would not be happy merely serving them lunch if your special skill—of keeping the peace—wasn't used. That's why they took it upon themselves to stage fights. It's very touching."

"I'm touched and humiliated at the same time. I don't think I can continue working here, now that I know this. And I'm not sure why you told me."

"I told you because I was afraid you'd figure it out yourself and decide to quit the job before giving me a chance to explain how important it is that you continue."

"Continue serving lunch?"

"And breaking up fights."

"Fake fights."

"Yes. The seniors have never been happier. You've given them a sense of purpose. They think they've given you a purpose in life and that without them you'd be falling apart."

"It'll be difficult for me to continue playing along with this."

"Yes. And therefore very rewarding. Please continue to give the seniors a sense of purpose by letting them think they're giving you a sense of purpose. That's a far greater gift than serving them lunch, which you do wonderfully well too."

Jack has been happy enough at that part-time job for the past five years. The seniors love him and the feeling is close to mutual. He has no immediate plans to leave.

Sure, Jack's willingness to go along with such an eccentric plan could be considered deviant behavior—but deviant in the most selfless and kind-hearted of ways. It shows such an endearing willingness to swallow his pride that I can't imagine him murdering a stranger over an offensive comment at a bar—even one directed at Lily. I know I could be wrong, but nevertheless I dismiss Jack as a possible culprit for now and turn my thoughts to Georgia, Penelope, and Lily to try to remember things they've said or done that could be indicative of their guilt.

I don't come up with any grand revelations.

THE NEXT DAY, I decide I must get some work done, must buckle down. I can't let my desire to protect Strad-the-Jerk damage my career. The movie director I'm working with left me a message asking where the hat was that I said I'd send him two days ago and if everything's okay.

No, things are not okay, but I must compartmentalize. Just because there's a problem in one life-box doesn't mean it has to create a problem in all my other life-boxes.

I settle down to my work, blank page in front of me, elbows on the table, head in my hands, thinking of hat for green outfit. I've hardly been at this for two minutes when the phone rings. I should have turned off the ringer. Forgot to.

It's Jack, saying he just got word from the forensic handwriting expert that Gabriel's letter is authentic.

I take this in. Jack then says there's a special way the killer could sneak in a weapon on the evening of Strad's death, even if I frisk everyone. And he describes the way.

After we hang up, the "way" haunts me.

I call for a meeting; I must discuss the way.

We meet for dinner at Penelope's place on the Upper East Side. We bring sandwiches.

Before we've even unwrapped them, I'm anxious and hence can't delay getting on topic: "It has been brought to my attention by one of you that women can hide weapons inside their bodies in the fashion of a tampon, and that the weapon can easily be accessed, especially when the woman goes to the bathroom."

"Typical that a man should think of this," Penelope mutters, looking at her shoes.

Jack seems taken aback by her guess, but doesn't deny it. "I'm a cop! That's why I thought of it. Not because I'm a man."

Georgia says to me, "Men can hide weapons inside their bodies in the fashion of a suppository. Don't tell me you're going to explore our crevices."

"I can't be explored," Penelope says softly, still gazing at her shoes.

Lily looks apprehensive as well.

"Don't be ridiculous," I tell them. "I'm not going to explore anyone. I just want you to wear pants, that's all."

"You mean so we can't whip it out in the middle of dinner?" snaps Georgia.

I nod and can't help laughing. "Everyone will wear pants, and everyone will get frisked, over their clothes, when they enter my apartment as well as every time they come out of the bathroom. In addition, Jack kindly offered to get me a metal detector."

NIGHTMARES WAKE ME in the middle of Tuesday night, less than three days before the dinner. Being a costume designer, I'm very aware of the nooks and crannies in clothing that can be used to hide a weapon, especially a tiny weapon such as a jugular-slashing razor blade. My fear is that the frisking and metal detecting won't be enough, that something will be missed. I need a backup plan, a more extreme safety measure I can resort to if necessary. After some thinking, I come up with one that is not ideal because it would make us seem strange in Strad's eyes, and we would hate for his opinion of Lily to be tarnished by something we do. So I will not use this extreme safety measure if I can help it, though it calms me knowing it will be at my disposal if I need it.

Chapter Nine

That evening, we're all sitting around in one of the TV studio's large dressing rooms, waiting to be interviewed live in about an hour.

Penelope breaks the silence with: "I got the result from my handwriting specialist. She said the same thing as Jack's guy—that her analysis concluded that it was highly probable that Gabriel wrote the letter. She said that 'highly probable' is the official term used and means 99 percent certain, and that that's pretty much as certain as it gets."

We all nod quietly, not surprised.

We perk up a bit when Peter Marrick comes in to greet us. Oddly, he seems more nervous than we are. But very charming nevertheless. He has the hiccups.

"I'm so happy to meet you," he tells us. "It's an honor to have a group like yours on my show."

We stand there, saying thank you and looking at him like dummies while he hiccups. We're a bit starstruck.

"I really admire what you do," he goes on. "I so wish I could be creative. But . . . let's save that for the show."

He chats with us a little more, asks if we have everything we need, then says he has to go to makeup.

Just as he's about to leave, still hiccupping, Georgia says, "Do you need help with that hiccup?"

"I may be open to suggestions."

Georgia says, "My method is infallible and can be used instantly. If I'm not remembered for my novels, I'll be remembered for my Hiccup-Stopping Method. If everyone knew it, no one on earth would ever again have the hiccups for longer than a few seconds."

What she says is true. Her Hiccup-Stopping Method is her most popular invention in our group. None of us has had a second hiccup in four years because as soon as we get our first hiccup, we use her method and the second hiccup is stopped dead in its tracks.

Georgia says, "The most remarkable thing about this method—considering how foolproof it is—is how unimpressive it sounds."

"Really? Sounds amazing. What's the method?" Peter asks, hiccupping some more.

"Stop moving and relax all your internal organs," Georgia tells him.

He laughs and hiccups again. "What does that mean—relax all my internal organs? Even my bladder? You want me to pee in my pants?"

This makes me laugh, which makes him laugh harder.

"No, not to that degree," Georgia says. "Just relax your stomach, throat, lungs, even peripheral things like your jaw and your shoulders. Do it now. Close your eyes if it helps. Let your body sort of go limp. The method works best if you use it right away as soon as your hiccupping begins, but even if you wait, like now, it'll still work. It'll just take a minute longer."

Peter closes his eyes but he can't stop laughing.

"If you laugh you're not relaxed. Stop laughing," she commands.

"Easier said than—"

"Don't talk! Just relax your internal organs."

Peter laughs some more, eyes still closed and hiccups still going.

Jack tells him, "It's true it's not going to work if you keep laughing."

"Okay," Peter says, and takes a deep breath and stops laughing.

His self-control impresses me. I'm still laughing.

He stays perfectly still. He has one more hiccup. And then he has no more.

He slowly opens his eyes. "That's dramatic. It's gone. How did you come up with that method?"

"I don't know. It just came to me one day. Maybe instinct," Georgia says.

Peter leaves the room, smiling at us before disappearing.

The segment on creativity is three minutes. At one point, in the middle of our live interview, Georgia says to Peter (and hence to the world), "I'm a very honest, blunt person, and let me tell you: My writing leaves much to be desired."

Jack quickly adds, "Anyone with half a brain will know that what she's saying means nothing. It's the normal thing writers and artists say when they're in the throes of self-doubt, which any decent writer or artist is in, much of the time. Plus, like many great artists, she's a bit bipolar . . . I mean, not clinically, but you know . . . so don't listen to a word she's saying. Her writing is pure genius and everyone knows it."

Peter nods. "What's it like being part of such a creative circle?"

"It can be difficult," Georgia replies. "One of us is extremely messed up. Far more than the rest of us."

"Really?" Peter chuckles. "You?"

"No. Why would you say that? Should I be offended?"

"Of course not. But then, who?" he asks.

"We don't know who. Hopefully one day we will."

Peter laughs again. "You guys are just fascinating. What is it that makes some people highly creative, like Georgia, Lily, and Barb, and others less so, like, perhaps, you and me, Jack?"

We stare down at the desktop thoughtfully, until Georgia says, "We're not at our best tonight. We're stressed and distracted because something's coming up in two days that we're really dreading."

I shoot her an alarmed look.

"What is it?" Peter asks.

"I wish we could tell you. It would make for good TV. But we can't, sorry," she says.

"That's all right. Eccentricities are permitted, forgiven, and even encouraged, where geniuses are concerned."

Georgia blushes. "Don't look at me. I'm a lackluster writer, which is something I discovered only recently after recovering some work I'd lost."

"I happen to know that the vast majority of people who've

read you would disagree. I also know that a lot of people who have regular jobs have artistic aspirations they've neglected. This can cause a certain amount of regret for them. What advice, if any, do you have for those people? Lily, Barb, Penelope, any thoughts?"

We each come up with some banalities along the lines of: it's never too late; no use regretting the past; pursue your dream even if it's just five minutes a day before or after work; what's important is making the time for it, etc.

Peter Marrick says, "Georgia's second novel, *The Liquid Angel,* is about a woman whose dream is to become a great artist. One day, to thank her for saving his life, a stranger kidnaps her for nine months and forces her, against her will, to become a great artist. Do any of you have anything to say about that?"

When no one answers, I say, "It's a story that appeals to a lot of people in artistic fields, especially people whose strong suit is not self-discipline. Lily and I have joked that what happens to the woman in that novel is not entirely unappealing. We sometimes have fantasies of being forced to work, when our own discipline is lacking."

"Final question," says Peter. "Is discipline enough? I have a friend, Bob, who claims he has no imagination, yet he wants to be creative. He dreams of doing some good art. Is there any hope for him?"

"No," Georgia says. "If he lacks imagination, there's no hope for him artistically. Imagination is the one requirement. Pretty much the only one, really. But so what? Lacking imagination has some great advantages."

"Like what?"

"Happiness."

"Really?"

"Sure. In a way, your friend Bob is lucky. So is my mother, who also claims she has no imagination. I think some of the sanest, happiest people are those with the least imagination. Paranoia, for instance, wouldn't get very far without it. Life is easier without it."

We go home after being bade a warm farewell by Peter Marrick. I'm sad I didn't chat with him at greater length during his few attempts at talking to me and the others. I wish we could have done the show when we didn't have a deadly dinner coming up.

WHEN I REACH my building fifteen minutes later, Adam the doorman opens my cab door for me, greeting me with: "Moonlight becomes you—total darkness even more."

The taxi driver looks at him, startled.

I blink, at a loss for words. I'm not at my sharpest tonight. I just stare at Adam, thoughtfully. He stares right back at me, just as thoughtfully. Not taking his eyes off mine, he breaks the silence softly, dreamily, with, "When I look into your eyes, I see the back of your head."

He's clearly unwell. I wonder if now is the time I should try to help him.

As I'm considering this, he says, "Sit down and give your mind a rest."

That unblocks me. "Actually, that's a good idea, Adam. Why don't we sit here together for a moment and talk?" I say, pointing at the little bench near the door.

The cab driver is still staring at us, which makes me uncomfortable.

Not budging toward the bench, Adam says to me, "I'm too busy. Can I ignore you some other time?"

A middle-aged couple passes us on their way into the building.

"Have a nice evening, Mr. and Mrs. Portman," Adam says, smiling at them pleasantly.

"Thanks, Adam. You too," they answer, smiling back.

As soon as they're out of earshot, I say, "When would be a good time for you to listen to me for a couple of minutes?"

"How about never? Is never good for you?"

"Then let's talk now, just for a minute."

"Sorry, I can't. But where will you be in ten years?"

Trusting he'll eventually run out of comebacks, I persevere: "Adam, there's a subject I'd like to discuss with you. It won't take long."

He takes two slow steps toward me until he's closer than I find comfortable. Looking amused, he bores his eyes down into mine and says intimately, "My, my. Aren't you a little black hole of need."

"Just this once. That's all I ask. It'll be quick."

"A quickie?"

I nod. "A short conversation."

"Hard to resist. But why don't we play house instead? You be the door, and I'll slam you."

"You're very quick-witted and clever, Adam."

"Your flattery repels me, Barb," he says. And immediately he hollers "Ow!" and holds his tongue in his fingers, as though in pain.

"What's wrong?" I ask.

"Your very name blisters my tongue."

I remember a similar line from my high school Shakespeare class and say, "And you're very well read, too. Listen, I want to help you. I know a therapist. I've seen her myself. I think she can help you, regardless of why you're doing this."

"Keep talking," he says, yawning. "I always yawn when I'm interested."

"This therapist might be able to uncover why you act and feel the way you do."

Looking at me thoughtfully, Adam says, "I see what your problem is. You suffer from delusions of adequacy."

"The cause of your unusual behavior might be emotional, chemical, psychological. It might be something you're not even aware of."

"Please breathe the other way. You're triggering my gag reflex."

"Okay, well, have a pleasant evening, Adam."

I walk to the elevator, concerned that his problem might be getting worse. He's becoming less inhibited, less careful. He allowed a taxi driver to hear him. Who will be next? Someone who might get him fired?

Once I'm in my apartment, my mom calls and tells me she saw the interview and that I was good, but that tragically the camera added ten pounds on top of the dozens of fake pounds already on me.

———

IT'S THURSDAY MORNING. Only one day left. The NYU students arrive. By three p.m., they and I have finished searching my apartment for weapons and have found nothing, which raises my spirits slightly. Maybe the killer is not as determined as I feared.

Late in the afternoon, I decide to go shopping. I need a change of scenery. I buy a cuckoo clock, in case we become complacent during the evening of Strad's death. Every hour, the bird will pop out and scream "Cuckoo" to remind us there is one among us. It'll keep our nerves on edge, where they should be.

THE DREADED FRIDAY has arrived. The effort of trying to think of and guard against every possible murder method has drained me.

In the morning, I decide to bake a lemon chocolate cake. I'm not a fan of the cake because I don't like cakes in general and Jack isn't a fan of it either because he doesn't like lemon, but the rest of our group loves it, and baking it usually helps me unwind.

As I'm grating the lemon peel, my phone rings. I assume it's one of my friends with a last-minute point of anguish.

But no. To my surprise, it's Peter Marrick, the news anchor.

"I just wanted to thank you for coming on the show," he says. "You were great. And your friends, too. Captivating, all of you."

"Thank you. It was fun doing it."

He then asks me if I'd like to have dinner with him some time, adding, "I so rarely meet anyone I find interesting."

He meets politicians, actors, scientists, some of the most important and powerful people in the world. I'm a little confused by his compliment, though I tell him I'd be happy to have dinner with him. He asks if tonight would work.

"Oh, I can't tonight," I reply. "I've got something I wish I could get out of, but it's impossible. Though I could have dinner another night." *Unless a murder takes place, in which case it might be some time before I'm up for dating.*

"How about tomorrow night?"

"Ah . . . tomorrow is not ideal either," I say, thinking I may have to stay in bed all day and evening to recover from tonight's stress. Or we may need tomorrow to hide the body. Or to prevent Lily from killing the killer. Or to deal with any number of other possible horrifications. "I can do Sunday, though. Or next week."

We settle on Sunday.

I get back to my cake. As I mix the ingredients, I think about how nice that was, talking to Peter Marrick. And rare. Ever since I've been wearing my disguise, men simply haven't shown any interest in me romantically—not that Peter Marrick's interest is likely to be romantic, actually.

Chapter Ten

When I'm done with the cake, I lock up all my cutlery, my hammer, my screwdrivers, and anything else that could be used as a weapon, such as items made of glass, that could, in a split second, be smashed and slashed across Strad's throat. I bought plastic cutlery and paper cups and plates for the dinner.

AT SEVEN, MY friends arrive, as planned. Strad is supposed to get here at 7:30 p.m., and the danger is supposed to start at eight. I thought it was best to get Strad here well in advance of the danger so that if he's running a bit late, he won't risk being assassinated on his way here by a hired gunman.

I frisk my friends carefully and then search them with the metal detector, which I practiced using on the NYU students yesterday. Everyone is wearing pants, as I'd instructed. No one sets off the metal detector, which means they didn't conceal razor blades on or in their bodies. It's nice to know I won't have to worry about them whipping out a razor blade when they go to the bathroom. I will only have to worry about them whipping out a piece of broken glass encased in a nonmetal tube inserted in their bodies in the fashion of a tampon or suppository. Frisking them every time they exit the bathroom should be enough to guard against such a danger. Metal detecting won't be necessary again.

I confiscate bags, cell phones, and shoes.

I then stand before my friends and say, "I want you to be extremely vigilant this evening. The killer could be swift. Be on the lookout for any abrupt movements from any of you, and be prepared to pounce. If the killer is Jack, we should be particularly alert because he's stronger than the rest of us and will be more difficult to restrain." They all nod, including Jack.

I continue with, "The rules are: No one goes near the kitchen area; no one near the food before it is served; from the moment it's served until Strad has finished eating, we should all keep a close eye on Strad's plate and glass to be sure nobody puts anything in them; everyone stays in the living room at all times, no wandering in the rest of the apartment; and nobody goes to the bathroom unaccompanied."

They all nod again. "Sounds good," Jack says.

"Oh, and let's not forget to try to act *natural*, for Lily's sake," I say. "We don't want him to think her friends are weirdos."

"I appreciate that," Lily says.

"Even if we're weirdos, we're still the Knights of Creation and he knows it," Georgia says, scornfully.

We wait for Strad as 7:30 approaches. It comes and goes. We look at one another. At 7:45 p.m., I instruct Lily to call his cell phone. She does, on speakerphone. He says he's on his way, had to take a cab because there's a problem with the subway.

I stare at my cuckoo clock as eight o'clock nears. I ask Lily to call him again. She does, again on speaker. He says he's two blocks away, that maybe he'll get out of the cab and walk the rest of the way because there's traffic.

"No!" I exclaim. If he's out on the street alone when eight o'clock strikes, who knows what could happen, what the killer might have planned. "No," I repeat, more calmly, and whisper: "Tell him not to worry, to stay in the taxi until it reaches my building."

She tells him this. He says he's now one block away. It's three minutes before eight. He says he'll see us soon. He says he can't wait. Lily hangs up.

I stare at my intercom, waiting for the doorman to buzz me. Finally, he does. It's Adam, and he softly says to me, "You clownish fool, someone is here to see you, don't ask me why. His name is Strad. I don't envy him. He's in for quite—"

"Send him up," I say, having no time for his disorder right now.

"Jee-*zuss!*"

"Real fast, please," I add.

"Fine, cunt," he says, and hangs up.

I look at the clock. We've got two minutes left before the danger starts.

Ten seconds left. He's still not here.

"CUCKOO!" shrieks the bird eight times at eight o'clock.

I hear a grim voice in my head saying, "And now, ladies and gentlemen, let the games begin."

Ten minutes go by, and still no Strad. Perhaps he got lost in the building. This is a common problem in my building, which is huge and consists of four towers, requiring visitors to take two elevators, which are separated by a long hallway and some turns.

I tell Lily this, to reassure her. She nods, chewing her lip.

Strad finally arrives at 8:11 p.m. and sheepishly confesses to me in the entrance hall that he got lost in the building.

"Yes, it's very complicated," Georgia calls out from the living room, her sarcasm unfair because it is.

Strad is carrying a shoulder bag, a violin case, a bunch of mixed flowers, and a bottle of red wine. He hands me the flowers and wine. "Thank you so much for inviting me," he says, following me into the living room. "You can't imagine how . . ." He stops mid-sentence as he steps across the threshold. He gazes around the living room at the masked and costumed furry mannequins. "Wow. Amazing. Wow."

"Aw, we love eloquent guests," Georgia says.

"Your decor is spectacular," Strad says to me.

"Thank you," I say.

He puts down his bag and violin case. He notices that none of us is wearing shoes, so he takes his off and puts them by the door.

Then he goes straight for Georgia. "Man, what an honor it is to finally meet you!" He takes her hand in both of his.

"Thank you," she says.

"No, thank *you*. For all your books. Spending this evening with you will be such a blast."

"A blast, possibly." She turns to the rest of us and asks, "Did we cover that possibility? That it might be a blast?"

"Many times," Jack says.

"And? What did we decide?"

"That it can't be a blast as long as he's with us."

It's true, we did cover the possibility of a small bomb and quickly realized that the killer would never use a method that had any risk of hurting the rest of us. As long as Strad is with us, no explosive would be used on him.

So I'm outraged at Jack and Georgia's unnecessary exchange and offensive double meanings aimed at insulting Strad. Have I not just told them to act normal? Do they not care how their weird behavior will reflect on Lily? I guess they don't, come to think of it.

Trying to hide my annoyance, I say, "I thought we decided not to be eccentric tonight?" I put a little water and Strad's flowers into a small plastic vase. "If I detect even a whiff of eccentricity this evening, you will not hear the end of it."

I take Strad's belongings (except for his violin case, which he'll need) and put them in my bedroom, because the killer might have cleverly hidden a weapon in Strad's bag or coat earlier.

I then pour the wine into a lidded plastic jug and I lock the empty wine bottle in my bedroom with all the other glass items.

Strad strolls around my living room, looking at the costumed mannequins. He stops in front of my ballet bar and asks me, "Why do you have a ballet bar if you don't use it?"

"What makes you think I don't use it?"

He looks me up and down. "Wild guess."

I feel slapped in the face on behalf of overweight people who do use a ballet bar. "The previous owner installed it," I explain. "She was a ballet dancer. And I do use it for my costume design work with actors."

"Fun piano," Strad says, standing in front of the mirror

piano. "The sound must suffer a bit in that kind of casing, but it's great-looking. Am I right, Lily, that the sound suffers?"

"Yes, it suffers," Lily says.

The thought of suffering reminds me that we're due for some, right about now. "Speaking of music, weren't you going to play a little something for us?" I ask him.

"Oh, yes, why don't you bless us with some of your music," Georgia says, with an impressive lack of sarcasm.

"Sure!" Strad goes to his violin case.

I follow him. He opens it.

"Can I see this case? It's so beautiful," I say.

"Sure."

I hold the case, caress the lining, examine it thoroughly inside and out and when I'm relatively certain that it's safe, I say, "And can I see your violin too?"

He hands it to me. I'm not sure what could be hidden in a violin, but why not be thorough? As for the rest of him, I didn't use the metal detector on him because I didn't want to freak him out. Plus, no one is supposed to touch him. If anyone stashed a weapon on him in advance and tries to pickpocket him during the evening, we'll put a stop to it before anything can happen.

I give him back his violin and he positions himself in front of the couch area, where we all take a seat.

Georgia raises her hand. "Oh, I've got an idea. Maybe Lily should accompany Strad on the piano. That would be so nice." Her motive is all too clear to me: she's hoping Lily's music will mask Strad's. But the pretext she gives is, "This way, Strad, you'll be able to hear for yourself if the piano suffers from its casing."

"Sure," Strad says. "If you want to join me toward the end, Lily. I'll signal you when I'm ready."

Lily nods and sits at the piano. He plays for ten minutes, which is mildly unpleasant, before he gives Lily the nod.

She starts improvising, and I don't know if my perception of her playing is influenced by my knowledge of her feelings for him, but her notes seem to coat his in silk. Her playing wraps itself around his in a manner that does not take us long to sense is rather erotic. Her sounds are caressing, clinging to his sounds, dripping from them, climaxing with them. Her notes are practically raping his notes, though the one thing they're not really able to do is to beautify them. Lily's power is not quite strong enough to counteract the mediocrity of his art.

When they're done, Strad plops into an armchair. "That was exhilarating! I don't think the sound from the piano suffered much."

"Oh, I think it suffered," Georgia says.

Jack starts talking to Strad about his acting ambitions.

Georgia walks by the low side table next to Strad's armchair without noticing that the bottom of her long cardigan is getting caught on the bouquet of flowers Strad brought me. Jack is the only one besides me who notices what's about to happen and lunges at the vase to steady it before it topples over and spills.

The only thing the three women notice is Jack lunging in Strad's proximity. Misinterpreting his abrupt movement as an attempt on Strad's life, they hurl themselves at him and he falls under their weight. On his way down, his lip and nose get smashed against one of my ottoman cubes. He is now face down on my thin rug, the women on top of him holding his arms and sitting on him like hens.

"Stop! Stop!" I cry, hurrying toward them. "Get off him. I saw everything."

They stare up at me, not convinced, and not getting off him. They're waiting for me to offer an explanation, which they know I can't give them in front of Strad.

"I order you to get off of him right now," I tell Georgia, Penelope, and Lily in a calm but commanding voice.

They finally obey, reluctantly. Not only can I not give them an explanation, but they realize they now have to help me come up with a fake one because Strad is watching us, horrified.

"Why did you just attack him?" he asks them.

Jack struggles to his feet, his nose and lip bleeding. He touches the side of his face, where he'll undoubtedly have a bruise.

He gazes down at the floor. There lie the flowers and plastic vase on the wet rug.

Strad looks at all of us, waiting for our explanation.

We stare back at him, stumped, having no idea what to say.

In the silence, the cuckoo clock tick-tocks like a metronome.

I try to buy us some time by fetching a paper towel and an ice pack for Jack.

Perhaps I could say the women thought Jack was headed toward the stereo, and he has terrible taste in music.

"Why isn't anyone speaking?" Strad asks. "Lily? Why did you pounce on Jack?"

Lily doesn't reply. Instead, she busies herself picking up the flowers and wiping up the spill.

I can't stand the silence anymore, so I'm about to blurt out my absurd answer, but just before I do, Georgia casually says, "Training."

I exhale softly, having complete confidence in her powers of fabrication.

"Excuse me?" Strad says.

"It's training." She shrugs.

"Training? To be what, Charlie's Angels?"

"No. We're training *him*. He asked us to attack him at unexpected times as part of his ongoing maintenance program. It keeps his reflexes sharp."

"Is that true?" Strad asks Jack, with a twinge of excitement.

"Yes. It improves my reaction time," Jack says.

"For what?"

"For my job. I'm a cop, you know."

"I thought that was over. I thought you worked at a senior center now."

"Only part time. I'm also an undercover cop."

"But I thought you couldn't be a cop because of your limp and your cane and the fact that you can't run."

"That's why it's a great cover."

"So you *can* run?"

"No, that's why it's a great cover."

"What's a great cover? Not being able to run?"

"Yes. That's what makes it really good."

"But how can you be an undercover cop if you can't run?"

"By doing special training, like you just saw."

"That makes up for not running?"

"More than makes up for it. You saw how intense it was. The

women did an excellent job, I must say. I'd been reproaching them lately for not going at it with enough conviction." He takes the paper towel and ice pack and presses them to his face. "I just never thought they'd attack me when a guest was here. Which, of course, is why it's the perfect time to do it." He chuckles and turns to his aggressors, giving them a thumbs-up. "Nice work, by the way."

Even though Jack is usually not the one who comes up with the ideas, he's quite good at riffing off them once they're out there.

Blood is still running out of his nose. He wipes it again with the now mostly red paper towel.

"I don't know, this seems weird," Strad says, shaking his head, looking suddenly skeptical again.

"It's a form of conditioning, like Pavlov's dog," Jack says. "When you get attacked and hurt on a regular basis and at various random times, you start jumping at the slightest abrupt movement because you know pain is coming. That jumping is a desirable state of conditioning."

"It is?" Strad says. "Like those kids who shield their faces if you make an abrupt gesture near them because they get slapped at home regularly? That never seemed good."

"But for adults it's good. Especially for cops. That's what average people don't realize when they watch those big Hollywood action movies. In those movies, it takes *a lot* to faze the heroes. But in real life, it's the opposite. The toughest, most effective guys, the best fighters, the police heroes, the army heroes—all the best ones—they jump at the slightest abrupt movement."

I'm struggling not to smile. My friends too. The tension has left their faces. You'd think the threat had left the room.

"Thanks again, guys," Jack says to his trainers, giving them each a high-five. He spins back to Strad. "Oh, and just so you know, they've asked me to put them through the same rigorous training, so we may be attacking each other at various times. Don't be too startled."

The three women chuckle uneasily.

I tell everyone it's time for dinner.

We move to the dining table. I serve them a cold meal of fancy sardines in herb sauce, which I bought already prepared from a nearby gourmet shop. I serve Strad last, and once his food is in front of him, I don't take my eyes off it. I can't believe he's the only person in the room I can absolutely trust.

We scare easy tonight. At one point Georgia sneezes. It practically gives me a heart attack. A few minutes later Penelope drops her plastic fork. We stare at her with terror.

Things get misinterpreted. The slightest sounds. If someone laughs, the rest of us hear it as evil and expect the worst.

"Wow, you guys are like jumpy, high-strung thoroughbred horses," Strad says. "You've really honed that flinching trait."

A few grunts is the only response.

No one tries to make conversation during dinner except Strad, but he doesn't get very far. He asks me about my costumes. I give him brief, bland answers. I'm not capable of more. The others don't seem to be either. So he gives up. The ticking of the clock is noticeable in the silence. There isn't even the familiar clanking of cutlery—typical of conversationless meals—since everything is plastic and paper. I spend long stretches of time in a sort of trance, staring at Strad and his plate, lost in thought, trying to make sure I haven't overlooked any killing methods or schemes the murderer might have come up with.

While Strad chews on his food, Lily, too, stares at him. But hers is a very different look from mine. Her look is one of adoration.

Strad gazes at all of us sitting there stiffly, and says, "Do you guys always have this much fun?"

Georgia can't help laughing.

When the fake bird flies out of the clock at nine, screaming "CUCKOO!!!" we all hit the ceiling except Jack.

"I saw it coming," Jack explains.

Three more hours to go. Why did I think marking the slow passage of time with this clock would be a good idea?

"Ah!" shouts Strad, slapping the table, which scares me even more than the cuckoo did, "I have been wanting to ask you something for ages, Georgia!"

"I'm all ears," she says.

"What in the world is the anagram for 'Whiterose' at the end of your novel *The Liquid Angel?* I've been racking my brains for months. I simply must know."

"Otherwise what? You'll die?" Georgia says.

He chuckles. "Uh, something like that."

"And we wouldn't want that, would we?" She pauses. "Which is why I've given you the answer."

"What do you mean you've given me the answer? No you haven't."

She turns to the rest of us, "Have I?"

We nod.

She turns back to Strad. "You see. I have."

"When?"

"A few seconds ago."

After a pause, he says, "You're not going to give it to me in a way I can understand?"

"Guess not," she says. "I'm a little sadistic, I suppose."

Nothing much but chewing goes on at the table for a while.

Strad gets up. "Where's the bathroom?" he asks me.

We all get up. He looks surprised and says, "No, please, you don't need to get up."

"It's all right," I say. "Jack, will you lead the way?"

"Certainly," Jack says, and proceeds toward the hallway. I keep an eye on Strad's plate until everyone has left the table. We begin escorting Strad to the bathroom.

"Uh, what are you guys doing?" he asks.

"Showing you to the bathroom," I say, trying to sound as casual as possible. "We're almost there."

We go through the hallway, turn a corner, and there we are, all crowded in front of the door.

"Please make way," I say, and open the bathroom door. I take a quick look, to triple-check that everything seems safe, and show him in.

Strad steps inside, closes the door, and we hear nothing. After about thirty seconds he says, not very loudly, "Are you still there?"

I don't answer right away, unsure what to say. Finally I answer, "Yes."

Softly, he says, "Why?"

After a pause, I say, "In case you need anything."

"I don't need anything. You can go back to your seats now. I'm sure I can find my way back even though I got lost in your building."

I don't think this requires a response, so I give none. We still hear nothing. Time passes and still we hear absolutely nothing. I get worried. Having him out of my sight makes me nervous even though I've searched that bathroom multiple times and found no danger. I imagine things. Impossible things, perhaps, but when they're dwelled on, they start to seem possible. I imagine a lethal gas seeping through the bathroom vent. I imagine a deadly electrical current connected to the metal faucet knobs and activated only when Strad is in the bathroom. I imagine that maybe I was not vigilant enough about staring at his plate and that now he's quietly dying from poisoning.

I'm straining to hear the slightest sound. My fingertips are against the thin wooden door that separates us.

And then I hear him say softly, "Are you still there?"

"Yes," I reply, almost as softly.

"I'm a bit uncomfortable with you all standing out there, you know," he says.

I nod and murmur, "We know." That wasn't meant for him to hear and I don't think he did.

There is the sound of the sink faucet going on, and a second later, the bathwater running. I have a preposterous vision of the killer having arranged for these faucets to turn on by themselves. The door would be locked, jammed, no way to unlock it, the faucets would keep running, no way to shut them off, and the tiny bathroom would fill up like a fish tank.

"Are you okay?" I ask through the door.

"Fine, fine."

Finally, despite the racket of the running water, we make out the sound of him urinating.

A few moments later, the water noises stop and he comes out of the bathroom, intact.

Relieved, I'm about to take him back to the table, when Lily says, "I need to go, too."

I give her permission.

"But I'm not sure I'll be able to, with you all standing here," she says.

Strad decides to make her feel more comfortable by masking her sounds. He fetches his violin and plays *The Four Seasons* by Vivaldi, right outside the bathroom door.

Upon her exit, I frisk her, prompting Strad to ask me, "What are you doing?"

"Just routine," I reply.

"I need to pee, too," Georgia says, and slips into the bathroom.

Strad plays "The Devil Went Down to Georgia."

When Georgia emerges, I frisk her very carefully.

"Did she steal anything?" Strad asks.

"Uh, it doesn't look like it," I say.

"You didn't frisk me," he says.

"Not yet."

As I'm about to give Strad his token frisk, I get a better idea. "Lily, frisk him." Why not give her some gratuitous pleasure?

She stares at me hard with embarrassment, and then slowly advances toward Strad. She pats his arms, from wrist to shoulder, then his chest. Her hands seem a little shaky as they descend toward his belly. She is carefully mimicking the way she saw me frisk her and Georgia—she does no more and no less. She strokes Strad's waist, his hips, his pockets—which are bulky, but she ignores them—then his legs and ankles. She walks around him and frisks him from behind. His back pockets have some bulk in them as well, but she does not explore.

"All good?" I ask.

"Yes," she says.

"This is surreal," Strad remarks to me, as we escort him back to the table. "You have me frisked, my pockets are bulging with things, and yet you don't ask to see what's in them. It could be your soap, you know. I could have stolen your soap."

"I trust you."

We take our seats and finish our sardines.

The time has come for the table to be cleared for dessert. The problem is, I don't want any of my friends to take the dirty dishes to the kitchen because of the opportunity it would give the killer to sprinkle sleeping powder on the fruit salad I've prepared (which is sitting on the counter) or in the coffee pot. We'd all fall asleep and the killer could kill Strad at his or her leisure. Or while setting the dessert plates, the killer could apply some poison directly onto Strad's plate or plastic spoon or fork.

One way to avoid these risks would be for me to clear the table, but this will not work either because I'd have to take my eyes off Strad's still unfinished cup of wine.

Therefore, there's really only one option that's completely safe.

"Strad, you may clear the table now," I say.

"Excuse me?" he says.

"We're ready for dessert. You can take the dirty dishes to the kitchen, and please don't eat out of anyone's plate."

He gets up, a little baffled, muttering, "Sure, I don't mind helping," and takes his plate to the kitchen.

He sees that no one else has gotten up. "Am I supposed to *help* or am I supposed to do it all by myself?"

"The latter," I say. "We prepared the meal. It's only fair."

"Oh, this is very original," he says, full of good humor. "The guest waits on the hosts. So this is what it's like having dinner with the Knights of Creation."

A few minutes later, I say, "Thank you very much, Strad. When you're done, you can set our dessert plates and serve us the fruit salad and lemon chocolate cake. Then if you wouldn't mind pouring us some coffee, that would be great."

"You really pull out all the stops when you entertain, don't you, Barb?" he says. "Not only do you bring out the fancy paper plates and plastic knives and forks and serve wine in these beautiful paper cups, but you ask your guest to clear the table and serve you." I think I detect a mixture of indignation and awe in his tone.

"You guys are so unconventional, it's delightful," he adds, taking my plate to the kitchen. He carries the plates one at a time, which drags out the process. He obviously hasn't had much practice helping clear tables. Three plates are still left. But that's okay, we've got all the time in the world.

We hear music. It's Strad's cell phone.

He answers it and hangs up after a moment.

"Now this is weird," he tells us, looking tickled.

"What?" I ask.

"There's a present for me downstairs!"

"Ignore it; it's a trick," I blurt.

"Who's it from?" Penelope quickly asks, undoubtedly attempting to cover up my strange comment, which I appreciate.

"She didn't say," Strad replies. "It was a woman on the phone, but I have no idea who. All she said was, 'Strad, there's a present for you downstairs.' And she hung up. And no number is showing up on my phone."

"I think it sounds fishy," Jack says.

I should have confiscated Strad's phone as soon as he arrived. In the last few days, it did occur to me that the killer might call Strad during this dinner—or rather, hire someone to call Strad—with some sort of pretext to lure him away from our protection. Nevertheless, seizing Strad's cell phone seemed excessive at the time. I regret my decision now.

A sudden, irrepressible urge to communicate my feelings to the killer overwhelms my desire not to sound strange in front of Strad. "I don't know what you're up to, but I don't like it," I say to the killer in our midst, whoever it is.

"What, you think I faked this call to get out of my domestic duties?" Strad asks me. "I didn't, I swear. I know I must clear the table and serve dessert, and I will. And I'll serve the coffee, too."

I'm afraid the supposed gift downstairs will be a small bomb, small enough to kill only the person who opens it. But I try to reassure myself that no member of our group—even the killer—would ever endanger any other member. A bomb—even a tiny one—is simply too risky. It must be something else, some other weapon or ploy.

My friends, too, are unsettled at the prospect of this gift being brought into the apartment. Georgia copies my technique of addressing the killer: she stares blankly into space and says to him or her, "I can't believe the gall you have to actually be attempting something right in front of our eyes."

Obviously this stunt does not clear her. She could still be the killer.

"I'm not attempting anything!" Strad exclaims. "I told you guys I would clear the table and I will, as soon as I get back from getting my present."

Penelope jumps on the bandwagon with her own blank stare and address to the killer: "Do you realize what you are doing to us? Don't you care about our group?"

"I do! I admire it greatly," Strad tells her. "I'd love to be a part of it. And you'll see, I'll be back before you know it."

Then Jack takes his turn addressing the killer, who could, of course, be himself: "If you do what you intend, don't assume we'll help you afterward. We definitely won't. You'll be on your own."

Strad squints, trying to understand. "You guys are not being clear. Is this about more than clearing the table and serving dessert? Is this about cleaning the kitchen? I can do that, too, if you want. It's not that much work to throw out paper plates and plastic cutlery."

Then I remember that even if it's a bomb, it can't go off after midnight because that was the rule KAY agreed to. "Strad," I say. "I want you to wait until the evening is over before you get your present. I insist on that."

"I'm sorry, I can't. I want to find out now what it is. I'll be just a minute."

I heave myself out of my chair. The others get up as well. I keep an eye on Strad's cup until all my friends have stepped away from the table.

"You didn't need to get up. I'll be right back," Strad says, putting on his shoes.

We gather around him near the front door.

"Wait," I say. "Let me call the doorman to make sure there really is a package. Maybe the call was a prank."

I pick up the intercom's receiver and I call downstairs.

Adam answers.

I begin, "Hi, this is Barb—"

"What do you want, ass-head? Make it quick. Your voice gives me ear infections."

"Did someone drop off a package for one of my guests?"

"Yeah."

"Really? No one? Are you sure?"

Adam is silent and confused for a moment, and then says, "Are you normally this stupid or are you making a special effort right now?"

"His name is Strad. You have no package for Strad?"

"I have it right here."

"Hmm. That's weird. We got a message saying a package was dropped off with you."

"If you're having a stroke or something that requires the defibrillator let me know by banging your head three times against the phone and I'll be sure to send the defibrillator up to you real slow."

"Okay, thanks." I hang up and turn to Strad. "He says there's no package."

"Really? Do you mind if I speak to him to be sure he didn't make a mistake?"

"Of course he didn't make a mistake. You heard how thorough I was."

"Yeah, but still. I want to make sure."

Clearly Strad won't let this rest until either he speaks to Adam himself or goes downstairs and looks for the present with his own eyes. There's no point in my trying to stop him. What's important now is that I not let him call Adam, who would inform him I've been lying, which could offend Strad enough to make him leave and no longer be under our protection.

"No, I'll do it," I say, picking up the intercom phone before Strad can respond, though I do catch the expression of frustration on his face.

Adam answers.

"Hi, it's me again," I say.

"Stop plaguing me."

"Sorry to bother you again, but could you please check in the back to make sure there isn't a package for Strad? Maybe it was dropped off earlier when Bill was at the desk, and maybe he forgot to put it in the system."

"What kind of game are you playing?" Adam asks me.

"Thanks," I say. I wait enough time for Adam to theoretically go to the back, while in reality he's treating me to a litany of insults. After a few more seconds I say into the phone, "Ah, you *do* have it? Great!"

"Leave me alone."

"Well, that explains it. Thanks for checking." I hang up.

"He does have it," I tell Strad. "Sure enough, it got dropped off when Bill was on duty."

"Great. I'll get it. Don't serve the fruit salad. I'll do it when I get back."

He walks out the door. We do as well.

"Be back in a jiffy!" he says, waving.

We flank him as he walks down the hallway.

"Why are you guys doing this? I'm not a moron; I won't get lost a second time. You don't even have your shoes on."

"That's all right," Jack says. "The person on the phone didn't say who they were or who the present was from. I'd stay as far away from that supposed present as possible if I were you."

"Jack is a cop," Lily adds. "He knows what he's talking about. Let's just go back to the apartment, Strad."

Ignoring her suggestion, Strad steps into the elevator. We squeeze in around him.

"It's wonderful to be escorted and embraced this way by your group, to be taken into your fold," he says. "You guys must like me. I feel cuddled by five mother hens. Does this mean I'm part of your exclusive inner circle, now? Am I one of you?"

We don't answer. When the elevator doors open again, we follow him down the long hallway to the second elevator. I'm in a trance, thinking that if we survive the opening of the present, I will take extra precautions for the rest of the evening, starting with his cell phone confiscation. I don't care how strange it makes me look. Appearances are nothing. Anyway, it's my apartment, my rules. And let's not forget that there is also my special backup precaution, which I was hoping to avoid using due to its extreme deviance. But perhaps the time has come.

We take the second elevator down and arrive in the lobby.

Wanting to be the first to examine the box for any suspicious signs, I move ahead of my friends and go straight to the front desk, behind which Adam is standing.

"Hi, Adam. Can I have that package, please?"

Handing me the box, he leans toward my ear and whispers, "Scumbag."

"Thank you so much," I say, smiling.

I haven't yet told my friends about the doorman's strange behavior these past few months.

I look at the writing on the box. There's no return name or address. Just the recipient's name, Strad Ellison, c/o my name, and my apartment number.

"When was this dropped off?" I ask Adam.

He looks at me and knows he can't insult me since my friends are next to me, staring at him, waiting for his answer.

"About half an hour ago," he says. "And I'm very sorry about the misunderstanding we had on the phone when I kept telling you the package was right here, and you kept thinking I said it wasn't. I'm glad we cleared that up, eventually." He looks at my friends.

"Yes," I say. Out of the corner of my eye, I can see Strad staring at me. "Who delivered it?" I ask Adam.

"A woman," he says.

"Did she give her name?"

"No."

"Did she say anything at all?"

"She said the package was for your guest, Strad Ellison. That's all."

"What did she look like?"

"Asian. Early twenties. Shoulder-length hair."

"Anything else you can remember?"

"No."

"Thank you, Adam."

He nods.

Strad takes the box from me. Luckily, it's sealed tightly, so there's no choice but to wait until we get back to my apartment to open it.

On our way up, I gaze at my friends' faces. By dint of imagining each of them in the role of the killer, they've each become the killer in my eyes.

Back in my apartment, I instruct everybody to go to the couch area and stay there while I fetch the scissors from my bedroom.

Upon my return, I inform Strad that I must be the one to open the box, that I never let anyone handle my scissors.

"I've been meaning to ask you something," he tells me. "You said earlier that you didn't want anyone to be eccentric tonight. So I'm wondering, is this your version of not being eccentric? What I mean is, are you usually even more eccentric?"

Not sure what to answer, I meekly settle for: "I'm not being that eccentric. It's just a habit I have with scissors."

"Why did you lie about my package?"

"It made me nervous. You didn't know who it was from."

Georgia says, "Plus, we were having such a good time, why interrupt the fun?"

"Okay, open it," he tells me.

"Everyone, step away," I caution.

I don't want anyone to make a lunge for whatever weapon might be in the box. And if it does turn out to be a bomb, the farther away they stand, the better.

"Farther," I say. They take another step back. "You too, Strad."

Everyone is now standing a good six feet away from me.

As I carefully cut the tape around the box, I start getting more worried that it might actually be a bomb.

"If you think you can zero in on your target with surgical precision, you are wrong," I say, speaking to the killer while staring at the tape I'm cutting. "Perhaps you *will* hit your target, but you'll hit us as well—yourself included—and me in particular. I'll be disfigured beyond recognition, which is okay with me, but is it okay with you? I'll be blinded, I may even get killed. So many of us could get killed. Do you really want to harm us this way? Is it really worth it?"

"Eccentric is not the right word," Strad says to Lily, who smiles politely through her fear.

I continue addressing the killer: "Think about it. You don't have much time. You better decide quickly because there won't be any turning back once the box is opened."

I glance at my friends. They all seem extremely tense, holding their breaths.

Penelope exhales suddenly and says, "I feel faint." She sits on the couch.

I've finished cutting the tape. I lift the flaps, push aside the crumpled paper, and see my face staring back at me from the bottom of the box. It's an antique-style mirror with a handle and an ornately molded frame. I take it out of the box.

The tension leaves the room like a change in cabin pressure. I pull the rest of the packing paper out of the box. Nothing else is in it. No bomb, no weapon.

I turn the mirror over. Beautifully engraved on the back is the name "*Strad*" and underneath it are the words, "*See Differently.*"

"See differently?" Strad says. "What's that supposed to mean?"

"Maybe someone wants you to see what kind of person you really are," Georgia says.

"Or maybe someone wants you to see the people around you in another way," Penelope says.

I puzzle over which of my friends sent this gift. It could have been any of them. It even could have been Lily, whose meaning behind the engraved words may have been: "Take a good look at yourself. Are you really so much more beautiful than I am?"

"Or maybe someone thinks you're vain," Jack offers.

Strad seems a bit disgruntled at these less than flattering interpretations. He finally suggests, "Or maybe someone thinks I'm a great guy and feels compelled to shower me with gifts."

"One gift," I mutter. "Hardly a shower."

"Oh, it's a shower. I call three gifts a shower. This is the third anonymous gift I've received." He plunges his hand into his jeans pocket and pulls out two silver objects: a lighter and a business card holder. They are both beautifully engraved in a similar fashion. The words on the lighter, right under his name, are "*Desire Differently.*" And on the card holder: "*Think Differently.*"

I just stare.

"I like these gifts," he says, putting them back in his pocket. "I just wish I knew who they were from. I haven't told anyone I was coming here today, so whoever dropped this off must have followed me here, or been hired to follow me. Unless . . . they're from one of you," he says, his gaze lingering on Lily.

We all shake our heads no, including Lily, who blushes slightly.

I return the scissors to my bedroom. Clearly these gifts have to come from someone in our group. If KAY's attack is only in the form of words engraved on a beautiful gift, I can handle that. The words aren't even an insult—just a gentle suggestion. Perhaps I've been overly cautious. I tell myself to relax a bit. I've known my friends a long time and I should have a modicum of faith that none of them would commit murder. I pause, catching an error in my thinking, which I grimly correct: or at least commit murder a second time.

As I reenter the living room, I see that Georgia has stepped away from the couch area, where the others are chatting. She is casually approaching the hand mirror, which I'd placed on a little table between two windows.

My leeriness comes swirling back.

"Georgia! What are you doing?" I bark.

She seems flustered—a rare occurrence. "Nothing, I just wanted to examine the mirror."

"Really." My tone reeks of skepticism.

"Don't let her!" This is Jack.

"Step away." I march over to the mirror. "Why are you so interested in it?"

"I'm not *so* interested in it," she says. "I'm just exhibiting a normal degree of curiosity."

I pick up the mirror and examine it. We were so relieved it wasn't a bomb, we forgot to be thorough. I turn it over, scrutinize the intricate molding.

And then I see something.

A tiny clasp that blends in with the molding. It's located on one side of the handle, in the nook where the handle meets the mirror. I spot an identical one on the other side. Each clasp is encrusted with one tiny red stone which I had noticed but thought was just decoration. I open both clasps and pull on the handle.

With a grave metallic sound, a steel blade slides out. What a moment ago was a harmless object of vanity is now a dagger and its sheath.

Chapter Eleven

Everyone gathers around me.

My lips clenched, I study my friends.

I see profound shock and stricken features.

I just can't tell which one's faking it.

"Not so close," I say, pointing the dagger at them. I wouldn't want anyone to grab it from my hands and stab Strad.

They back up.

"Wow, look at that," Strad says, oblivious. "How cool!" He takes the knife and mirror from me. "It's an even better gift than I thought. Too bad I don't know who it's from."

"Yes, it's a shame," I say, trying to unwrap Georgia's soul with my eyes.

She gives me a little shake of the head to deny her culpability.

Far from being too cautious, it's clear to me I was not nearly cautious enough. Drastic revisions of plans need to go into effect immediately.

"If you don't mind, I must put that in the bedroom," I tell Strad, tugging on the dagger and sheath.

"Why?" he says, letting them go.

"It's my knives and weapons phobia."

"Why are you guys so scared of me?" he asks. "I'm not going to hurt anyone!"

"Oh really?" Georgia replies, her tone dripping with sarcasm.

I notice Lily reacting with a barely perceptible cringe.

"And I need your cell phone, too," I tell Strad.

"And what's your pretext for that?" he asks, plopping it in my palm.

"Disliking interruptions." I look at the assembly. "Couch area!" I order, pointing.

They shuffle to the couch.

I carry Strad's gift and phone to my bedroom. Despite being deeply shaken up by the dagger's unsheathing, I'm still not sure I want to resort to my special backup safety method. So I hold off for now.

I return to the living room with a nagging feeling that I've overlooked something.

And then it occurs to me.

"Strad, show me your other gifts again," I say.

"Why? You want to take those away too?"

"Please, I just want to see them."

He hands me his silver lighter and business card holder. I scrutinize both. After fiddling with them for a few moments, I discover a very well hidden razor blade built into the structure of each one. Once the blade is slid out, it remains attached to the object, which has become its handle.

"CUCKOO!" shrieks the bird ten times in the most obnoxious manner possible. It's ten p.m.

"You are cuckoo, Barb, to have bought that clock," Georgia says, clenching her heart with her hands.

"Those are fantastic gifts!" Strad says, thrilled to behold the hidden weapons.

I don't share his enthusiasm. I visualize what could have happened tonight if I hadn't discovered those blades. Maybe after dinner, while sitting on the couch having coffee, Strad would have taken out his lighter, lit a cigarette, and tossed the lighter onto the coffee table to await his next cigarette. (I would have allowed him to smoke since our priority this evening—his protection, not our comfort—requires him to stay with us till midnight.) My friend the killer would then have gotten up to stretch his/her legs, casually picked up the lighter "to look at it," pulled out the blade, and sliced Strad's jugular. Same thing could have happened with the business card holder if the opportunity had presented itself.

Who knows what other weapons the killer might have stashed or smuggled in, or simply have access to—starting with his or her own body, for Christ's sake! I hadn't thought of it till now, but here it is: what if the killer is a secret martial arts black belt and can inflict a lethal blow in a split second?

"Sit!" I order my friends, pointing to the couch.

I carry Strad's silver gifts to my bedroom.

It's clear to me I've got no choice but resort to my special backup method now.

I return from my bedroom holding four pairs of handcuffs I bought a couple of days ago.

I drag four chairs from the dining table to my ballet bar, which is parallel to the table, a few feet away from it. The fact that the bar is sturdy, horizontal, height-adjustable, and bolted to the floor makes it perfect for what I have in mind. I lower it to child level. I position the chairs side by side, behind the bar, and instruct my friends to take their seats.

They obey, only a little surprised. I handcuff their left wrists to the bar. They will be comfortable; their forearms can rest on the bar, which hovers a foot above their laps.

"What in the world are you doing?" Strad asks me, alarmed.

I've already come up with my excuse, so I confidently deliver it: "I'm about to serve the chocolate cake."

"What does that have to do with handcuffs?"

"They go wild for that cake. Like beasts. I always have to handcuff them when I serve it."

He stares at me.

"If I don't restrain them, there'll be no cake left for you," I explain.

He still just looks on, not responding.

I continue—might as well prepare him: "And they must remain in the restraints not just for dessert, but until the end of the evening or at least until the effect of the cake has worn off. It takes a while."

"The cake's that good?" he finally says.

"Quite good."

"I look forward to tasting it." He frowns. "Why are you lowering the blinds?"

"It can get ugly once the cake kicks in, even with the handcuffs on. I'd rather the neighbors not see." The truth is, the possibility of a sniper has only now dawned on me.

I also discreetly unplug the doorman intercom. I don't want

any more announcements of presents waiting downstairs, or, God forbid, visitors—hired visitors, hired killers, or even just innocent visitors who might be shocked at the sight of a dinner party with handcuffed guests.

I serve each of my friends a piece of chocolate cake and some fruit salad on a plate on their laps under the bar.

They begin eating the cake.

Strad watches them and starts laughing. "You guys remind me of cattle at the trough. It's so degrading. Geniuses in chains. Well, at least some of you. I've got to take a photo of this. I brought my camera, actually. It's in my bag."

My friends look at him aghast, their gaping mouths full of chocolate cake. They turn their faces to me like spectators following a tennis match. In my court is where they think the ball is now. I'm sure they're imagining this photo plastered all over the Internet.

"Are you out of your mind, Strad?" I say. "I'm horrified you would even suggest such a thing."

"No need to get hysterical. I won't take a photo, then. No problem. Actually, I'm honored that you're letting me see your inner sanctum, your secret weirdness."

Returning to the kitchen to cut Strad a piece of cake, I warn him: "And remember, stay away from them. They've had their first bite. They're under the influence."

"They seem very well-behaved to me."

"They know they better be or they won't get seconds."

Strad and I take our seats at the table, facing the others. I nibble on my pear. He smokes and tastes the cake. He compliments me on it.

Strad tells us he read parts of Georgia's novels aloud to his various past girlfriends.

"Oh, terrific," Georgia says, sourly. "And how did they like them?"

"Depends on the girl. Some of them didn't quite have the mental capacity to appreciate your work."

"Really? You dated some dumb girls?"

"I've had my share."

"Why?"

"They had other things going for them."

"Like what?"

"Phenomenal looks." Strad chortles smugly.

"That must be thrilling, dating a good-looking cretin," Georgia says.

Penelope scornfully snorts.

"It can be, for a time," Strad says.

"I suddenly feel less flattered that you like my books," Georgia says. "Sounds like you've got bad taste. And you're very shallow."

He seems hurt, and in that moment, I catch a glimpse of what is the real problem with Strad (and by the same token, what the problem is for Lily): Strad is a somewhat endearing asshole. He's a generally amiable guy with some odious opinions.

He finally responds to Georgia's accusation with, "You feel that way because you're a woman. It's different for men. A man has to be physically attracted to a woman. If he can't get it up for her, what is he supposed to do, shove it in with a stick?"

We're all a little shocked. I steal a glance at Lily. She's staring down at her plate, looking extremely uncomfortable.

Georgia recovers first and says to Strad, "Don't worry, you're not the only one in this room who has bad taste in romantic partners."

"That's good to hear," Strad says, smiling at Jack with complicity. But then, noticing that Jack doesn't return his smile, he says, "May I ask who it is?"

"No, you may not." And then, after a beat, Georgia says to him, "Could you go for me?"

"What do you mean?"

"You know, could you date me?"

He seems stunned. "You mean, considering how charming and charismatic you've been with me?"

"Whatever. Could you?"

"You mean if I could imagine there wasn't a torrent of hostility coming from you to me?"

She rolls her eyes. "Just answer."

"Well, I can't imagine it."

"Why do you think you always date physically beautiful women?"

"I like 'em."

"Yes, but why aren't you capable of falling for someone with other attributes?"

He looks mildly exasperated and doesn't answer.

I glance at Lily, sitting there frozen and looking as though she wishes she could disappear. I disapprove of beauty conversations taking place in front of her, and yet, now that my pet peeve is being bounced about, I cannot, will not, be left out of the dialogue.

"Strad," I say, "there are other aspects to a person. Even other *physical* aspects that can be sexy—apart from beauty."

"Yes, of course. But . . . like what?"

"Anything!" I snap impatiently. "Body language, for example."

"Body language doesn't do it for me."

"Then pick another."

"None of them do it for me. What do you want me to do?"

"I don't know, practice. Eventually, you may acquire the taste. You may even wonder how you were ever satisfied with the straightforward, simple, dumb kind of beauty."

Strad replies, "Most men don't get turned on by 'other attributes.' In fact, if you want the truth, those 'other attributes,' especially brains, talent, higher education, accomplishments, impressive jobs, often make a beautiful woman *less* sexy in the eyes of many men. Not in mine—I'm not that way. But in the eyes of many. They would never admit it, of course. Anyway, why are you all pickin' on me?" He turns to the only other man in the room. "I feel persecuted, Jack. Help me out here a little, will ya?"

Jack sighs. "What can I say? Many guys can get turned on by other attributes. Most jerks can't."

"Et tu, Jack? What's going on here? Anyway, you're full of it. I'm sure you go for the best-looking women you can get, and you probably do pretty well getting the better specimens."

Georgia yanks on her handcuff. "Specimens? Are you for real?"

"Sorry, poor word choice," Strad admits. He leans toward me

and says under his breath, "I'm glad she's chained, by the way."
He turns back to Georgia. "I'm not an artist with words, like
you, Georgia, but you know what I mean."

Georgia says, "Many years ago I met a guy at a dinner party
and I thought he was really ugly. Pale skin, very thick lips, pre-
maturely gray frizzy hair, puffy slit-eyes like a toad's, and I was
horrified when he sat next to me. Within probably five minutes
of him talking to me, I was utterly charmed, completely under
his spell to the point that I asked the hostess if he was single.
The hostess said he was gay. That didn't stop me having a crush
on him for years."

Eyebrows raised, Penelope says, "That's funny, the same thing
happened to me in college. There was a guy in my drawing class. I
found him utterly repulsive. He was short, fat, had greasy stringy
black hair plastered on his balding sweaty head. He compli-
mented me on one of my drawings. Then I bumped into him in
the coffee shop and we had a snack together. During that snack I
developed a massive crush and started finding him beautiful. We
became friends. My crush lasted for months, maybe years."

"What happened?" Lily asks. "He didn't like you back?"

"He was gay."

We all laugh, even Strad.

"I don't suppose that's ever happened to you," Georgia says to
Strad.

"No, I've never had a crush on an ugly lesbian," he replies.

"Come on, I'm serious. Haven't you ever developed feelings
for someone you weren't attracted to at first?"

Frowning in mock concentration, he says, "Oh, dear, I'd have
to give it some thought when you're not all looking at me."

But we keep on looking. Even Lily. She's clearly very interested in the topic.

Strad finally says carefully, "I don't recall if that's ever happened to me. But I'm sure it could, under the right circumstances."

Penelope waves me over.

"What is it?" I ask her.

"I need to whisper something to you."

I bend down to her level. Cupping her free hand around her mouth, she whispers in my ear, "This only just occurred to me. The weapon could be a tiny poisoned glass dart blown out of a tiny straw smuggled in the hem of a garment. It could be done one-handed with the hand that's not cuffed. Strad is not safe right now."

I blanch. She's absolutely right. The metal detector wouldn't have picked up a tiny glass dart and straw, and neither would the frisking.

Penelope warning me of this method seems to indicate that she's not the killer.

On second thought, if she were the killer, she'd still have plenty of reasons to tell me of this method. In a flash, four possible reasons go through my mind, and I'm sure there are more:

1) She wants to divert my attention away from another method she's about to use.

2) She is curious to see how I would have protected Strad against this method, had she thought of using it.

3) She wants to make herself appear more innocent.

4) She knows that by telling me about this method, she is forcing me to increase Strad's protection, which will escalate

the weirdness of the evening to a degree that might cause Lily to finally lose any remaining hope that Strad could ever fall in love with her, which will help her move on with her life.

Barely breathing, I say, "Strad, get up."

"Why?" he asks, getting up.

"Come right this way." I lead him out of the room and around the corner, while shielding him from the others with my body as much as possible. I bring him his chair. "Sit down."

He sits. From my seat at the table, I will be able to see both parties while they won't be able to see or hurt each other.

This is only a temporary solution because I'm sure Strad will not want to stay behind that corner for two whole hours. Maybe not even for two whole minutes. Therefore, I must come up with a better system to protect him from possible darts. I wish I could ask Georgia for ideas.

Luckily, it doesn't take me too long to come up with one. I set myself to work immediately.

I open the living room closet and withdraw the big sheets of transparent plastic I bought to protect my furniture when my apartment was painted a few months ago.

"Why am I around this corner?" Strad calls out to me.

"Punishment," I reply.

"Oh. Was I bad?"

"No. They were bad." My new location hides me from his view as I unfold the sheets of plastic.

"What'd they do? They didn't seem so bad." As an after-thought, he adds, "Apart from ganging up on me and telling me what a jerk I am."

I don't answer.

He says, "Anyway, how is my sitting around this corner *their* punishment rather than mine?"

I open a drawer, looking for my roll of transparent masking tape. I reply, "I'm depriving them of the sight of you."

"Is the sight of me that good?" he asks.

"They thrive on it."

"Perhaps I should just go home, then. That would deprive them of it very effectively," he says.

"No!" I exclaim.

"Why not?"

I don't know what to say. I hope my silence will alert Georgia to come to the rescue.

She does, with: "Barb's kidding. We weren't bad. This is just a game we like to play called Hide the Guest."

Still hidden from Strad's view, I climb on a chair and start taping one end of a plastic sheet to the ceiling, letting the rest hang like a transparent curtain. This creates a dart-proof partition between my friends and the dining table.

While I do this with a few more sheets, until all my friends are behind plastic, Georgia explains the game to Strad: "You have to try to remember what each of us is wearing and what we look like, including eye color, hair color, presence or absence of glasses, etc."

From behind the corner, he sounds mildly interested in this game. But then she has to ruin it by adding, "The point of the game is to test your level of self-centeredness."

I kick my socked foot in the direction of her face, intentionally missing her by only an inch, which sobers her up temporarily.

I finish taping the last bit of plastic to the ceiling. Just in time, too, because Strad says, "You know what? I don't really like the sound of this game. I'm sure I'd be terrible at it, so I'd rather just have a normal remainder of evening with you—"

He stops mid-sentence as he emerges from around the corner and beholds the plastic curtain with my friends watching him through it. And me, still atop my chair.

Stupefied, he asks, "What are you *doing*?"

"We've entered the phase of the evening called Partitioning," I say.

"It's totally creepy-looking," he says. "It looks like you're setting up some sort of weird execution."

"Oh, no, on the contrary. I'm about to serve them seconds. They go so wild for seconds, they often throw their cake."

We keep the conversation going for another hour. Jack throws most of his cake at the curtain to support my story. Not being a fan of lemon, it's no big sacrifice for him. The others merely throw large crumbs. No one attempts to shoot darts, thankfully, not that it would matter much with the plastic sheets.

When the cuckoo finally screams twelve times at midnight and the danger is over (according to KAY's rules), my friends really start acting mad. They cheer and clank their chains, demanding to be freed.

I unlock their handcuffs. They all, except for Lily, shake Strad's hand, saying, "Congratulations." Penelope even says, "Congratulations, you've made it."

"Into the group?" Strad asks, his face lighting up. "You know, it did occur to me that this might be some sort of initiation. If you tell me that I have made it into the Knights of Creation, you'll make me a very happy man."

"No, I'm sorry," Penelope says. "I just meant that you made it through this strange evening. There is no such thing as 'making it into the Knights of Creation.'"

Strad is disappointed though he takes it well. In fact, he doesn't seem to be in any hurry to leave, now that everyone is so cheerful and authorized to go to the bathroom unaccompanied. We move to the couch area and Strad says he'd like some more coffee, but asks if he can get his phone back to quickly first check his messages.

I get him his phone. He's surprised to see he has three new ones.

As he listens to each one, our attention is drawn to his gasps and facial expressions, which become progressively more despondent.

He finally turns off his phone and says, "Barb, you ruined my day, possibly my life, by taking my phone from me. I have to go."

"Why? What's wrong?" Lily asks.

He speaks quickly: "First, some chick tells me there's a fantastic film audition I'd be perfect for, in an alley. She gave me the address. It's just a few blocks from here. She said she spoke to the casting people about me and they really want to see me, but it has to be soon because they're closing casting at midnight, no exceptions. She said not to bother coming after that. She left me that message at ten o'clock. It's now after midnight."

"In an alley?" I ask faintly.

"Yes."

I can't believe what a close call that was. I took Strad's cell phone into my bedroom right before the cuckoo scared us at ten. If I'd waited another ten minutes, Strad would have answered the call and gone.

Strad glares at me. "The second message was from someone saying there's a leak from our music store to the basement apartment and that if I don't get there in the next hour, they'll have to get a locksmith to force the door open because the super's not there."

We don't comment.

"The third message is from someone who says he's a friend of my friend Eric, and that they're both at a party and just met this chick who's unbelievably beautiful and who wants to meet me because they've been talking me up to her, but I'd have to go there right away because she's only staying ten more minutes and doesn't want to leave them her number. So he tells me to hurry on over. The message was left an hour ago. That woman might have been my future wife. And now she's probably gone."

I'm all too aware that each scenario could have led Strad to a probably deserted place, perfect for slaying him. If we'd accompanied Strad to the location, the killer among us would have committed the act personally by grabbing a weapon that was possibly stashed ahead of time at the scene or along the way. If we'd let Strad go alone, some hired killer might have done the deed.

Strad gets ready to leave, but as he begins putting on his shoes, he cries "Argh!" and withdraws his foot immediately from his loafer. His toes have something gross-looking on them. Hard to tell what. He slides his hand into the shoe to investigate and extricates a smelly mash, which I recognize as sardines from our dinner. There's no mistaking it, thanks to a little sardine tail sticking up in the air.

"Why is there fish in my shoe?"

No answer from anyone.

"Who did this?" he asks.

I apologize profusely and say, "One of us has a serious mental problem and likes to leave this kind of gift for people he or she likes. Like a cat who brings a dead rat to its owner."

"Which of you?"

"We don't know."

He dumps the sardines in the trash, washes his hands, cleans out the inside of his loafer, and leaves me his dirty sock.

About to plunge his other foot into his other shoe, he thinks the better of it and checks it with his hand. Instead of sardine mash, he pulls out a little piece of paper that he reads aloud: "If I could have, I would have." Strad looks at us, clearly waiting for an explanation and a quick one.

"God only knows," I say, shaking my head. "I'm sure it was meant in the nicest possible way. But as I said, serious mental problem." I circle my temple with my finger, hoping that will be enough to satisfy Strad.

"If I had to guess, I would guess it's you." He approaches me, searching my face. "You've been acting like a lunatic all evening."

"That was necessary," I say. "But this wasn't me."

He sees it's pointless to argue with me. He grabs his things and his engraved gifts, which I've turned over to him. We say our goodbyes and he departs.

As soon as I close the door, I grab Georgia's arm to get everyone's full attention, especially hers. I hiss at them all: "My compliments to whichever one of you is responsible for those voice messages he received. But it's now after midnight. I hope it is understood that nothing, *nothing* bad will happen to Strad at any of these locations he may go to. Or anywhere else, for that matter. Now or ever. One of you is clearly a psycho, but I hope even psychos can have a sense of honor. You gave Gabriel your word that Strad would not be harmed after midnight tonight, KAY." I look at one after another. They stare back at me.

"Well, I'm not the killer," Georgia says, "but if I were, I would absolutely keep that promise. And I tend to think the actual killer will have that same decency."

The others nod uncertainly.

She says, "I think we should get back on the horse immediately and have one of our Nights of Creation as soon as possible. Say, tomorrow night. I'm free."

We look at each other but no one answers.

She says, "If we don't make a big effort to regain a sense of normalcy right away, things could stay awkward between us forever. And that would be a shame because I love our group. I know we all do."

So we agree to meet the next day for a Night of Creation.

Chapter Twelve

The following morning, Lily calls and thanks me for the "unbelievable amount of effort" I put into protecting the man she loves. She says she'll never forget it.

I'm glad I didn't schedule my dinner with Peter Marrick for tonight. I need this whole day to rest and unwind, though I did some Internet research on him and learned he's thirty-five and won the Emmy for local news five years straight. In addition to anchoring the local news, he anchors the national news when the usual anchor is out, and he does regular special reports for *Newsroom Live*, the weekly current events show. As I already knew, he got a huge amount of attention nationally when he saved the three children from the fire. Soon afterward, he appeared on *The Ellen Show, Letterman*, and *The View*. He (along with his singed hair) was in *People* magazine's 100 Most Beautiful People. The article under his photo talked about his "inner beauty." He did a series last year about poverty in America that won a Polk Award, after which *Time* magazine selected him as one of the hundred most influential people in the world. All of this is a little intimidating. I love talking about current events but I've never had to hold a conversation with someone this well versed in world affairs.

Not wanting to get any more nervous than I already am about my dinner with Peter tomorrow night, I decide to distract myself by going to Strad's store to find out if I was right about the voice messages being part of an elaborate plan to kill him. I bring him his sock, which I've cleaned twice to get rid of the sardine smell. I ask him if everything turned out okay with the leak from his store.

He places his palms on the counter and leans toward me. "You're not going to believe this, but it seems that every single one of those messages was a prank."

"Really?" I say, trying to look surprised.

He tells me there was no flood in the music store, no audition in an alley, and no beautiful woman at a party. In fact, no party.

This grim information chills me, even though it's what I expected.

I must stop obsessing about Strad's near murder. It's in the past, he survived.

This evening, during our Night of Creation, I'm too tired and stressed to work on the hat. Instead, I read a script for a film I've been asked to costume design—not sure I'm interested. But it's hard to tell, because I have a hard time concentrating. The fact that one of my friends is a killer is something I have to live with—not comfortably, but I have to endure it, because the alternative is worse. We all have to endure it. We don't talk about it.

Nevertheless, I do watch my friends. And I notice them watching one another, too. I wonder if we'll ever find out which of them did it. I wonder if we can live with never knowing. In truth, that may be the only way we can live with it.

We are all completely crazy to have decided not to tell the police. We are spending large amounts of our lives with a homicidal maniac who could, at any time, decide, on the spur of the moment, to kill anyone, kill all of us, kill strangers. We are crazy and I assume my friends realize this. I wish I could express it to them, but I don't want to because I'm afraid my argument will be too convincing. I don't want them to decide we must tell the police.

THE NEXT DAY, Sunday, I design the hat. I can sense right away that I'm back. I know what a hat is today, and I'm able to judge my own work. It's a good hat. That little hat is a huge load off my conscience. I spend the rest of the day designing ballet costumes that are due in two weeks. I get all sixteen costumes done.

Thanks to my productive day, I'm in a decent mood as I sit down to dinner with Peter Marrick at Per Se. We're seated near large windows with a beautiful view of Columbus Circle and Central Park.

I'm glad I did my research on Peter because after we place our order and the waiter has explained the detailed history of the three kinds of butter on our table, I'm able to turn to Peter and say, "I watched your interview with the Chinese president on YouTube. It was very impressive."

"Thanks. Being on *Newsroom Live* gives me some great international opportunities." He chuckles. "After I got an interview with him, every Asian leader wanted to talk to me."

I hope he's not going to expect me to know the names of any of those presidents. I have an urge to put on a seatbelt because I sense we are about to launch into a detailed conversation that might require a knowledge of the minutiae of world politics. But I've got nothing to worry about. Suddenly appearing uninterested in the topic, he veers off and tells me he always dreamed of being creative but somehow never had time, life just whizzed by, propelling him in the direction of TV journalism.

To my surprise, he asks if he can join our group, the Nights of Creation, for just one evening.

"Oh," I say, startled. "It's nice you'd want to. I'll ask them. I know they loved meeting you."

"Thanks." He smiles and takes a sip of wine.

"Would you be working on an art project, if you came?"

"Yes."

"Great. What would it be?"

"I don't know." He tears a piece of bread.

"What art form would it be?"

"I don't know," he says, buttering his bread.

A bit embarrassed for him, I softly say, "I just mean, would it be, like, painting, or music, or writing, or sculpting . . .?"

"I know. I don't know," he replies, just as softly. We gaze at each other. Then he whispers to me, with a sad, dreamy air, "I must sound like an idiot."

"Not at all!" I say, thinking he sounds a bit strange. "Which art forms have you tried in the past?"

"Practically none. In school, I drew a bit in art class. And I learned to play the recorder when I was ten."

I nod. "Were you good at either?"

"No. But I was a total beginner."

I laugh, and nod again. "Do you have a good imagination?"

He looks away quickly. "Probably not." He raises his arm high in the air to flag the waiter, which I sense is to hide his discomfort. He orders another bottle of water, even though ours is still three-quarters full.

Feeling sorry for him, my mouth starts uttering words without my brain having completely approved them. "You can come to our Night of Creation. No problem. It'll be fun. I'm sure the others will be fine with it. We have one tomorrow night, if you're free."

He says he is, and thanks me. He seems happy.

Since we set foot in the restaurant, everybody's been staring at us. Perhaps they're surprised that this famous news anchor is having dinner with someone so conspicuously unattractive.

But Peter seems completely oblivious to the stares and very much at ease with me as his dinner companion.

During dessert, Peter says to me, "The truth is, I think I haven't got an ounce of imagination."

When I did my research on him yesterday, I found out he's been married once. Since his divorce three years ago, he's been linked to a couple of women, but nothing serious.

"Do you like being an anchor?" I ask.

"I like it. I don't love it. When you're an anchor, you cover events. You don't create them. You report on contributions. You don't make them."

"Reporting on contributions is a contribution, isn't it?"

"Such a minor one."

"I disagree. Plus, you're so good at it. How did you become so successful if you weren't that interested in your work?"

"Of course I was interested. It's easy to be interested in a big, fat soap opera—which is what local, national, and world events are, you know. If I could go back and do things over, I might have preferred to become one of the notable people who is notable for something other than reporting on notable people."

I nod, understanding.

After dinner, he hails a cab for me, smiles down at me, and says, "See you tomorrow." He kisses me good night on the cheek. It leaves me feeling weak.

When I arrive at my building, Adam the doorman says, "I should change my shift. Seeing you so close to my bedtime gives me nightmares."

I don't mention that we have that in common.

THE FOLLOWING EVENING, my friends arrive early to our Night of Creation so that we can watch Peter on the six o'clock local news before he joins us. They're excited I've invited him, and it works wonders to lighten the mood, which frankly was a bit weighty last time, when all we could think about was which one of us was the killer.

We wait for Peter. He finally bursts into my apartment carrying a large drawing pad and exclaiming, "My friends!" with such an air of relief and yearning, it makes us laugh.

When he sees my mysterious, dim, cavernous living room filled with upright, human-sized animals wearing my costumes and masks, he falls silent.

"Oh my God. This place is amazing," he says, walking in slowly, taking it all in. "I've never seen such a beautiful room."

I'm glad he finds it beautiful. Everyone finds it striking but not everyone finds it beautiful.

"These costumes are gorgeous. Are they your creations?" he asks.

"Yes."

"It's like walking into a fantasy land of imagination, of endless possibilities. No wonder your friends like to work here. Did you put this whole decor together yourself too?"

"Yes, but the lighting is what makes it work, and that was done by a lighting designer friend of mine."

He looks at me and laughs. "The lighting? So on top of being astonishingly talented, you are also breathtakingly modest."

During the session, he draws imaginary landscapes, but his output is low and his skill is poor. Georgia whispers to me in the kitchen, "If he spent less time gazing at you and more time turning that gaze inward, he'd boost his productivity. If you want to help him, you should sleep with him. It would get that sexual tension out of his system and allow his creative juices to flow."

I laugh her off. "If you spent less time surfing the Internet and more time working on your novel, perhaps you'd boost your productivity."

"I can't. My novel makes me nauseated."

"Then write a new one."

"I can't. I've put too much time and work into this one. I can't just abandon it."

Peter seems endearingly concerned that Georgia hasn't

been able to write since she lost her laptop and got it back four days later.

He asks her, "If your laptop had been returned to you more quickly, say after one day, do you think you'd be experiencing the same difficulties with your writing now?"

"I don't know. Why?"

He turns away. "I'm just always interested in how creativity works."

"It's not like I do *no* writing. I do write in my journal."

"That doesn't count," Peter says. "Not to belittle journal-writing, though. I wish I could keep a regular journal. I've tried it, but I can never stick to it for more than a few days. I should give it another shot at some point."

We invite him to join several more of our Nights of Creation. He seems delighted.

Peter Marrick

Sunday, 12 November

I started showing up early for the Nights of Creation, hanging out with Barb in her kitchen, just talking. She's a fascinating person. I'm charmed by her focus on her work and by the wildly imaginative drawings that result from that focus. I'm charmed by her sense of humor. I'm amazed by how much she cares for her friends and by how much they adore her.

Now that we're becoming closer, I know I should tell her I'm the one who found Georgia's laptop in the taxi—

that I know she's wearing a fat suit and a wig, and that underneath it she's drop-dead gorgeous. But I don't want to hurt or frighten her, and I don't want to make her angry. More than anything, I want to keep spending time with her.

Barb

Peter Marrick comes early to our Nights of Creation, week after week, and he stands in the kitchen with me. I don't know why. He's subtly flirtatious, yet doesn't ask me out on another date. I have absolutely no idea what's going on in his mind, no idea what he's feeling. He's a mystery.

Georgia, too, has noticed his strange air, and she remarks to me in private one day, "He seems a little tortured."

"I know," I tell her. But I have to admit I enjoy his company.

Lily hasn't been making much progress on a piece of music that will beautify her for the man she loves. She works on it all the time, including every time we meet for our Nights of Creation. As the days pass, she gets more frustrated and depressed.

I know that the killer promised never again to try to kill Strad, but every time Lily exhibits extreme sadness I worry that the killer won't be able to resist the urge.

Midway through Peter's eighth Night of Creation with us, when we're focused on our work and Penelope has just broken, very gently, yet another small pot, Lily gets up, lifts her piano bench in the air, and lets it drop on the piano. She smashes the sides and back as well.

We stare at the spectacle in utter shock.

Without its mirrored coating, the piano is ugly. Its surface is matte brown with patches of exposed glue.

After we've cleaned up the mess and everyone has gone home, I call Lily before going to bed to make sure she's okay. She doesn't answer but calls me back a few minutes later and tells me I just saved her life. She explains that she was playing at her piano, feeling in the pits of depression, and her hands started turning reflective again. It began spreading up her arms and she knew that this time she wouldn't have the strength to stop it and it would kill her and she didn't care. Hearing my voice leaving her the message is what gave her the strength to stop the progression.

THAT EVENING, PETER calls me. He says he was very disturbed by the incident of Lily smashing her piano and that he's worried about her.

This is not the first time he has seemed caring about my friends, which is something I really appreciate. He's kind and gentle and strikes me as a genuinely good person. I'm particularly touched that he is concerned about Lily's well-being, as she is the one I'm the most anxious about.

"I wonder if there's anything anyone could do to help her snap out of it," he says.

"If you get any ideas, let me know." And then I remember he doesn't have much imagination.

We move on to more pleasant topics. Peter is in no hurry to get off the phone. He seems to enjoy talking to me and getting to know me. But our conversation ends with no suggestion that we get together outside the group.

He probably can't overcome his lack of attraction to my appearance.

"AN INTERVENTION," PETER declares. That's the idea he comes up with a few days after our conversation.

"Like for addicts?" I ask.

"Yes. Because that's what she is. She's addicted to a person."

It's true. The day after smashing her piano, Lily went right back to trying to beautify herself through her music. She worked on this impossible project not only on her home piano, but on her now ugly, naked piano at my apartment. Gone is the energy she was infused with when practicing on Jack and then on herself. She plays slow, melancholy pieces. Now that every reflective surface of the piano has been shattered, we're afraid she'll treat us as her mirrors and ask us for progress reports on her looks. The last thing we want is to have to say, "No, you don't look any prettier yet."

MY FRIENDS AND I decide to give Peter's idea a shot. On the day of the planned intervention—the first Monday after Thanksgiving—Lily is sitting at her ugly naked piano, striving for the impossible, as usual. She thinks this is one of our regular Nights of Creation.

As a group, we approach Lily. I put my hand on her instrument and say, in a formal voice, "Lily, we would like to speak to you."

"Yes?" she says, looking at me without stopping her playing.

"On the couch."

"Really?"

I nod.

The music dwindles and stops. "What's it about?"

"Come this way."

She takes a seat on the couch. Peter and I sit on the ottoman cubes in front of her. The others sit on either side of her.

Peter will be making the speech. He told us in confidence that he prepared one, so we decided to let him be the main speaker, since the intervention was his idea. I hope it'll be good.

Leaning toward Lily, his elbows resting on his knees in a casual pose, this is what he says to her: "You know, in my line of work, I'm out and about in the world a lot. I go to fancy dinner parties and I see women who dehumanize themselves, who treat themselves as though they're pieces of meat. They objectify themselves. And as if that's not bad enough, they don't even do it for themselves, they usually do it for someone else: for a man. It's really sad."

"Okay," Lily says, appearing uncertain as to what he's getting at.

Peter remains silent, until she says, "And? What? You think I do that?"

"Only you know," Peter answers.

"I don't do that," she says.

"These women see themselves as merchandise." He pauses and looks at her meaningfully, letting his words sink in. "They get facelift upon facelift upon nose job upon cheekbone implant upon breast augmentation upon liposuction upon lip enhancement. It seems to me the only way these women are able to subject themselves to so many procedures is by viewing their bodies as nothing more than material possessions. Can you imagine how hard that must be on their spirits, to see them-selves as nothing but meaningless, lowly objects? They may not realize it, but consistently thinking of the external appear-ance as both supremely important and also as an object whose uniqueness and differences are not valued or appreciated and must therefore be butchered and uniformized has got to wear the spirit down on some deep level."

His words express how I feel so perfectly, they make me want to cry.

I have to admit I'm intrigued by him. And I'm starting to like him very much: for this speech, for his effort, for recogniz-ing Lily has a problem, and for caring enough to do something about it. I like that he took the initiative on this, that despite knowing her less well than we do, he took a more forceful step than we have ever taken with her. He's the first person outside of our group that I've been drawn to in a long time, since before Gabriel died.

Lily is listening to him very attentively. She appears genu-inely interested. I think Peter is making progress, which is not surprising considering how persuasive his argument is.

"And it requires a lack of self-esteem, too," Jack adds, "even though these women often try to claim the opposite. You know, they like to profess that it's *because* they value themselves that they do all these cosmetic procedures. But that's just spin."

Peter continues: "What I'm getting at, Lily, is that you are such a beautiful person, intrinsically. You shouldn't try to alter yourself to accommodate the tastes of a shallow prick who's unworthy of you. You're a great artist. Do you know how much

I'd give to have even a fraction of your talent? This may sound corny to you, but my advice is love yourself and love the people who love you, not the others."

I'm nodding in agreement. The others are, too.

The most thrilling part is that Lily is nodding, too. Peter's words seem to be getting through. And I don't think she's just being polite.

Lily raises her index finger to interrupt Peter, and says, "Wow, you're saying some very interesting stuff. You're really helping me put things into focus. You're so right on every front."

"You see my point?" Peter says.

"Oh, God, totally!" she replies, getting up. "Can we continue this a bit later?"

"We haven't finished!" I cry.

"I got the gist of it, though," she says. "But please, keep talking. I can still listen." She walks over to her piano, sits, and goes right back to playing—completely undeterred.

We stand around her piano. Through the filter of my frustration, her music is hell to my ears. "Why are you doing this?" I bark.

"Don't mind me."

In a whisper, I ask Peter if this is common, the alcoholic getting up in the middle of an intervention and going straight to the liquor cabinet.

"I'm sure it happens a lot," Peter says.

I turn to Lily. "Have you even heard a word Peter said?"

"Yes, every word," she replies, clearly reabsorbed in her playing. "And I will give it some serious thought."

Jack says, "Lily, do you see that getting up in the middle of Peter's talk is a symptom of your disease?"

She nods. "I'm sorry. But you know how it is ... when the impulse takes you."

"The impulse to what? Destroy your life?" Penelope pitches in.

"I can play and listen at the same time. I'm a good multitasker. You guys can keep talking to me, if you want." But her eyes are downcast, and she doesn't really seem to be listening to us.

We ask her to please stop and pay attention.

"I am!" she claims. She has an intense expression on her face—a look of deep concentration. But her gaze seems to be turned inward. As I speak to her, she nods mechanically while playing.

And then I stop talking. An unsettling sensation has quieted me.

Still nodding, she says, "Go on, I'm listening."

But I don't go on.

"You were saying?" she says.

I just gaze at her. Words are meaningless now.

Then she asks, "Has the cat got your tongue? I'm all ears, keep talking."

"It doesn't matter anymore," I finally manage to murmur.

And the reason it doesn't matter, the reason I have been silenced, is that the unthinkable, the impossible, has begun.

Beauty is crawling all over Lily like a disease. It is clawing at her face, chewing her features, transforming their shapes, harmonizing their lines. It attacks her flesh, takes hold of her skin like a rapidly-moving cancer, leaving behind pure loveliness. Waves of delicacy wash over her. Ripples of symmetry soften her. Layer upon layer of grace sweeps over her entire countenance.

I shake my head a little, to make sure I'm not hallucinating. I blink.

We need the tape recorder.

The melody is fast and inescapable. It's an ocean of notes crashing around us in my living room. Gorgeous and delirious.

This has got to get recorded. Before it's too late. Does Lily even know what's happening to her—what she's achieved?

I finally manage to tear my eyes away from Lily, who no longer resembles the Lily who entered my apartment tonight. I look at my friends.

Jack is fetching the small recorder from the bookshelf nearby and comes back with it on tiptoes, turning it on. He holds it out of Lily's sight, so as not to distract her—not that she would notice anyway; her eyes are closed.

She still hasn't looked at us since she sat at her piano. We, on the other hand, can't stop looking at her—with the solemnity of country folks watching a spaceship land. Her beauty continues to increase. She looks like an angel.

I've never seen anything like this, beauty of this magnitude. I had no idea it existed.

And suddenly, the angel speaks. "I'm tempted to look into your eyes to see if anything has happened. But I'm afraid of being disappointed again."

"Open them," I say.

Slowly, she does. The effect is spectacular. Her eyes are turquoise, large and clear.

There is no model, no actress in any movie I have ever seen who is as exquisite as Lily right now. When I'm not wearing my disguise and men look at me, if they see even a fraction of the beauty I am seeing right now, I forgive their shallowness. There is power in beauty. That's the tragedy of it.

It's hard to imagine that Lily can't decipher from the looks on our faces the extent of her success. If we were cartoons, our mouths would be hanging open wide in awe, our lower jaws on the floor.

But because we are human and because Lily has endured months of failure, her insecurities aren't permitting her to read our expressions with any degree of accuracy. So she seeks out an answer in a roundabout way. "Does this piece need to get recorded?" she asks.

"Yes," Jack says, lifting the recorder within her line of vision. "It's on."

A smile appears on her lips and her music takes off again, free and wild. She's done it and—at last—she knows it.

She plays for a while longer and says, "Time to see the rate of the fade." She stops playing, gets up and goes to the ballet bar. She stands with her hand on the bar, facing the narrow full-length mirror at its side.

She seems startled by her reflection and takes a step closer to see better.

"You've succeeded," Georgia tells her. "Probably beyond what even you imagined, right?"

"Yes," Lily says.

As the seconds pass, Lily's loveliness lessens. "The fade is even more rapid than I expected," she says.

Within a minute, every hint of beauty has left her.

"Now I just have to see if playback works as well as live," she says, and asks us to hook up to the speakers the recorder containing the musical hallucinogen.

We do, and turn on the music. She studies her face as her beauty returns. The porcelain skin, the delicate features.

"Peter," she says, looking at him in the mirror, "thanks for helping me. It's completely thanks to you that I succeeded."

"How?" he asks, baffled.

"You made such good points. The women you spoke about, who alter themselves drastically—you said they objectify themselves, that they see themselves as merchandise. You made me realize how important that is. I wasn't doing it very much, and that was the problem. You helped me see that. So I lowered my self-esteem until I saw myself as no more significant than an item sitting on a shelf—a ceramic pot Penelope might break and put back together. I told myself that I'm like any other object in this world that I must beautify, just an ugly pot."

"Wait," Peter says, looking at me. "I can't believe my ears. I was making the absolute opposite point."

"Which was then reinterpreted by an artist," Georgia says.

"Before, I wasn't focusing on the right things," Lily says. "But as soon as I tried Peter's idea of looking at myself as an object, bam! I gained a sense of distance from myself, which freed my mind to come up with this new solution: depth. So that's what I went for. The music enables you to see past my unfortunate physical appearance."

"Past it? So what are we looking at?" Jack asks.

Lily doesn't answer. Her silence is puzzling until I understand what she's reluctant to state because of her modesty.

"Her soul," I say.

"Her inner beauty," Georgia adds.

Blushing slightly, Lily says, "Yeah, it wasn't shining through. Not even slightly. I don't know why. My physical appearance is very opaque, in addition to being ugly—an unfortunate combination."

"So you performed . . . a kind of . . . musical peel?" Penelope asks.

"Yes, exactly."

"What now? Do you have a plan?" Georgia asks.

"I have a fantasy. One of you will call Strad and offer to set him up on a blind date. He will agree. He and I will have our date at the Barnes & Noble in Union Square, in the coffee shop on the third floor. I will ask the store to play my beauty music on that day, instead of my book music, which they usually play. That's how the whole thing would begin."

"The whole thing? So you're thinking there will be a 'whole thing'?" Penelope asks.

"Well, that was the point, wasn't it?" Lily says.

"How can you have a relationship with someone if the music always has to be on?" Peter asks. "What if he wants to take you out where no music is playing? Is this stuff covered in your fantasy?"

"Yes. I'd wear a mask."

"A mask?"

"Yes. Or just avoid going out. But if I can't avoid it, I'd wear a mask."

"Won't he find that strange?" Peter asks.

"Perhaps. But in my fantasy, he accepts it. And plus, people are often strange."

"And you wouldn't mind living your whole life this way?" I ask.

"Maybe not. And that's an interesting question coming from you, Barb."

"What if he finds out the truth?" Peter says. "What if you're at home with him one day and for some reason the music stops and he sees you're Lily?"

"Maybe his love could survive the truth."

"What if it couldn't?" Penelope asks.

"Maybe it won't be the truth anymore."

"What do you mean?" Jack asks.

"Maybe by then I will have improved the music to make its effect permanent. Even through silence."

Georgia claps her hands once. "Okay, who's going to make the call? I hope it's not me because the thought of setting you up with that creep is hard to bear."

"I'm not quite ready yet," Lily says. "There are two things I have to take care of first."

AN HOUR AFTER my friends leave, I'm surprised that Lily comes back to my place to speak to me one on one.

She asks me if I could make a mask for her to wear sometimes, if she's ever out with Strad. She says she wasn't able to find a nice one that fits her because her eyes are too close together for any normal mask. She says there's only one she found that fits her, and she pulls it out of her bag. To my horror, it's a mask of the Wicked Witch of the West, from *The Wizard of Oz*. The face is hideous green rubber with a hook nose topped by a big mole. The witch is wearing sunglasses—cheap sunglasses attached to the mask. I turn the mask over and see that each eyehole is huge, the size of the entire lens of the sunglasses, which explains why she bought it. Big eyeholes can accommodate a greater variety of distances between people's eyes.

"You're right, this is not exactly the kind of mask you want to be wearing when you're hanging out with Strad," I say.

"I'm going to wear it at the start of my first date with him."

"Why?" I ask, stupefied.

"I want to experience what you experience when you take off your disguise at bars."

I PUT EVERY other project on hold to make the mask. I shouldn't, but I can't help it. I'm so excited by what has happened. And it's all thanks to Peter. Lily will have a chance to taste one of life's greatest joys: romantic love; unrequited love suddenly requited—something she might never have been able to experience if it hadn't been for Peter helping her access her greatest powers. He was her source of inspiration. And he wasn't even trying. He *was* trying to do the exact opposite—convince her to give up her insane project and unhealthy obsession with Strad. If he'd succeeded at that, it would have been good. But this new outcome is even better. It may not be as healthy, but it's much more delicious.

I could make a perfectly decent mask in an hour, but I want this mask to be inspired. I want it to be jaw-droppingly beautiful, ethereal, majestic. And most of all, I want it to be white. I have a vision of Lily in a white mask, which doesn't make it easy for me because white is my weakest color. White masks always come out bland at my hands. Especially the feather ones, which is the kind I want Lily's to be. I try to talk myself out of that color, but fail.

I work on it all night. Can't stop. It always makes me feel good to do things for Lily, and she never asks for anything, so the opportunities are rare.

In the morning, I sleep for a few hours and then get back to work on the mask. One reason it's taking so long is that I keep pausing to daydream about Lily wearing it and taking it off for Strad while the music is playing.

I continue working all day, and by the evening, I'm practically done. This white mask rivals—possibly even surpasses—my most beautiful colored masks. I had to make the eyeholes close to each other, though doing so would reveal Lily's biggest facial defect. So I made the eyeholes huge, touching in the middle and extending far to the sides, in a sort of infinity symbol, which turns out to be the mask's most stunning feature. I covered the eyeholes with a mirrored surface (the type of glass used for mirrored sunglasses). It's essentially the same concept as the mask she already has—but attractive. Lily will be able to look out, but anyone trying to look in will only see themselves.

THE SECOND THING Lily takes care of is asking Barnes & Noble for the special favor she is hoping they'll do for her. They refuse, claiming a whole day is too long to play her mysterious "other" music instead of her brilliant book music, and that their sales would suffer excessively. But then Marcy Singer, a very kind store manager, succeeds in getting permission to play that "other" music, as a "very special favor," from two to three o'clock, on any afternoon of Lily's choice—but only one single afternoon.

Lily is pleased. One hour seems more than adequate to get her fantasy started.

THE TIME HAS come to make the phone call. No one wants to be the one to make it, though everyone wants to listen, including Peter, so we gather at my place to decide who will do it.

But first, I can't resist showing Lily and the others the white mask I've almost completed. When they see it, they gasp.

To my great pleasure, Lily says, "I never expected you to make something this amazing!" She touches it lightly with her fingertips.

They all stand there admiring my mask, which cannot go on long enough for my taste.

"It's reminiscent of a mask one might find in Venice, only more unusual," Penelope says.

"It's your best work," Jack states.

"Possibly," I reply, pleased. "I don't know what possessed me."

"You don't? I do," Georgia says. "What possessed you is the same thing that possessed me last night: inspiration. Caused by Lily, her perseverance, and her magical success. When I got home, after I got over my initial despair that I would never be able to create art that came even close to rivaling hers, I decided to emulate her. Just for the hell of it. Just to see what happened. So I got a bucket and placed it next to my chair in case I needed to throw up, because, as you know, every time I even *think* of trying to write since I got my laptop back, it makes me want to vomit. I sat there and actually attempted to write."

"And? Did you succeed?" Peter asks.

"I'm not saying I produced anything on Lily's level. But it was like before I lost my laptop. As though I'd never lost it. And to me, that feels like magic. It's all I could hope for."

"I'm so happy you're writing again!" Peter exclaims, hugging Georgia, to our surprise. "What a relief! All is right with the world." His hug lifts her off the ground.

Lily thanks me again for the mask. I tell her I can't give it to her just yet because I need one or two more days to add a couple of finishing touches to it.

"It looks pretty finished to me," Penelope says. "Be careful not to spoil it. I know that sometimes when I overwork a ceramic piece, it turns out worse rather than better."

"Really? That's interesting," Jack says, strolling over to my shelves. "Where's that nice ceramic box you made for Barb a few weeks ago? That was such a beautiful example of having not overworked a piece. And it had such a nice clasp."

"Thanks, but I didn't make the clasp, remember, only the box."

We move on to the question of who will call Strad. As expected, they all say they'd rather not, which only leaves me. I'd rather not, too, but I cave in.

On speakerphone, I dial Strad's number.

"Strad, Barb," I say, when he picks up.

"Hi Barb," he says.

"I'm calling to set you up on a blind date."

"Oh." A cautious pause. Then, "Who is she? What does she look like?"

His question surprises me, which surprises me.

"She is a knockout," I tell him.

I give him Lily's new cell phone number—the one she got for this occasion.

To our pleasure, he calls her just a few minutes after hanging up with me. Lily answers her cell on speakerphone, so that we can all hear. She adopts a slightly deeper voice than her natural pitch.

He asks her a few perfunctory questions. She tells him she's my new assistant. That's what we settled on in advance, along with her new name, "Sondra Peterson," which she picked as an homage to her favorite top model from the sixties.

They make plans to meet on Sunday at two o'clock at the coffee shop on the third floor of Barnes & Noble in Union Square. Just like in Lily's fantasy.

Before they hang up, he says, "How will I recognize you?"

"I'll be wearing a mask."

Silence. "Why?"

"Why not? It's as good a way as any to be recognized."

Silence. "And then you'll take it off? I like being able to see who I'm talking to."

"Yes, I'll take it off."

PART

TWO

Chapter Thirteen

Carrying a shopping bag containing her two masks, Lily goes to Barnes & Noble for her two p.m. blind date with Strad (she tells us all about it later). Customers in the store have already been under the influence of Lily's "beauty" music for a few minutes, so she gets admiring stares when she enters, which she finds unsettling. It's the first time in her life she's out in public and beautiful.

She takes the escalator straight to the third floor and hides behind some bookcases to spy on the coffee shop area. She wants to wait until Strad arrives and seats himself before she makes her appearance.

Three minutes later, she sees him ambling into the coffee shop area. He looks around, searching for someone wearing a mask, sees no one, chooses an empty table, hangs his jacket on the back of the chair, and stands in line to buy a snack.

Lily decides that she will make her entrance when he's back at his seat. She feels more nervous than she expected.

While she waits, a young man tries to start a conversation with her. No one ever tries to pick her up, so at first she doesn't realize what he's doing. When it finally occurs to her that asking her what is her favorite time to come to Barnes & Noble is a weird question, she says, "I'm sorry, I can't talk right now," and turns back to her object of interest, who's paying. Strad carries a hot beverage and a plate with a pastry on it to his table. He looks around again, then at his watch, and sits.

Now is the time. Her apprehension has grown. Trying to calm herself, she takes a deep breath.

She pulls out of her shopping bag the green mask of the Wicked Witch of the West wearing sunglasses. She puts it on.

Before she has a chance to take her first step in Strad's direction, there is a tap on her shoulder and an "Excuse me" behind her. She turns. It's the same guy again. He jumps with fright, looking aghast.

She lifts up her mask. "What?"

He holds up a book. "This is my favorite novel. Have you read it?"

She thought she'd made herself perfectly clear to this guy.

"I'm sorry, I'm in a relationship," she lies, "and in the middle of something important. I'd really be grateful if you would leave me alone. I'm sorry." She replaces the mask over her face, hoping it'll frighten him away.

He raises his hands. "Shame. But okay," he says, and walks off.

Strad is now sipping from his cup and reading a magazine.

Lily steps out from behind the bookcase just as a group of people are walking by, headed toward the coffee shop area. She goes with the flow.

Strad looks up from his paper, scanning his surroundings again. He does a double take. He has spotted her behind the approaching heads. His eyes are locked on her mask and he's not smiling.

He rises from his chair and gives her a courteous nod as she nears. She nods back and stops in front of him. He mumbles hello, says it's nice to meet her. He indicates the empty chair. She sits.

The first thing he says when they're seated is, "Don't get me wrong, I appreciate your sense of humor. But they do say first impressions are very important." He laughs. "I guess you haven't heard that?"

"They're not that important."

From the start, the fantasy is not going exactly as she had imagined. There's a different feel to it. First off, the coffee shop is loud. More so than usual. Her soul-baring music is not easy to hear above all the noise. This worries her. She wonders if her music's transformative power will be diminished or maybe even canceled.

As a result, the thing she has been looking forward to the most—the removal of the mask—she now begins to dread.

Her anxiety is not helped by what Strad asks her next.

"Do you know Barb well?"

"Not that well. I only started working for her recently," she says, the first of probably many lies.

"Why do you think she wanted to set us up? I don't entirely trust her motives. I think it's a trick to teach me a lesson. She disapproves of a couple of my views. They all do, that bunch." He shakes his head regretfully. "Too bad, really. I admire them."

He will certainly feel tricked if she takes off her mask and he sees his ugly former colleague Lily sitting in front of him instead of beautiful Sondra. This could happen because of all the racket masking her music. To make matters worse, children are crying at three different tables around them. Unbelievable. It's not romantic. What bad luck.

She suddenly wishes she didn't have to take off her mask. Maybe she'll simply refuse to take it off. She has a right to change her mind. Perhaps she'll just arrange to see Strad another time, someplace safer, more familiar, such as Barb's apartment. These thoughts are calming her. And she decides right then that, in fact, she won't take off her mask. There. She feels much better now.

"God, it's so loud here," he complains.

"I know."

"This cake is great. Here, have a bite," he says.

"No thanks, I'm not hungry."

"It would make me so happy if you would taste it."

Her anxiety returns. Obviously he's trying to get her to take off her mask.

She will give in without giving in. "Okay," she says.

She takes the fork he's handing her, on which rests a piece of tart, and lifts the bottom of her mask just enough to slide the bite into her mouth.

She chews and releases the mask to where it was. "Mmm. It's good," she says.

Lily glances at Strad. He is solemn. Clearly he's disappointed that she hasn't removed her mask as she'd promised she would. Well, tough.

Taking it upon herself to get the conversation going again,

she says, "So, Barb tells me you're a musician. What kind of music do you play?"

"Wait," he says. "I'm still recovering."

"Recovering?" she asks, puzzled.

"Yes," he says, gazing down, looking almost pained.

"From what?"

"That glimpse of your chin," he replies, softly.

She doesn't respond.

"I think I'd like to get together again, based solely on your chin."

"Ah." She doesn't know what else to say. All she can think about is how relieved she is that the music worked well enough on her chin. And not only that, he wants to see her again. Things could not be better.

They chat about various things. He tells her about the evening he spent having dinner with the Knights of Creation at Barb's apartment, and how they attacked Jack and then were handcuffed for dinner to a ballet bar and then were sectioned off for dessert by a transparent plastic sheet hanging from the ceiling. Lily tries to react as though she wasn't there. But conveying amusement and amazement while masked is not easy and has to be done entirely with voice and body language, which she does as best she can by flinging her head around and laughing loudly.

Then Strad moves on to the topic of Lily's music. "I wouldn't be surprised if that's her music playing, right now," he says, finger pointing up, ear cocked. "That's if you can hear it above all this howling. God, you'd think we were in a day care center.

Anyway, if that's her music, probably before we leave here today we'll have bought at least five books each."

Lily laughs. "Really?"

"Oh yeah, you'll see. Lily's got phenomenal talent."

Suddenly, a floor manager appears at their table.

Lily and Strad stare up at him, wondering what it's about.

The manager leans toward them and says, in a hushed voice, "Excuse me, your mask is upsetting the children. I've had a few complaints from mothers. Would it be too much to ask you to please remove it? I apologize for the inconvenience."

"Oh, I'm sorry, I didn't realize I was the cause of the crying," Lily says.

The manager nods sympathetically, waiting for her to take it off.

Lily frantically wonders if her music is loud enough to work its magic. It did okay with her chin, apparently. But she's gripped by an irrational fear that now the effect won't work.

She's tempted to tell the manager, "In my bag I have another, much more attractive mask that the children might prefer. Could I just switch masks in the bathroom?"

But why postpone the inevitable? She did not spend weeks struggling to create music that would beautify her just to keep her face hidden.

She prays that when she takes off the mask, Strad will not recognize her. If he sees Lily, the embarrassment would kill her.

She lifts the mask and puts it in her shopping bag. "No problem. Out of sight, out of mind," she says.

Both men are staring at her. They look dumbstruck.

The manager regains his wits first, and says to Lily. "You know, you look very familiar. Do I look familiar to you?"

Lily studies his face. He's in his late twenties, dark hair, glasses, nice-looking. "I don't think so," she says.

"Hmm. Could I have your number or give you mine so we can figure out where we might have met before?" He chuckles, mock sheepishly. "Otherwise I know it's going to nag at me."

Strad snaps out of it. "You must be joking. We're on a date. Please leave us alone."

"Apologies." The manager leaves.

"Can you believe his lame pickup line?" Strad tells her.

She smiles.

"It's so quiet now. It really was your mask causing all the crying." He attempts to shake his head at her flirtatiously, but he seems nervous. He glances around. His smile fades. "Do you always have half the people in a room staring at you?" He adds in a whisper, "Especially the male half?" He attempts another flirtatious look of reproach.

"Let's ignore them," Lily says.

They talk about various things. His childhood. Hers—partly made up so it won't match Lily's. He asks her about her tastes in everything. He tells her about his music and acting ambitions.

Their conversation is interrupted by the approach of a distinguished older man with a warm, intelligent face who hands Lily a book. "Excuse me. I just want to give you a copy of my autobiography that was recently published. I hope you'll enjoy it." His accent sounds French.

Lily hesitantly takes the book, entitled *This Is Not an Autobiography*.

"Oh. Thank you," she says.

"You're quite welcome," the man replies, bowing to her and then to Strad before walking away.

Lily opens the cover and sees a handwritten message to her: "For the stranger who spoke to me without speaking. I'd love to know your thoughts on this—or on anything. Danny." And a phone number is scribbled underneath.

"Do you mind if I take a look?" Strad asks.

Lily gives him the book.

He reads the message, snorts, and tosses the book on the middle of the table.

Lily picks it up and reads the back cover, which seems to annoy Strad, who says, "So who the hell is this guy?"

"This says he's a legendary French photographer."

"Yeah, bullshit."

"The photo looks like him," she says and quickly puts the book down, not wanting to annoy Strad further.

They resume their conversation, which gets interrupted ten minutes later by yet another man—this time a tall and extremely good-looking one.

"I don't believe this," Strad mutters through clenched teeth.

The man looks down at Lily without saying a word and places a little piece of paper on the table in front of her. She picks it up. It reads: "You deserve the best. Let's have coffee." His phone number is underneath.

She chuckles nervously and looks up at him. He smiles at her before strolling off.

With an air of indifference (in order to calm Strad), Lily lets go of the paper. It flutters to the tabletop. Strad reaches for it, reads it, and, with scathing disdain, calls out after the man, "What are you, a male model or something?"

The man pivots on his heels and comes back to the table. "Pardon?" he says, looming over Strad.

Strad does not hesitate to stand and confront the man, even though this man is taller than he is. "I said, 'What are you? A ridiculous male model, or something?'"

The man takes hold of Strad's jacket lapels, pulls him close, and talks to him intimately. "And what do you think *you* are, you pathetic, greasy, ugly, creep?"

Strad struggles free and then charges the man. They both crash into some empty chairs. They wrestle on the floor, throwing punches. The floor manager rushes over, tries to make them stop. People shout. Toddlers resume crying. Lily is distraught. But not nearly as distraught as she is a moment later when she realizes that the music has abruptly changed. She looks at her watch. The favor-hour is over. The book music is back on. And now her appearance is undoubtedly starting to change in people's eyes.

She springs from her chair, grabs her shopping bag, and runs to the escalator, leaving the French photographer's book and the possible male model's phone number on the table, far too in love with Strad to be interested in other men's advances.

"Sondra!" Strad shouts. He loses interest in the fight, struggles to his feet, and rushes after her.

She hops onto the moving staircase and flies down the metal steps while putting on the beautiful mask I made for her—in case Strad catches up with her. She looks back and sees him leaping onto the escalator just as she's getting onto the next one. A group of people are in his way, slowing down his pursuit. Soon, Lily is out of sight and too far away to be caught. Strad gives up. He goes back up to the coffee shop to retrieve his knapsack with his wallet, then walks across Union Square, straight to my apartment.

When I open the door for him, he looks frazzled, frantic even.

"Barb, I'm afraid I made a bad impression. I think I scared her away. I got into a fight with a guy. It was stupid of me. But jerks kept coming on to her. I couldn't take it anymore. She's so beautiful. Barb, she's amazing."

I gaze at the few cuts on his face and hands. I won't pretend they don't bring me satisfaction.

I decide I will take this opportunity to explain Lily's frequent wearing of a mask, so he won't question it in the future. Giving him a look of concern, I reply, "Yes she's very beautiful, but fragile."

"What do you mean, fragile?"

"You'll see, if you get to know her. Her beauty is taxing for her, as I'm sure you can imagine, now that you've witnessed the excessive attention and advances she has to deal with all the time. It's a heavy burden to bear. As a result, she has erected certain defense mechanisms."

"Like what?"

I answer by looking past him, into my living room. Strad follows my gaze, which lands on my large, brown, swivel easy chair with its back to us.

Slowly, the chair turns, revealing Lily wearing the white feather mask.

Strad's eyes open wide.

I move to the stereo and turn on the special music.

"I'm sorry I made such a fool of myself," he tells her.

Lily makes no response.

"I apologize for the fight at the bookstore. I hope I didn't freak you out too much. I don't usually get into fights. I'm not a violent person, I swear," he says.

Lily languorously swivels the chair, disappearing behind its back once more. When she reappears, she is unmasked.

The music has had enough time to take effect. Her inner beauty is exposed in all its radiance.

Her lips, curved in their deliriously lovely way, spread into a mischievous grin. "You didn't freak me out that much."

MY FRIENDS COME over the following day for a Night of Creation. When Lily has finished regaling them with her account of her bookstore date, we work. Peter is drawing in his pad, frequently glancing at me, as usual. I'm not looking at him much, but I'm thinking about him—and not entirely happily. He seems attracted to me, and yet he hasn't been doing anything about it. He must not be as interested as he seems, and it must be my disguise that's preventing him from wanting to take things further. It's disappointing. I hoped he might be different.

In Central Park at nine p.m., two days later, Strad is waiting for Lily where they decided to meet for their second date: along the edge of the lake in a secluded spot at the foot of some rocks.

He's been waiting five minutes.

Suddenly, he sees her at the top of the rock formation behind him, wearing her white mask. She looks majestic standing there, gazing down at him. He waves at her.

With a minimal gesture of the head, she motions for him to join her. Before he can, she backs away until she's out of sight. He scrambles up the rocks to find her.

And he does. She's leaning against a tree, waiting for him.

"You're wearing your mask again," he says, surprised.

She nods.

"I guess you wear it a lot?"

She nods.

"How come?"

"I can't talk about it now. I'm sorry."

"Oh, that's okay. It's great to see you again. Or at least to somewhat see you again," he says, as they begin to stroll. "How've you been?"

"Well. And you?"

"I hardly know," he murmurs.

"Oh? Is something wrong?"

"I'd rather not talk about it right now. It is *so* nice to see you again."

"Thank you. Have you had dinner?"

"No. I haven't had much appetite lately," he says, looking off into the distance.

Georgia had predicted that "He will barely eat and he will barely sleep. Your face is not one from which one recovers quickly."

Lily glances at him. He does look rather tired and gaunt. She feels a surge of joy.

That's why Lily had to ask. Curiosity. Not because she wanted dinner, which she couldn't eat anyway, with her mask.

Eventually, they sit on a rock at the edge of the lake, in the obscurity. The side of his body is touching the side of hers.

"May I take off your mask?" he asks.

"No, I'm sorry."

"Why not? I mean, I understand that with your looks, wearing a mask attracts less attention than not wearing one, but right now we're alone. No one will see you."

"Except you."

"Why would that be a problem?"

"Now is not a good time."

"What a shame. I don't even remember what you look like." She chuckles.

"It's true," he says. "Hasn't that ever happened to you—you think about someone so much, you can no longer remember their face clearly?"

"Yes, I know what you mean," she says.

"So." He pauses, grins at her. "When will I get to see your face again?"

"I'm not sure, yet. I often wear a mask. I wear it at many expected times, and at some unexpected times."

"I see. And do you have an aversion to being touched?" he asks.

"No."

"Really? Could have fooled me. You're completely covered. Even your hands. I can't see any of your skin."

"That's because it's cold," she laughs.

"The only part of you that's not covered is the back of your head. Do you mind if I touch that?"

"I guess not."

"Turn around."

She turns her back to him.

She feels his hands softly separating her hair, pushing it forward over her shoulders.

"There's your skin," he notes.

He runs one finger along her part, and over her nape, sending shivers through her body. He gently kisses the back of her neck.

At the end of the date, he asks her if he can see her again tomorrow, if not sooner.

He stares at her frigid, feathery expression. He doesn't know it, but on the other side of the mask, she's smiling.

ON TV, I hear a line that strikes me as a perfect comeback to most of the insults my doorman throws my way. So I decide to try a new technique: give him a taste of his own medicine.

I seize my opportunity the next day, when I come back from running errands and Adam says, "The aberration of nature has returned."

I stare at him squarely in the eyes and reply, "Whatever's eating you must be suffering horribly."

His face turns red, as though he's been slapped. "That's very insulting," he says.

"You mean compared to all the charming things you say to me?"

"Whatever. Cocksucking bitch."

"I'm sorry, Adam, I didn't mean to offend you. Good night."

"You fucking curse on society," he says to my back.

Okay, that experiment didn't work too well.

Now I'm back to my original plan: give him the name of my therapist.

———

FOR THEIR THIRD date, Lily and Strad go to a bar. They pick a cozy couch to settle themselves on, in front of a fireplace. Strad orders a glogg. Lily orders nothing.

"Because of the mask?" he asks.

She nods.

"But you could lift it slightly to sip a drink, the way you did at the bookstore when you tasted my tart. I wouldn't see anything except maybe your chin, which I adore."

Without her special music playing, her chin would be its hideous receding self—the last thing she wants him to see. She sticks to ordering nothing.

"It would be so wonderful to see your face in the light of this fire. Do you think that might be possible at some point before we leave?"

"Oh, no, definitely not."

He laughs. "What does the removal of your mask depend on?"

She shrugs.

"Okay, let me guess. Does it depend on your mood?"

"No."

"Does it require a magic word? Like 'please'?"

"No."

"Does the moon need to be full or absent, or somewhere in between?"

"No."

"Does it depend on your menstrual cycle? No offense."

She laughs. "No."

"Do I need to give you a gift?" he asks, taking a small lily from a vase on the table and handing it to her.

She takes the flower. "No."

"Do I need to touch you a certain way?" he asks, stroking the side of her head, just behind the feathers of the mask.

"No," she says, leaning slightly into his hand.

"Do we need to be somewhere in particular?"

"Yes."

"Where do we need to be?"

She shrugs.

"Okay, I do think we're getting warmer. At least now I know I need to take you somewhere," he says, stroking his chin thoughtfully.

"No."

"No?"

"No. *I* need to take *you* there."

"Really? You're feeling an urgent need to take me there? That's great. Let's go!"

She laughs.

"Can we go to the place where the mask comes off?" he asks.

She studies him. "Yes." She gets up.

Lily leads him to her apartment. Fortunately, she doesn't have to worry about him remembering it as "Lily's" apartment, because it's not the same apartment he visited a couple of years ago when he lay on her floor and told her he'd fall in love with (and marry) any woman who could create music that beautified the world.

Nevertheless, she is worried. She's afraid that something in her home will give away her true identity. She spent the last few days taking precautions, guarding against this danger. She removed her name from the buzzer. She carefully hid all her mail and documents with her name on them. She moved her piano and musical books to a tiny spare room, and locked the door.

She never in her life had kept any photos of herself on display—not seeing the point of living among reminders of her ugliness—but still, she made doubly sure before Strad came over that she hadn't left a snapshot lying around. She had discovered, through experimentation, that the music she'd created to beautify herself also beautified photographs of herself—but as the music might not be playing during the entirety of Strad's visit, the last thing she wanted was for a photo to be changing throughout the evening, depending on whether the music was on or off.

When Strad and Lily enter her apartment, she closes the door behind them. She turns on her soul-stripping music, which is wired to play in all the rooms whenever it's turned on (except the bathroom, unfortunately), and waits until she's sure the music has taken its effect before removing her mask. She opens a bottle of wine and they sit together on the couch.

Seeing him reclined there, she becomes sad just looking at him, at how beautiful he is to her, at how often she's dreamed about him, at how much she loves him. She is painfully aware that his happiness at sitting here with her, his desire to touch her, is not something she was born to experience in the natural world.

She must have looked sad, because he finally asks, "Are you okay?"

"Not really," she says. "I'm a bit overwhelmed."

"I'm not attractive enough for you, right? I know I'm not good enough for you."

"No, you're wrong. I find your face very moving."

"Are you mocking me?"

He looks at her and sees tears in her eyes.

"You're not," he says, perplexed.

She shakes her head.

He descends upon her. They kiss passionately, each with their own personal desperation. He basks in the sight of her face, running his fingers through her hair, devouring her with his eyes, and then with his mouth, and again with his eyes. Before long, they move to the bedroom. He undresses her quickly. Even though their passion is frantic, every second is slowed in her mind, and she has time to relish the caresses. She hugs the body she craved for years, the body that never wanted her and still wouldn't if she hadn't worked beyond sanity to warp reality.

Afterward, he notices blood on the sheets. "Oh. You have your period?"

"No," she says.

He frowns. "That's strange," he mutters. And then he opens his eyes wide and looks at her. "Were you a virgin?"

"Yes."

"Why me?"

"You're my type."

"No one else was your type before me?"

"Not so much."

"I hope this isn't some elaborate and cruel prank because I'm not so bad of a person to deserve it."

Chapter Fourteen

During the next two weeks, Lily and Strad see each other almost every day. He treats her with tender devotion. She never dreamed he could be so gentle and loving.

He's always touching her, caressing her, which she loves. She's hardly ever been touched before. In fact, she was so touch-deprived that she used to derive inordinate pleasure from the handling of her hands during a manicure. And now he's constantly grabbing her around the waist, kissing her, hugging her, cupping her breasts, and then jokingly saying things like, "Oops, I'm sorry, am I molesting you? You'd tell me if it bothered you, right?" They laugh. To her, it's heaven.

When she's home with a bad cold, he brings her large containers of wonton soup and urges her to drink a lot of it. He buys her homeopathic medications, takes her temperature and gives her foot rubs.

When they go to parties, they stay in a corner, people-watching and whispering. She finds his take on everyone entertaining and witty. Much whispering is done about them, too, of course, as she's wearing a mask. They have such a great connection.

Why couldn't this kind of connection have existed if she hadn't become beautiful? Why is it that a connection that seems to have nothing to do with looks—because it feels so much deeper than that, like a connection of minds and souls—is actually entirely dependent on looks?

She realizes she may be in for some serious suffering once he discovers the truth about her—and she does think he will learn it, sooner or later, one way or another, perhaps even from her.

She and Strad are so often together that she doesn't find many opportunities to work on the piece that will give permanence to her new beauty.

Much of their time is spent at her place; that's where she feels most comfortable replacing her mask with her music.

"I love making you laugh; you're so beautiful when you laugh," he tells her. "But you're so beautiful when you don't laugh, too. And when you look sad."

She laughs.

Strad notices she always has the same piece of music playing. Granted, it's a very nice piece, and long, and with lots of variations, but still. He asks if he can choose the music, from time to time. She says no.

"That's not totally fair," he says.

"I know. But it's my only unfair thing. You can have one, too, if you want."

"Can I choose all the movies we watch?"

"Yes."

"And all the TV programs?"

"Yes."

Each night, she insists on sleeping alone in her bedroom. She gives him the choice of sleeping on her foldout couch or going home. She sees no alternative—she practiced sleeping with her mask on, but found it too uncomfortable. As for the option of letting the music play all night, she wouldn't get any sleep, too worried that the music might stop for whatever reason.

Most nights, Strad chooses the couch. After two weeks of this arrangement, he becomes more persistent in his questioning. But Lily remains evasive.

He tells her he'd like to take her to the birthday party of a friend of his. She says okay. He says he'd like her to go without the mask. She says that's impossible. He gently but firmly wants to know why. She says she will try to tell him soon.

He knows she's a fragile soul—just as I had warned him—and he loves that about her. To be with a girl possessed of beauty so great that it has screwed her up to this degree is thrilling. Girls of this sort are rare. Guys lucky enough to get those girls are even rarer. Strad got lucky. He knows that. Nevertheless, he wants to understand her better. So he keeps asking questions.

On her end, Lily has been trying to come up with plausible explanations, though without much success. Narrative invention is not her forte. She knows that sooner or later she'll have to ask the expert for some ideas.

OUR WHOLE GROUP, including Peter, is gathered at our beloved restaurant, Artisanal, for our annual holiday dinner. We're seated at a round table.

"Strad wants to know why I always wear the mask outside our apartments. Any thoughts?" Lily asks Georgia.

"I'll think about it and try to come up with something," Georgia says. "But I have to warn you, it'll have to be melodramatic and sentimental to be effective with Strad. You may balk."

"I won't."

As soon as my friends start digging into their cheese fondues, they perform their usual gesticulations and noises of ecstasy.

Peter looks at them, startled. "Oh, my. What a beneficial group to be with."

"What do you mean?" Georgia asks, munching happily.

"Years ago I met a tribe in Africa who believed that you can derive more benefits from being in close proximity to someone experiencing pleasure than you can from experiencing pleasure yourself."

"How could that be?" Penelope asks.

"They claimed that people who experience physical pleasure emit vibrations—pleasure vibes—that are beneficial to people around them. Anything that pleases any of your five senses or that simply makes your body feel good will cause your body to exude these invisible pleasure vibrations that are therapeutic to others."

"So having sex must be the most beneficial," Jack says.

"No, actually, sex is the one pleasure that doesn't work that way."

"Why not?"

"Oh, I can't remember exactly the reason. It was something about pleasure vibes staying within. They claim that's what makes orgasms so powerful: the vibes are trapped, and so the pressure builds and builds until it explodes. But it's an internal explosion. Nothing escapes. Except fluids, of course, but no vibes."

"So, what specific benefits does the tribe believe one gains from being exposed to someone's pleasure vibes?" Penelope asks.

"Every benefit you can think of. They say you'll feel better, look better, sleep better, think better, be happier and more energetic," Peter says. "And maybe that tribe does benefit from practicing this philosophy because they were possibly the healthiest, most charming and appealing people I've ever met. Present company excluded, of course."

"Well then, let's indulge, for the sake of bettering each other!" Georgia exclaims. She dunks a potato into the melted cheese.

"You should know, though, that the tribe believes that the pleasure vibes work even better if one person is emitting them, and another person is completely passive, just receiving them. That's because if both people are experiencing pleasure simultaneously, then their outgoing pleasure vibes will tend to get in the way of each other's incoming ones."

Peter changes the topic, asking us what we're all doing for Christmas. We go around the table, answering this question.

When it's Penelope's turn, she says, "I don't know. Christmas Eve is in three days and I still haven't heard from my parents. And yet my rent has been paid. Clearly my dad hasn't stopped supporting me."

"You should call them," Georgia says.

"I don't feel like it."

"What will you do for Christmas?"

"I don't know."

Jack suggests that she spend Christmas with him and his mother at the senior center where he works. "If you're lucky, you might even get to see me break up a fight," he adds.

Penelope has tears in her eyes—perhaps at the thought of spending Christmas at a senior center.

"Or you could spend it with me and my family!" Georgia and Lily offer, almost in unison.

"That's very nice of you guys," Penelope says. "Maybe I'll spend it at the senior center. A little volunteer work might make me feel better. Thanks, Jack."

Georgia barks at me, for the whole table to hear, "Why are you staring at Peter so intensely?"

"I'm not staring," I lie. She caught me.

"Yes you are," she says. "You look like you're devouring him with your eyes. Especially when he's not looking."

My face feels hot.

"Plus," she continues, "you're as red as a tomato right now, which I think is a sign that I'm correct."

I feel the roots of my hair prickling under my gray wig.

Peter gazes at me.

"So? Are you going to explain?" Georgia asks.

I'm too flustered to resort to anything but the truth. "I was just wondering how much pleasure Peter was deriving from his food and whether he was emitting any pleasure vibes."

"Why only Peter?" Georgia challenges, still loudly. "Why not the rest of us?"

Not knowing what to say, I finally, lamely answer, "I guess because he was the teller of the story."

Peter startles us by taking out his wallet, placing a few large bills on the table, and rising.

"Hey, Peter, what's going on?" Georgia asks, chuckling uncomfortably.

Peter walks over to my side of the table and extends his hand to me.

Addressing my friends, but looking down only at me, he says, "I hope you all don't mind if Barb and I leave. She's in need of a demonstration, and I, being the teller of the story, want to give it to her."

"You mean you'll do something pleasurable to yourself while she watches?" Georgia asks.

Peter laughs. "Yes, something like that." His hand is still waiting for mine.

I glance at my friends, hesitant to leave them in the middle of dinner. But they don't seem to mind. They're smiling at me.

I finally accept Peter's hand and we leave the restaurant.

Once in his apartment, he gestures for me to sit on the huge white couch. I do, admiring the sumptuous living room with lots of glass surfaces.

He takes care of a few things in the kitchen and comes out with a small tray. He positions a chair right in front of me, very close, and sits on it. His seat is slightly higher than mine, so he is looking down at me somewhat, his legs open to accommodate mine between his. Our calves are touching.

He picks up a chocolate truffle and bites into it and chews it slowly, looking at me like I'm the next truffle he's about to relish.

He then takes his iPod, puts the buds in his ears, and makes his musical selection. He goes back to gazing at me intently, while I hear the faint tinny noise emanating from his earbuds. It sounds like classical. Something passionate. Wagner, perhaps.

After about three minutes he selects another piece of music

and another piece of chocolate and consumes both while we stare at each other for another two minutes.

"Do you feel anything?" he asks.

I chuckle and say, "Yes," though I doubt the excitement I'm experiencing has as much to do with his emanating pleasure vibes as it does with my anticipation of what might happen next.

He switches off the iPod and pulls his earphones out of his ears.

He stares at me for a few more seconds and says, "I saw you bite into a bruschetta, once, during one of our Nights of Creation. You closed your eyes and leaned your head back, reveling in the taste. As I observed you, a feeling I'll never forget coursed through me—a feeling so spectacular, it felt like a drug. And I thought, *Our world doesn't pay enough attention to that feeling. Almost as though it hasn't been discovered yet. Maybe that tribe really was onto something.*"

I smile. We are silent, our eyes locked. Now is the time. He will lean toward me. He will touch me. He will kiss me. He will be the only man who has ever done this since I started wearing my ugly disguise after Gabriel's death.

He starts moving. He picks up his iPod, searches for another song, and puts his earbuds back in his ears, saying, "I bet this one will sound great to the sight of you." He listens to it while staring at me.

He is trying to torture me. That must be it. I am so drawn to him that were I to move toward him, it would simply feel as though I'm letting gravity take me. But my policy specifies that he has to make the first move because I need to be utterly convinced—I need irrefutable proof—that he wants me in spite of how I look to him with my disguise on.

When the song ends, he places his iPod on the coffee table next to his chair and says, "That was very pleasurable, listening to music while staring at you."

"Great. I look forward to reaping the fruits of your pleasure," I joke.

He nods. "Now, during this session I've derived pleasure from each of my senses." He pauses. "Except for one."

"Is it an important one?"

"Yes."

"So what are you going to do?"

This is the moment. This is the very moment when he is going to make a move to indulge his sense of touch.

He answers, "I'll make sure it's not neglected next time."

How it is that he brings the evening to an end without anything having happened is a mystery to me. It must be my teeth. Or my fat, my gray, my frizz, my brown contacts, my glasses. Perhaps I should take them all off. No, I can't believe I'm even thinking this, after my resolution—after Gabriel. My throat tightens at the memory of him.

Peter says he'd better call it a night because he has to get up early the next morning. He offers to escort me home. I tell him that won't be necessary. He kisses me on the cheek and I leave.

I decide to walk home to clear my head. My apartment is 45 minutes away, but the air isn't cold for December and I'm wearing a big coat over my bloat wear.

"You look a bit hot and sweaty," Adam notes, opening the

lobby door for me. "When you get upstairs, why don't you cool off by opening your window and sticking your head out, feet first?"

Of course, he doesn't know that my best friend killed himself by jumping out a window. I doubt he would have made that comment if he'd known—despite his disorder.

THE FOLLOWING EVENING, Strad and Lily are walking to his friend's birthday party when he suddenly takes hold of the edge of Lily's mask and tentatively begins to lift it off her face.

She grabs his wrist. "Never," she says.

"Oh, come on, won't you let me?" Strad pleads.

Lily shakes her head. "No one ever takes off my mask. Only I do that, when and if I choose to."

"I think I'm going to go home. I'll see you tomorrow, maybe."

"What's wrong?"

"I'm feeling a bit sad."

"Why? Because I won't take off my mask?"

"That's just a symptom. The spot I take up in your heart seems . . . so small. It's hard for me to get used to that."

"What makes you think so?"

"Your unwillingness to be truthful," he says, leaning against a lamppost. "You allow me to believe things that are completely inconsistent with ways that you act, and you don't bother explaining the inconsistencies, as though I'm not even worth the trouble."

"What inconsistencies?"

"You let me believe that you absolutely *have* to wear a mask in public so that you won't be harassed by strangers, but then why do you put it on when I go to the bathroom in your apartment?

It insults my intelligence. Also, you refuse to take off your mask to go to this private party, and yet you took your mask off at the bookstore on our first date. So why can't you take it off now as a special favor to me? My friends aren't going to pester you the way those jerks did at the bookstore."

Head hanging, shoulders drooping, Lily says nothing. She can't explain to him that she puts on her mask when he goes to the bathroom because there's no music in the bathroom and when he emerges from it, he'll see her in all her ugliness; he'll instantly recognize her as Lily until the music's power takes hold of his brain again.

He continues. "I want to help you find another way to deal with the problems you're struggling with that make you wear the mask."

"That's not likely to happen. I've been wearing a mask for fifteen years."

"You have?" He pulls her to him and tenderly whispers in her ear, "I knew there was more to it. Things didn't quite add up. Please open up to me. I want to know you." He kisses the edge of her ear. "Will you tell me? Let's forget about the party and go home."

She nods. They walk back to her place. In her mind, she's rehearsing Georgia's concoction. She dreads using it. When she first heard it, she cringed and was tempted to ask Georgia to make it more literary, but Georgia had already made it clear she wouldn't, that it wouldn't be effective on Strad.

Strad and Lily go straight to her bedroom. She turns on the music. A minute later, she takes off her mask. She lies next to Strad on the bed.

He strokes her hand. "Tell me everything."

She gazes at him for a long moment and then takes the plunge into Georgia's fabrication. She describes at length a torrid history of sexual abuse that supposedly happened up to and including the age of eight, and that involved many pedophiles: her swimming instructor, her neighbor on vacation one summer, an art teacher, etc. The offenses were never genital penetration—because, as Strad knows, she was still a virgin their first night together—but it was everything else. Lily tells him she had an uncle she adored, who'd never laid a finger on her, until one day when he became one of the others. He couldn't bear the guilt of what he did to her, and what he did to her again twice, and what he knew he would continue doing to her, so he killed himself.

Strad looks too shocked to respond.

"And that," says Lily, "was when I started wearing the mask."

Strad puts his arms around her and seems very distraught.

She, too, is upset, though over the fact that this crazy story was what she had to resort to. And it's not even over.

She pulls away from Strad. "He left a suicide note confessing to my mother that he'd been molesting me and that he was killing himself mostly for this reason. I couldn't believe he would do that to me—that on top of traumatizing me with his abuse and traumatizing me with his death, he was exposing our disgusting secret. He himself was conveniently escaping the shame of it through death, leaving me to bear it. I wanted to die, too."

Strad is staring at her, looking quite upset.

Lily continues. "I refused to take off the mask. I wasn't only wearing it to stop attracting sexual abuse, I was also wearing it out of shame. When my parents tried taking it off by force, I had a fit. I told them that if they didn't let me wear it, I'd find another mask and glue it to my face with Superglue, or I'd cut up my face. They were horrified. They sent me to therapy, which was useless. Finally, there was one shrink who did help, though only a little. Now I'm going to explain to you those inconsistencies that offended you."

"Okay. Thank you," Strad says.

"After three months, the psychiatrist found an alternate way to make me feel safe. I was only eight years old, keep that in mind. He made me listen to a piece of music and said that whenever that piece was playing, I'd be protected. He claimed the music had properties that would make people around me inoffensive and relatively normal-acting in the face of my looks."

Strad strokes Lily's hair.

She continues. "My parents were thrilled, at first, that the therapist was able to add the musical piece to my derangement. They thought I was on the road to recovery. What they didn't realize was that my progress toward mental health would stop right there. They had to learn to live with their daughter either masked or accompanied by music, and they got so tired of both that sometimes it was hard for them to decide which they could bear. To this day, things haven't changed. I can live either behind the mask or behind the music. I can choose between my two prisons."

"But now, as an adult, I assume you know the music doesn't protect you."

"On some level I know that. But on an emotional level I still believe in it. I need it."

"What a sad story." He pauses. "I don't mean to sound nitpicky, but I still don't understand the bookstore. You took off your mask, yet I assume your special music wasn't playing."

"Yes, it was, actually."

"How did you manage that?"

"Connections."

Strad nods.

"Now you know. I'm very screwed up," she says. "It's hard for me to have a normal life. That's why Barb thought we might be a good match. Most men wouldn't stand for my lunacies, but she thought that you—because you value physical beauty so much—might be willing to . . . or be able to . . . overlook these huge psychological aberrances."

He hugs her. "Thank you for being open with me about your past. It all makes so much sense now."

Georgia never fails, Lily marvels to herself.

OVER THE HOLIDAYS, I spend a few days with my mom in her house in Connecticut, just the two of us. We have a nice time. She hasn't mentioned my fake fat since I went to the Excess Weight Disorders Support Group, that one time. I can tell it takes some effort on her part, but I appreciate it. Instead, we talk a lot about her upcoming trip to Australia in March, which is a topic I much prefer.

I devote a large portion of each day to working on some designs for the dream sequence of a new movie. And I dedicate the rest of the time to fantasizing about Peter. I'm feeling optimistic. He said he would not neglect his sense of touch at our next meeting. Who would say that if they weren't interested? Only a sadist. I think he's interested.

In the end, my mom can't help herself. Right before I'm about to go back to the city, as we're standing at the living room window staring out in silence at the countryside, she says, "Barb, you'll never find a worthwhile guy if you keep wearing that disguise."

I'm sure my mom would find Peter Marrick worthwhile. In the window, my own reflection is staring back at me with a tiny, hopeful smile.

Chapter Fifteen

Strad tells Lily it's been three years since he's been with a woman who made him want to take a vacation with her. He suggests they go on a trip for two weeks to the Puerto Rican island of Vieques. Then he says, "Why not leave tomorrow?"

Excited by his spontaneity and enthusiasm for her, Lily agrees to go on vacation with him the next day. Worried that the airline might not let her wear a mask, she insists they take separate flights. She says she always travels alone.

MY FRIENDS *SANS* Lily come over for a Night of Creation. I've been daydreaming about Peter a lot since he gave me that frustratingly incomplete demonstration a few days ago, so it stirs me even more than usual when he walks through the door and kisses me on the cheek.

While we work, the room is quiet without Lily here playing her piano. Half an hour into our session, I go to the kitchen to get some juice. Peter joins me.

Softly, so the others can't hear, he says, "Can I see you tomorrow evening?"

I don't answer right away, wondering how I'll survive twenty-four hours until then.

"Please say you can see me tomorrow," he whispers, leaning against the island, his back to our friends. His smile is so seductive I nearly drop the knife I picked up to cut a lemon. He adds, "We need to finish that demonstration I started. One of the five senses was missing, remember?"

"Yes, I remember." I clear my throat. "Okay, tomorrow."

"Thank God," he says. "Otherwise we'd have to wait a week because I'm leaving after tomorrow to visit my dad in California for five days."

"Oh."

"And that would be too long to wait, don't you think?"

That he's showing this much interest in me moves me deeply. My gray curls shield my face as I lean over my lemon and answer "Yes," casually.

"We can hear you!" Georgia hollers, and then mutters to herself, "Where is Lily when we need her to mask the noises of love?"

She resumes her typing, but louder.

I LOOK FORWARD to Peter's visit with utmost anticipation. But he calls me in the morning to let me know that sadly he will not be able to come over tonight because of unforeseen work obligations. He says he's very disappointed and can't wait to see me when he returns from his trip, in six days.

After we hang up, I wander from room to room, stunned, like a human being dying of thirst having just been told the water will not arrive today as promised, but possibly after I'm already dead.

I get back to my work in a daze. It takes me a while to regain my focus.

AS LILY REPORTS to me later, the first few days in Vieques are heavenly for her and Strad. She wears her mask by the hotel pool and on the beach. She even swims with it a few times, trying not to wet it too much.

People stare, of course. But Strad and Lily don't care. In their rooms, she doesn't wear the mask, only the music.

Strad feels protective of her. He's attentive to her psychological and emotional needs. The more she gets to know him, the more she loves him.

BACK IN NEW York, I've been having an intense e-mail correspondence with Peter while he's away visiting his dad. Our exchanges are flirtatious and titillating. I can hardly sleep. I spend most of my days smiling or snickering to myself while working, reminiscing about the last message sent or received.

I can't wait for him to get back, can't wait for him to indulge his sense of touch. I wonder what first move he has planned, how he will touch me, how he will kiss me, how he will undress me, how surprised he'll be to encounter my fake fat under my clothes, how astonished—though not overly ecstatic, otherwise that would make him shallow—he'll be to discover I'm attractive by every conventional standard, not only by his open-minded, evolved, and big-hearted one. For the first time, I will take off my disguise out of love, not out of hate, like I do in bars. And then I can keep it off, because I will no longer be searching for my soul mate. I will have found him.

My friends have remarked that since I've met Peter, I've stopped going to bars and doing my stripping ritual. It's true, I've lost the urge to rub shallow men's faces in their own superficiality.

PETER RETURNS FROM his trip, and our long-awaited reunion is that same evening, during which he will complete his demonstration by delighting his sense of touch. I'm very excited, imagining his caresses.

When he walks through my door, right on time, he gives me a big hug and smiles at me, saying, "I missed you." He's lightly stroking my gray curls with the tips of his fingers. I'm glad my wig is made of real hair.

We position ourselves just like we did at his apartment, with me on the couch and him on a chair facing me, close.

He opens his bag and pulls out a piece of fabric. He begins stroking the fabric—red velvet—while staring at me.

Needless to say, this is not the kind of touching I expected.

After what feels like ten minutes (but maybe it was just one), I say, "Is it still good?"

"Remarkably."

"You'd think the pleasure of touching that thing would wear off after a few minutes."

"Hasn't yet. It's really very soft."

I nod. Maybe if I act ever so slightly bored, that will nudge him in the right direction. So I lean my head back and gaze past him, as though momentarily lost in thought.

After another minute, he says, "Well, that was great." He puts his piece of velvet back in his bag.

I smile and nod again. And wait. He does nothing.

"So, is the demonstration complete?" I ask.

"I think so. At least for now. I mean, one can always do better, I suppose. There are always more pleasures one can come up with."

I wait a moment, hopeful, but he still does nothing.

I laugh, worn out. I could try to nudge him a little more, but I'm tired of it, so instead, I say, "You know, you're a bit strange."

"I know," he blurts. "The reason is . . . there's something I need to tell you. But I don't want to, because it's something about me I'm not sure you'd like."

Everyone has secrets these days—I think of KAY's secret identity, whoever KAY is, of mine, of Lily's.

"Really? You'd be surprised, I'm very open-minded," I say.

"Maybe not as much as you think."

"What is it? I'm sure I've heard worse."

"If I tell you," he says, "I don't think you'll want to see me again."

"Now I'm intrigued. Why don't you tell me?"

"The consequences could be dire."

I don't insist because I don't believe him. I think it's the classic: *It's not you, it's me.*

And I'm starting to think he's the classic guy, like all those guys I've met at bars. He can't get past my teeth, my fat, my gray, my frizz. I suspect that's the secret thing he knows I won't like about him—the fact that he's not attracted to me.

He says he should be getting home because he has an early day tomorrow, and that it was lovely to see me. He leans forward and gives me a kiss on the cheek, and then he's gone.

ON LILY AND Strad's seventh morning in Vieques, they are sitting on her balcony, her legs resting on his. Her music is playing just inside and is very audible from where they are, so she's not wearing her mask. But she's holding it on her lap, just in case.

The empty breakfast dishes are on a low table in front of them. Lily is staring out at the ocean.

"You seem melancholy," Strad remarks, brushing a strand of hair from her face.

"No, I'm fine," she says, smiling.

But that's not quite true. What she's thinking about is the one flaw in their happiness: her dishonesty.

Yet what can she do? Nothing, if she wants their relationship to continue.

Looking down at her beautiful mask, she thinks about how much she hates it, about how much she wishes she didn't have to wear it. And she thinks about the guilt. And the fear. Guilt about lying to Strad. Fear of being discovered. Plus, the mask is uncomfortable to wear. And the music is annoying.

Her confidence has been soaring lately—foolishly, she knows. She's been thinking that perhaps he'd still love her if she revealed she's Lily. After all, their great times together seem based on so much more than just her looks. Maybe beauty matters only at the start of a relationship, when it sparks the initial interest. But each time she formulates this thought, she beats herself up about the stupidity of it. The thought, however, comes back: Strad *was* very nice about her childhood sexual abuse story. Very supportive and understanding. Isn't there a chance he might be equally understanding if she revealed her true story, which in a way is no less tragic: extreme ugliness, no romantic or sexual interest from anyone, ever. And once again she can't believe how dumb she is to think he'd be understanding. He already knows Lily. Has he seemed charmed by her plight? Did he court her? No.

They go parasailing together over the ocean, both under the same parachute. People stare at Lily in her white mask. Afterward, they lie on chairs on the beach, reading and people-watching, commenting to each other about the beachgoers' swimsuits, flirtations, affectations, and reading material. They laugh and play in the water, touching each other naughtily, and return to the hotel.

Lily heads for her room, which is adjacent to Strad's. She's the one who insisted they have separate rooms so that she could sleep without her mask or the music on.

Strad stands behind Lily as she slides her electronic key in the lock. She pushes her door open and gasps when she sees what's inside. The room is filled with flowers, bouquets resting on every surface. A little dinner table that wasn't there before is beautifully set for two.

She looks at Strad. He admits responsibility and tells her a bath has been run for her if she feels like one before their dinner here at eight.

Strad goes back to his room. Enchanted, Lily steps into the hot bath. She's never had rose petals floating on her bathwater before. She takes off her mask and places it on the floor, within her reach. The music is off. She closes her eyes and enjoys the silence.

After her bath, she dons a pretty yellow chiffon dress and lies on her bed, waiting for dinner. No further preparations are needed. Her music is the only makeup she wears. Applying regular makeup on top of her musical makeup mars perfection, as she discovered recently when, out of curiosity, she tried it.

Strad knocks on her door at eight. She turns on the music, puts on her mask, and opens the door. He's dressed in an off-white linen suit. Very charming, she thinks. Once his brain is certain to be under the influence of the music, Lily unmasks.

Dinner is brought to them, and when they are finished eating and laughing about the fun day they had, Strad leans back in his chair and says, "A big part of who I am, as a bastard, is my desire to show off my beautiful girlfriends to my friends, acquaintances, and enemies, in order to arouse their envy."

This takes Lily by surprise, and she half expects him to say, "Therefore, it's not going to work out between us, and we better call it quits."

Instead, he says, "But I'm so in love with you that none of that matters anymore."

He reaches into his pocket and pulls out a little black velvet box, which he hands to her. She opens it. Inside is a beautiful diamond ring.

He goes down on one knee and says, "I would love to spend the rest of my life with you. Will you marry me?"

Lily is shocked by the proposal. And happy. But something is holding her back from giving him an answer.

Nevertheless, the awkward silence is not painfully long, because Strad has more to say. He sits back in his chair and declares he wants to help her get over her mask-wearing. He says he'll go with her to therapy if she wants, because he'd like to help her achieve a normal, mask-free existence—for her sake. If she doesn't want to, that's fine. He will happily marry her and spend the rest of his life with her masked and put to music.

Lily still doesn't know what to say, except, "Thank you. I'm incredibly honored. Would it be okay if I gave your beautiful proposal a little thought?"

"Really?"

"Yes."

"So . . . you're not sure?" he asks.

"It's just . . . that . . . my situation is very complicated, as you know. I have issues I need to consider."

"Of course."

WHEN LILY IS alone later that night, she calls me. She doesn't want to talk about herself yet, she just wants to be distracted from her problem. She asks if things have progressed between Peter and me. She's the one person to whom I've confessed my attraction to him.

"Not really. He says there's something about him he thinks I won't like," I tell her.

"What is it?"

"I don't know. But I suspect it's just an excuse and that the real problem is my disguise."

"That would be disappointing," Lily states softly.

"I'm tempted to take it off."

"That's major. And funny because I'm tempted to take mine off, too."

"Why?"

"Do you disapprove?"

"No, I'm just surprised."

"Why would you be? You're thinking of taking yours off."

"Yes, but I'd be doing it to see if his lack of interest is due to my appearance. And if it is, I can forget about him. You'd be doing it to . . . I'm not sure why you'd be doing it."

"To see if his love can survive my appearance."

I refrain from pointing out that if she puts her happiness at risk, she might also be putting Strad's life at risk. I don't remind her that there is a killer among us who's had trouble tolerating Lily's unhappiness and whose promise not to try harming Strad again may not hold as much weight as we're all hoping it does.

THE NEXT DAY, Lily and Strad try to have a good time, but they're both so tormented for their own reasons that they can't enjoy themselves. They drive around the island in their little white Jeep. They aren't able to take much pleasure at the sighting of wild horses roaming like stray dogs along the sides of the roads.

They stop at a deserted beach and sit, in silence, on a rock. The ocean is calm, barely making a sound.

Strad speaks. "I have a surprise for you the day after tomorrow, in the evening. It's something I've planned since I booked this trip. It's one of the most extraordinary things you could ever imagine."

Lily smiles. "Sounds exciting."

A few minutes pass.

Looking out at the ocean, Strad gently says, "So, do you think you might be getting closer to making a decision about my proposal?"

"There's something about me you might not like if you knew it," she says, inspired by Peter's words to me.

"What is it?"

"I'm not sure I feel comfortable talking about it."

"Well, then, don't tell me. Just accept my proposal."

"It's something you'd want to know."

"The only thing I want to know is if you'll marry me."

"You wouldn't feel that way if you knew what it was."

"I can't imagine anything you could possibly reveal that would change my mind or lessen my enthusiasm."

"And yet, that's exactly what I'm afraid will happen—your enthusiasm will be lessened. To put it mildly."

"And you know what *I'm* afraid of? That that's just an excuse. That you're the one who's not very excited about marrying me."

"What I'm not excited about is the prospect of accepting a proposal that might not exist if you knew the truth."

"Then why don't you tell it to me so I can prove you wrong?"

Lily doesn't know what to do. There are so many good reasons to tell Strad the truth, such as: How can she fool him forever? Does she really want to live that way? And is it fair to him? Isn't it better that they deal with the truth now? And isn't it better that she be the one to tell him rather than risk having him find out some other way?

Sometimes she's on the brink of telling him, such as when they're lying tensely on towels on the beach.

She succeeds in talking herself out of it.

As a way of discouraging herself further from entertaining such a self-destructive notion, she considers asking him what he thinks of Lily, physically. His answer—if it doesn't outright kill her—is bound to ensure her silence. But she doesn't ask him for lack of courage.

She tries to be more upbeat about her circumstances. She reminds herself that it's not really so bad having always to wear a mask or to play the music. Plenty of people are still able to enjoy life despite having to live with a cumbersome piece of equipment like a wheelchair, an oxygen tank, or how about a pouch attached to a hole in the abdomen through which they defecate? Lily saw a documentary on that, once. Even though the show convinced her that colostomy pouches are not as terrible as most people think, wearing a mask is better, Lily reasons. Many people with colostomy pouches find true love, she is certain of it—and no, not necessarily only with another person who has a colostomy pouch.

So she does nothing.

MY FRIENDS COME over for our scheduled Night of Creation. In the middle of the evening, when everyone is working and I go to the kitchen to get some coffee, Peter joins me there as usual and whispers, "Now that I've given you a full session of my pleasure vibes, I believe it's your turn."

He doesn't cease to surprise me.

"Can I come and collect tomorrow after lunch?" he asks.

"Uh, okay."

"Will you arrange to have pleasures you can indulge in while I bathe in your vibes?"

"Sure."

LILY AND STRAD make love that night, but it's a quiet affair, tinged with sadness.

"Are you okay?" she asks.

"No."

"What's wrong?"

"Give me the bad news, if that's what it is. I can't take it anymore. I need an answer. If you don't want to marry me, please just say so. Put me out of my misery."

"I can't just say yes," she says, pulling away. "I lied to you."

"About loving me?"

"No."

His face lights up. "Well then nothing else matters." He embraces her again. "I'm very forgiving of liars, being a great one myself. I've lied to countless girlfriends. Never to you, of course. But I know that lying doesn't always come from bad motives. I don't hold it against you. What did you lie to me about?"

"My mask."

"Is that all? I don't care. What was the lie?"

"Everything I told you about it. The reasons why I wear it."

"You mean you weren't sexually molested as a child?"

"No."

"So why do you wear it?"

"That's the thing. That's what I'm having trouble telling you."

"Then don't tell me. I don't care why you wear it, and I don't care *that* you wear it. And plus, I'm sure the truth is not that bad."

"No, it's not that bad. But to you it may be worse than to most."

"I don't know what sort of misconception you have about me, but I'm very average."

THE NEXT DAY, Peter comes over to my place at three. I was hoping to get a lot of work done before that so that I wouldn't feel guilty about taking the rest of the afternoon off, but I was unable to focus on my work. I was in a trance, completely stoned on the love hormones coursing through my body. I got almost nothing done.

"Did you stock up on some pleasures?" he asks.

"Yes, I have a couple that could do the trick. And I skipped lunch so that I'd experience maximum pleasure during the session."

"That's very nice of you."

I don't mention that skipping lunch did not succeed in making me hungry. The stronger my feelings for Peter have become, the less appetite I've had. As a result, I've lost weight recently, which was not something I especially needed.

I arrange my pleasures on a tray. We settle ourselves in the same way as last time—me on the couch, Peter on a chair facing me.

I first take my iPod from the tray and start listening to the French pop song "Un Jour Arrive," which I happen to be fond of at the moment. I open my bottle of Petite Chérie perfume and hold it under my nose, feeling the intoxicating scent of pear and spices dance under my nostrils to the romantic melody.

Peter is watching me carefully. I don't take my eyes off him.

There is only food left on my tray of pleasures. Before the end of the first song, I put down the perfume and transition to goat cheese on a cracker. I don't generally like cheese, but that particular goat cheese is one of my favorite foods. Even though I'm not hungry, I do my best to savor it, luxuriating in the delicious sharp flavor. Peter's gaze is intense and seductive. I try not to let my attraction to him distract me from my task.

"Am I any good?" I ask.

"Remarkable," he says.

He says nothing more. And neither do I. We are sitting motionless, looking at each other. Now is the time, the ideal time, for him to kiss me.

I wait. But nothing happens.

I start feeling sick with disappointment. He is toying with me.

Or maybe he does want to make a pass at me, but can't bear the look of me.

I can't take it anymore. He has almost passed my test. He is almost there. He is clearly interested in me romantically.

That's why I get up and bend down to kiss him on the cheek—a pass so slight it can hardly be called a pass at all. It's more of an encouragement, a nudge, to help him cross the finish line.

Looking alarmed, he pulls away before my lips touch his skin.

I'm shocked. I clearly misread him. He had no intention of making a move, ever.

Humiliated, I decide to put an end to his little game right now. I will take off my disguise and present him with his own shallowness as I have done countless times to men at bars.

I start unbuttoning the top buttons of my large man's shirt that covers my gelatinous jacket.

When Peter sees me about to undress, he leaps out of his chair and grabs my wrists—not out of passion, as I imagine it might be for a second—but, to my horror, out of panic, to restrain me from proceeding. He is *that* disgusted. Well, I'm glad I found out now instead of letting it drag on.

"Don't do that," he says, rebuttoning my top buttons. "Please. Not right now."

"Okay, forget it, Peter. I get it. I'm not your type. Perfectly understandable." I pull away, confounded by his aversion and too sad to complete my punishing procedure.

"No, you don't get it," he says. "It's just that there's something I must tell you before—"

"Yes, I know, something you're afraid I won't like about you."

"Yes, exactly."

"So tell me."

"Can I tell you tomorrow? It has the potential of upsetting me very much. If I tell you now, it might be hard for me to anchor the news tonight, whereas tomorrow I've got the whole day free. I could come over for dinner and tell you. We could order takeout."

I agree to let him come for dinner the next day.

IN LATE AFTERNOON the following day, on my way out to Whole Foods to get a few delicacies for our evening, Adam the doorman says, "Oh, Barb, I've been meaning to ask you, are your parents siblings?"

Every time he insults me, which is every time he sees me, I feel guilty that I have neglected to give him the name of my therapist. It's just that there's always so much going on in my life, so many friends to be concerned about, and Adam is never at the top of my list of priorities.

AT SIX, LILY goes to the lobby of the hotel to meet Strad for the surprise he has planned for her. She's wearing a bathing suit under a casual outfit, as he instructed. And of course, her white feather mask.

As she waits for him, she paces the lobby, lost in thought, again wondering if she should tell Strad who she really is. Fortunately, he has seemed willing to wait a bit longer for an answer to his marriage proposal, now that he understands the situation is less simple than he thought.

A van picks them up and takes them to an electrically powered pontoon boat. A few passengers board the boat. Lily and Strad join them at the bow.

The boat promptly departs, carrying them over the black sea, along the coast, and into a bay.

The guide tells them that this is the biobay—one of the most magnificent bioluminescent bays in the world. He explains that the water glows around anything that moves because it's filled with microorganisms that light up when disturbed. He says the glow is only visible on a very dark night with no moon, such as tonight.

The passengers start gasping and shrieking with delight at the beauty of the natural light effects in the water.

Unfortunately, Lily is unable to see anything because of the dark glass covering the eyeholes of her mask. It's like wearing sunglasses at night. The glass is not detachable, but even if it were, she would not, for anything in the world, remove this important part of her mask which prevents the ugly proximity of her eyes to each other from being seen.

Squeezing Strad's arm affectionately, Lily gently informs him of the problem, apologizing for her mask spoiling the surprise he had planned for her.

Strad slaps his forehead and curses himself for his over-sight. "What a shame," he says. "But come here. Let me at least describe to you what you're missing."

He turns her toward the water and stands behind her, gently pressing himself against her. He's holding onto the railing on either side of her.

In her ear, he softly says, "As our boat advances, the fish are darting out of its way, causing the water to light up in blue-green streaks. It looks like bolts of lightning tearing through the water. They create wild jagged patterns."

Lily is saddened by the startling description she can't see.

She can hear the other passengers saying things like, "It's just extraordinary! I've never seen anything like it."

Strad guides Lily to the back of the boat.

"Wow," he marvels, looking at the wake. "Can you see this at all?"

"No. What?"

"The wake glows."

The boat stops to give passengers a chance to take a swim.

Many of them jump into the water, creating luminescent splashes.

Lily wishes she could see it, swim in it, marry Strad, tell him the truth, take off her mask. She would love to dive into the luminescent water like a carefree person who can experience the beauty of life even though she herself is not beautiful.

"You should go for a swim," she says.

"Are you sure?"

She nods.

He strips down to his bathing suit and jumps into the bay.

People cheer at the glowing splash he creates. Lily sees nothing except black on black. She remains motionless, gazing down, lost in thought.

She hears a young woman in the water exclaim to her friend, "Oh, look at all the tiny sparkles trickling down my arm!"

And that's the moment Lily makes a decision.

Strad comes out of the water, dripping. "I was doing water angels. They glowed," he says.

Lily smiles, forgetting that her smiles are never seen behind the mask.

"Strad," she says, with a solemnity that gets his full attention, "tomorrow I want to have a wonderful day with you. And tomorrow night, I will keep my mask on all night so that we can sleep in the same bed for the first time. And the next morning, I will tell you the truth."

Strad lifts her up in the air and twirls her around. "That's fantastic! Thank you!" He gently lowers her. "And after that will you agree to marry me?"

"If you still want me to."

I SOAK IN a hot bath, trying to relax before Peter's visit. I then slip into my fake fat and put on some attractive clothes in very large sizes. By attractive, I mean a huge pair of beige pants made of a dressier fabric than my usual sweat pants. And an extremely large turtleneck made of a silkier cotton than my everyday ones. I then put on my gray frizzy wig, my yellowish crooked teeth, my brown contacts, and my fake glasses.

When Peter arrives at eight p.m., he looks a little tired and pale. He says he has no appetite and asks if I would mind if we waited to eat. I say fine, since my stomach happens to be in knots, too.

We're standing at the small island that separates the kitchen from the living room, and I decide to get something off my chest before we even sit down: "I'm sorry I got annoyed yesterday. The truth is, I love our friendship. So if things stay the way they are between us, I'll be more than happy."

He looks at me seriously, gives a brief nod, and says, "I won't be."

"Oh no?" I ask, genuinely surprised.

"No. At least . . . it wouldn't be my preference."

A smile escapes me. "I see," I say, "but at the same time you shouldn't force yourself. If you feel more comfortable with things the way they are, I understand."

"I'm not more comfortable. I'm uncomfortable."

I chuckle. Joy and relief unwind every muscle in my body. "What is your dark secret?" I ask.

"Telling you will be disastrous." He pauses. "But . . . much as I've enjoyed our relationship the way it's been, I really can't go on like this. I have to tell you the truth."

He goes over to the window and gazes down at Union Square. I follow him there. He moves close to me until the space between us is small and intimate. Looking at me sadly, he says, "I want you to know that this thing you don't know about me is substantial."

"So what? There's something substantial you don't know about me," I say.

"Unfortunately, no. I don't think so. That's my secret, you see. My secret is that I know yours."

The tension snaps back into my body. Barely breathing, my pulse racing, I carefully ask, "What secret is it that you think you know?"

"I know that when I touch you, like this," he says, putting his fingertips lightly on my shoulders and running them down my arms, "you feel nothing."

He walks behind me. "That when I bring my lips this close to your hair and whisper to you, you don't feel my breath in your gray curls." He puts his hands on my shoulders and turns me around. "That were I to wrap you in my arms, you would hardly feel a thing because you've created a partition between you and the world."

He lets go of my shoulders.

"How long have you known?" I ask, my eyes filling with tears.

"Since I found Georgia's laptop in a cab."

Stunned, I listen as he explains how he allowed himself to open Georgia's diary document and stumbled upon descriptions of me and my friends and saw photos of me without the fat suit. He says since meeting me, he fell for me like he'd never fallen for anyone, and that's why it didn't feel right to let our relationship progress without my being aware of everything.

I don't respond.

"Is this problematic?" he asks.

I nod. Tears start running down my cheeks.

"You see, I knew it."

I say nothing.

He says, "I could easily have fooled you by pretending I didn't know the truth about your true appearance and—"

"You mean as you have done?"

"Uh . . . yes. Except, I could have continued and allowed

things to progress. But as my feelings for you deepened, it became harder for me to choose this dishonest option."

He pauses, waiting for me to say something, but I can't. I'm too upset.

"My conscience was getting in the way, you understand?" he says softly.

I nod, unable to speak.

"Because you mean so much to me," he says.

I quickly nod as tears keep spilling, and I finally manage to say, "Can we continue this another time?"

"Really?" he asks, concerned.

"I'm sorry, I have to lie down now. I don't feel great." I start walking out of the living room. "Please let yourself out."

"Barb, can't we talk about this a little more?"

"Sure, later," I call out, going to my bedroom.

But he comes after me. "No, wait, Barb." He takes my arm before I reach my bedroom door. Touching my gray curls, he says, "I admire the system you've devised to ensure that your beauty won't be the cause of your happiness. And I know I didn't meet you the right way, but isn't it better to have met you the wrong way and to love you the right way than the reverse?"

I say nothing.

Not giving up, he says, "I'm sorry I found out about your real appearance. I'm sorry because it robbed me of the opportunity to prove that I could pass through your filtering system."

After hesitating a long time, I gently say what I know to be the truth: "You wouldn't have passed. If you had believed I really was fat, gray-haired, and the rest, you never would have become interested in me."

"How can you be so sure?"

"Because of my years of experience."

"If I'd gotten to know you as I have, I would have fallen for you. As I have."

"You wouldn't have had the slightest interest in getting to know me in the first place. And even if you had, you wouldn't have been able to think of me as anything but a friend."

"My feelings for you now have nothing to do with your looks. In fact, I don't care if I never see your physical beauty again. You could wear your disguise all the time if you wanted to."

"I do."

"Yes, but I mean you could *keep* wearing it if we were involved. And I mean *all* the time—even during the most intimate times."

I can't help laughing through my tears. "It wouldn't be very practical."

"I wouldn't care."

I shake my head and quickly enter my bedroom and lock myself in, saying, "Please let yourself out."

I hear the front door close, and then for a long time I hear nothing but my sobs.

Chapter Sixteen

I 'm at home, up late working on costumes for a historical drama. Deeply depressed by Peter's revelation, I'm doing my best to lose myself in work, which is not going well, when the phone rings. I pick up because this time the caller ID says "Out of Area," not "Peter Marrick," as it did three times today already.

I answer Lily's question with the truth: yes, Peter has now told me his secret. And no, I cannot accept him.

In the silence, I hear her breathing. And in her breathing, I hear her anxiety.

"What's his secret?" she asks.

I tell her what it is.

"Maybe you just need a little bit of time to think about it, and you'll come round to accepting it," she says, full of hope, almost as though she's arguing her own case.

"You know I can't, Lily." I wish I could add something to comfort her. But I can't, because I feel dead.

After Lily hangs up with me, Strad joins her for their first night of sleeping in the same room.

They make love, snuggle, and Strad drifts off to sleep. But Lily lies awake, weeping silently inside her mask.

Strad wakes up to the sound of her crying. He's kind and gentle. He says, "Are you sure you don't want to get it over with now, and just tell me what this big skeleton in your closet is? I hate to see you like this." He's hugging her, stroking her hair.

"No, no," she says. "Not yet."

She feels suffocated by her mask, so she turns on the music and takes off the mask. Strad has no trouble going back to sleep, but she only briefly dips into slumber. The hours pass and the music is becoming unbearable to her. Unlike the mask, which asphyxiates only her lungs, the music is suffocating every pore of her being. And yet, the thought of its elimination tomorrow—and of the mask's—is even worse.

She rushes to the bathroom, overcome by a surge of nausea.

When she emerges, pale but no less ravishing, Strad is awake, propped up on one elbow, watching her with concern. He taps the mattress. She sits. He pulls her to him, holds her in his arms. Using much patience and reassurance, he tries to convince her *not* to tell him the truth about her mask, since it's clearly making her so miserable; not to worry about anything, and to just accept his marriage proposal.

She finally agrees.

LATER THAT MORNING, they drive around the island with the top down, her hair and her music blowing in the wind. Reclined in the passenger seat, her head relaxed against the headrest, she's holding the mask firmly on her lap, just in case. It caresses her hands with its soft feathers made alive by the breeze. And she caresses it back, no longer hating it—at least not today, not right now. She's engaged to Strad and she's rarely been happier. He was right; not telling him her secret was the correct decision. All she had to do was embrace this state of things.

They stop for a picnic on a deserted beach, settling down in the shade of a cluster of palm trees. Lily positions her travel speakers next to them and puts a heavy rock on her mask to prevent it from flying away.

Strad looks blissful, feasting his eyes on her exquisite face framed by the turquoise ocean behind her.

THEY SPEND ALL afternoon in her hotel room with the music playing. They make love, they laugh, they talk about their future. He then settles himself in the easy chair and takes a couple of old magazines out of his beach bag to browse while he waits for her to get ready to accompany him to the pool.

"I love you. I adore you," he says to her.

"I love and adore you, too," she says, smiling at him.

As she rubs sunscreen into her arms and legs, she notices that something in one of the magazines grabs his attention. He places it down on the ottoman and pores over it. Lily sees him scratching the page with his thumbnail, as though he's trying to get something unstuck. He's frowning.

"What in the world is this," he mutters. He picks up the magazine again to look at it more closely, and that's when she sees its cover.

She freezes. She knows what he's looking at.

As vividly as the previous moment represented a life of romantic bliss for Lily, this moment embodies its end.

Strad is looking at a picture of his transcendentally beautiful girlfriend, Sondra, in the magazine, and clearly wonders why the picture is in an article about Lily Stanton, his supremely unattractive musician friend, and why even the caption under the photograph so confusingly reads: Lily Stanton at her piano.

It's not as though she hasn't known the risk of photos—hasn't known that photographs of herself get beautified by the music just as effectively as her physical self does, and that when the music stops, her beauty on paper fades just as quickly as it does in the flesh. She knew she could never let Strad have a photo of herself because as soon as he took it home with him, away from the music, it would no longer look like the woman he loves but like his ugly ex-colleague. She has guarded against this risk by hiding all photos of herself and forbidding Strad to snap any new ones, ever. But it hasn't occurred to her that one day, on his own, he might stumble upon a photo of her in an old magazine, and that this might happen while the music was playing. That day is today. That time is now.

Strad tries one more time to remove what he thinks must surely be a photo of his girlfriend Sondra stuck on top of Lily's photo, because he *saw* the original photo on this very page before packing the magazine in his suitcase and it was unmistakably a photo of Lily. "I don't get it. Am I dreaming?" he asks.

"In a sense, you are," she answers.

They stare at each other wordlessly for a long while. Finally, he says, "I don't want this to be a dream."

"It was the only way possible."

He slowly turns his gaze to the music player, and she can see in his face that he finally understands. He reaches for it. He's about to stop the music, but she says, "No, please don't. Not like this."

And so he doesn't. Instead, he gets up and says, "I need to be alone for now."

"I understand."

He goes to the door.

"Strad," she says.

He turns to her.

"Don't take the magazine." She knows that if he does, he will gawk at the hideous photo as it emerges in the silence outside her door.

Guessing her fears, he says, "I've seen Lily before, you know."

"I know. But never through the eyes of her lover."

He places the magazine on the bed and leaves.

AN HOUR LATER, she knocks on Strad's door. No answer. She calls the front desk, asks if he's checked out. He hasn't. She goes looking for him. She finally sees him, alone, in the business center, gazing at a photo of her—as Lily, not Sondra—on the Internet. And while he's staring at the screen, he's humming her music. She's tempted to tell him it's nearly impossible to activate the illusion by merely humming the melody. But she steps away from the door without saying anything and without having been seen.

She goes back to her room, buys a plane ticket so she can depart the next day for New York, packs, checks out, and takes a taxi to spend the night at a different hotel.

That night, she goes on the pontoon boat to the biobay. She swims in the luminescent water, looking down at the shine of her movements. She floats on her back, sinking her ears under the surface so that people's shrieks of joy are silenced. Tears run down her temples and disperse in the liquid light as she stares at the black sky. She lifts one arm out of the water and admires the glitter sliding down her skin.

Even after she leaves the bay, she will try to continue bathing in the beauty of existence. She will let the universe embrace her, since no man will.

ON THE PLANE back to New York, Lily tells herself that if Strad e-mails her or leaves her messages, perhaps she won't return them. Perhaps it's for the best. Their relationship might have worked out for a while, but now that he knows, how can it?

THERE ARE NO e-mails or messages when she lands. Nor are there any later that evening.

She calls me and we talk about her trip.

Worried about her, I suggest we get together. Lily says she's tired and will visit me tomorrow evening instead.

WHEN LILY ENTERS my apartment the following evening, I scrutinize her. In addition to her customary ugliness, there are lines of stress on her face, and an expression of resignation that amplifies the overall sorry effect.

The first thing she says to me is, "Strad doesn't care."

"What do you mean?"

"He hasn't called."

"It's only been two days. And plus, you left suddenly. Maybe he's afraid you might not want to talk to him after the way he reacted. Maybe he thinks he has a better chance of explaining himself in person."

"He's made no attempt to see me in person either."

"Maybe he needs time to think about things, figure out what he'll say, especially if he happens to want to continue the relationship. It's possible," I tell her.

"Why are you trying to get my hopes up? You usually do the opposite."

"It's for your own good when I do the opposite. To manage your expectations."

"And you no longer care about my expectations?"

"Yes I do."

"So why are you doing this?"

I answer by looking past her, into my living room. She follows my gaze, which brings her to the large swivel easy chair with its back to us.

Slowly, it turns.

And Strad is revealed.

In Lily's ear, I whisper apologetically, "He persuaded me to let him do this."

I tell them I'm going out for an extended errand. And I leave.

What happens then, I'm told later:

Strad gets up and walks over to Lily. She has an urge to hide her face, but she remains motionless.

Without saying a word, he gently kisses her lips. And then he kisses her more passionately. He envelops her and buries his face in her hair.

"Isn't this great?" he whispers. "We can go to my place and listen to some of *my* music, for a change."

She laughs, crying a little.

He gives her another long kiss and takes her hand and pulls her out of the apartment. They fly out of the building.

AT LEAST THAT'S how Lily describes the scene when she calls me the next morning. She says last night was the happiest of her life. "And to think that just the night before, I was so depressed I almost died."

I grunt sympathetically until I realize she's not just using an expression. "You almost died?" I ask.

"Yeah. I was playing at my piano, feeling devastated, and my hands started turning reflective again. Clearly it's the depression that triggers it. It hadn't happened in a long time, many weeks. The reflectiveness spread up my arms. I couldn't stop it. I didn't have the will. And when it got past my shoulders and started spreading onto my chest, I could feel I was dying. And part of me just wanted to let go, let it take me, and be released from the burden of living. I can't tell you how difficult it was to muster the will to stop the process. I managed it this time, but barely. If it ever happens again, I'm not sure I'll be able to stop it. Hopefully, I'll never be that unhappy again."

THE NEXT DAY, I'm finally ready to return Peter's calls. I'm still just as disillusioned by his secret and by the fact that he's not a valid exception, or if he is, there's no way to be certain of it now.

But in early afternoon I gather my courage and dial his number.

He picks up. I ask him if we can see each other, to talk.

He comes over an hour later.

We sit at my dining table, nothing to drink before us. Neither of us wants anything.

I begin with, "I can never bypass my rule."

"I know. You told me," he says.

"But I miss you. And I was wondering if we could be friends. Just friends. But good friends."

"It won't be easy for me."

"I'm not sure I believe you. And actually, there's something I've been wanting to ask you."

"What?"

"Why did you torture me?"

"When, specifically?"

"All the time. Like when you came over with your piece of red velvet."

"Yeah."

"And when you kept canceling or postponing our appointments."

He nods. After a pause, he says, "It was all very calculated. And very difficult."

I stare at him.

He says, "You're sort of right that I was trying to torture you. It was an elaborate ploy to get you to . . ." He seems unable to finish.

"Get me to what?"

He looks embarrassed. "I thought that if I could increase your desire and your frustration you'd be more likely to forgive me for knowing what you really look like, once you found out I knew. It didn't work, of course."

We talk for hours. When we get tired, we lie on the couch, one of us at each end of the sectional. We keep talking for most of the night, covering countless topics.

The last thing he says to me before we finally fall asleep on the couch is, "Okay, I guess we can be friends. I've missed you. Having you in my life in whatever capacity is better than not having you at all."

Even though I can't be his lover, I love him more than ever.

PETER AND I get together frequently. It's usually my initiative, sometimes his.

It comforts me to be with him. So I keep asking him to come over.

When he points out, pleasantly, the abundance of my invitations, I simply say, "I like to be with you."

He never turns me down. The few times he can't make it, he makes a counterinvitation, usually for earlier or later the same day.

I CATCH MYSELF staring at him when I think he's not looking. But sometimes he catches me. Like the time we were sitting on my couch, watching a movie, and I thought the angle would make it impossible for him to know I was gazing at him, and he said, "Why are you staring at me like that?"

Blushing, all I could say was, "You have good peripheral vision."

"Yeah. So why are you?"

"Just looking at what a good friend you are."

His eye twitched.

———

WE MAKE A point of not getting together on Valentine's Day to avoid the romance aspect. But we make up for it by seeing each other five evenings in a row after that.

I don't know what Peter did on Valentine's Day. I don't ask. As for me, I stayed home working.

FINALLY, ONE DAY, when I call Peter—as I often do to ask him if he wants to come over and hang out—he tells me, "You don't understand. It's very difficult. I am practically delirious. I could get killed crossing the street because I have fantasies and I don't see the cars."

"Fantasies?"

"Yes, fantasies!" he barks. "Fantasies of running my fingers through your gray curls until your wig falls off. Of peeling that strangely erotic gelatinous monstrosity off you and enlacing you in my arms. I even have fantasies of *not* peeling that thing off you and enlacing you in my arms anyway and making love to you with that thing still on."

To this, all I say is, "Please come over. I miss you."

"Okay, I'm here," he says, an hour later, covered in snow and carrying takeout sushi.

We watch a movie chastely on the couch. We eat, and chat for an hour about this and that. He goes home.

AND THEN, I feel it slipping. A sadness sets in. He's less talkative. More pensive. Our frustrating nonsexual relationship seems to be taking a toll on him, and I get a sense it's affecting other areas of his life as well. He's less interested in his job. He skips network meetings. His anchoring of the news is detached and glum. I'm worried. I don't want to be responsible—even indirectly—for any damage to his career, health or happiness.

Maybe it's selfish of me to want a friendship from him. Maybe I should let him go.

But I can't. I tried it, didn't like it.

A COUPLE OF days later, when I'm in Peter's neighborhood, I call him to see if he'd like me to stop by and say hello.

He hesitates. "Yes, actually. Why don't you come over. I'd like to talk to you."

At Peter's place, we sit on the couch. He looks at me sadly and says, "The time has come for me to stop seeing you."

I'm taken off guard. "But, you're not 'seeing' me. We're not dating. We're just friends."

"I know. I gave it my best effort, but friendship with you doesn't work. Not for me."

I don't respond.

"It's better for us this way," he says. "My frustration at wanting more from our relationship outweighs the delight of your company. In fact, the more delightful your company is, the more unpleasant it is for me to be in it."

Even though I'm heartsick, I decide to respect his decision.

As I head back home, I try to persuade myself that he's right and that it was too hard for me, too. I'm so downtrodden that when I enter my building I hardly hear Adam the doorman telling me I'm a shameless display of genetic deficiency. And he throws in "Vile serpent" for good measure.

I KNOW I should move on with my life, try to forget Peter, but I keep pondering our situation, wishing we could remain in each other's lives.

And that's not the only thing I'm tormented by. I'm also saddened by Lily's relationship with Strad, which hasn't been going well for quite a while now. Since Vieques, he remained nice enough and adequately loving and affectionate, but there was a faint sadness that hung over him most of the time, that Lily couldn't help but sense. And he hasn't mentioned marriage since Vieques.

He sometimes makes insensitive comments, which Lily tries not to take personally because she knows she's not the only one he's done this to. She often heard him complain about having to walk on eggshells around various customers, friends, and family members, even way back when she used to work with him in the musical instruments store. When she mentioned this to Georgia, Georgia replied, "Walking on eggshells is what stupid people call the effort required not to offend someone. For smart people, not offending takes no effort."

Lily knew Strad wasn't stupid, otherwise she couldn't have fallen in love with him. But as for his emotional intelligence, it did seem a little higher when she was beautiful.

Lily has gone back to trying to compose a piece that will beautify her permanently. But her heart's not in it. The prospect of manipulating love through unnatural means doesn't appeal to her as much as it once did.

Even though she fails to compose that piece, in the process of trying she ends up developing a different and hugely significant musical skill: the ability to beautify—and create a desire for—things even when they're not there.

Yet Lily is barely interested in her new stunning accomplishment. She's preoccupied by her relationship with Strad.

Georgia, on the other hand, is very affected by Lily's achievement. "You dwarf me, Lily," she tells her. "It's demoralizing.
Every time I get over it, you come up with some new and even
greater accomplishment that makes all of my accomplishments
seem even punier than before. For example, today I was going to
tell you guys that last night I finished writing my novel, but now
it hardly seems worth mentioning."

We explode with congratulations and cheer. We ask her if we
can read it. She says not yet, but soon. She says she e-mailed it to
her agent this morning and wants to wait and hear her reaction.

GEORGIA DECIDES THAT she will throw a party at my apartment in
two weeks to cheer Lily and me up. She says she's also secretly
throwing this party for herself to celebrate the completion of
her novel and because she hasn't had a party in a while and it's
overdue.

Georgia has mixed feelings about the parties she throws,
which she always holds in my apartment because of space con-
siderations. She invites lots of people from the literary world,
yet she has trouble tolerating them. But she can't help inviting
them. It's a compulsive need—wanting to be in the loop while
loathing the loop.

LILY'S RELATIONSHIP WITH Strad continues to go downhill.

There is one thing, especially, that really bothers her.

One night, before they go to bed, she brings it up. "I see you,
sometimes, staring at a photo of me while listening to your iPod."

He looks uncomfortable, feigns not knowing why she'd point that out.

"I know that on your iPod you have the music that changes my appearance. Is that what you were listening to?"

Doing some quick thinking, he answers, "Yes, actually. I find it exciting that my girlfriend is such a virtuoso."

"Really? It didn't seem to do much for you that time we went to the Building of Piano Rooms and I—as Lily—beautified the pen. It didn't make you interested in me romantically."

"It *did* do a lot for me. But we'd been friends for so long . . . I didn't think of you romantically back then . . ."

"And now?"

"Let me show you." He kisses her and takes it from there.

She's touched by his effort to be nice, but it feels forced.

Lying in bed afterward, she wonders if maybe she's simply spoiled. After all, up to about a month ago she'd been made love to by a man who thought she was the most beautiful woman in the world. It makes a difference.

She's grateful at least that he doesn't ask her to go back to the way things were: with the mask or the music on always. She'd find it humiliating.

But Lily knows their problems have to be faced. Therefore, she decides she will confront him with the beautiful version of herself one last time. She hopes his reaction, whatever it will be, will help her figure out what should be done about their relationship.

So the next day, she takes Strad to the Building of Piano Rooms, pretending it will be fun to redo that old afternoon that didn't go the way she'd hoped.

At the front desk, Lily asks for the same room as before. It happens to be available. It's just as small and bare as she remembers it. Strad sits in the white plastic chair, much closer to her than that first time.

For a few minutes, she plays him various short pieces, nothing special. And then, she launches into the piece that beautifies her—the one so familiar to them both.

She watches his face. She can practically see, reflected in his eyes, the hideous mask that is her external appearance lifting from her face.

His eyes fill with tears. He's clearly devastated by the sight of the girl he was in love with.

Instead of stopping, Lily continues playing passionately until his tears have been running long enough that he won't be able to deny them.

When Lily stops, she turns her back to Strad, not wanting him to gape at the gradual return of her ugliness.

"I'm sorry to be crying," he says. "I don't know why you had to play that piece."

"Because we have to face things."

"What things?"

"The fact that you're unhappy."

"I'm not unhappy. And I love you."

"I don't think it's the right kind of love."

"It's a deep love."

She turns around and looks at him. "It's not a helpless, passionate love. It's a responsible love."

"So what? I love you."

"But not the way you did."

After a long pause, he finally murmurs, "Maybe not exactly the same way."

Gently, she says, "And it's because of how I look."

He flinches. "The way you look makes no difference."

"Oh? Because you don't want it to? Or because it really doesn't?"

"Because you're the same person."

"Not visually. And I know that matters to you a lot. You can't change your nature."

After a long while, he replies, barely audibly, "I don't know. Maybe you're right. I feel I've lost the person I was in love with. As though she vanished or died."

Lily nods, resigned.

Suddenly, Strad seems to backtrack. "But it doesn't matter because you didn't vanish. You're here, the same person. In fact, the beauty I saw and fell in love with was your soul."

"But you no longer see it."

"Maybe not with my eyes, but I see it with my heart, with my mind."

"But it's not the same, is it? For you, it's not the same."

He can't speak, can't contradict her. He looks miserable. He lets his head drop, in complete abjectness.

Softly, she adds, "I think it might be best if we stop trying to make our relationship work. We should accept that it's over."

Hardly raising his head, he nods.

They leave the piano room—she feeling many times worse than she did upon their first disappointing exit.

When they step out onto the sidewalk, he hugs her. In a choked whisper, he says, "I'm so sorry."

When he releases her, she smiles at him weakly and walks away.

Strad doesn't move. He watches her go. From the back, she looks the same as when he loved her.

HEARING ABOUT LILY'S breakup sinks me deeper into the dumps. Having finished reading Georgia's novel only adds to my sadness, even though I loved the book. It's a funny yet pessimistic novel about a love triangle—a one-directional triangle of unrequited love. It explores attraction, appeal, and desire. It's about how even the most obsessive love can be fickle, as illustrated when the direction of the love triangle changes.

The book's final message is that no one ever really finds true love, because such a thing doesn't exist, but that people can have happy lives anyway, thanks to good friends.

It's called *Necessary Lunacies*.

It left me more hopeless about ever getting over my romantic block regarding Peter, though more hopeful that he might be open to resuming contact with me.

I call Peter and invite him to Georgia's party tomorrow night, even though I know I'm disregarding his wishes.

He says he doesn't want to go.

I plead with him gently, tell him I'd like to see him.

"I don't know," he says.

I ask him to at least think about it.

But he won't commit to doing even that.

After hanging up, feeling powerless, I decide to turn my attention to something I've been neglecting for too long.

I pick up my therapist's business card and go down to the lobby.

I hand the card to Adam the doorman and tell him he should see this therapist, that she's very caring. (I should probably see her again myself, but I'm always too busy.)

He strokes the card thoughtfully between his thumb and forefinger and says, "Thank you, but I prefer a softer kind of toilet paper."

"I just want to help you, Adam."

"You have helped me, actually, by giving me this card. I know I can stop trying to prove myself wrong."

"About what?"

He doesn't answer, but his face looks flushed and his eyes look slightly wild.

I say good night uneasily and go back upstairs.

PART

Chapter Seventeen

To my relief, Peter does show up at the party the following day. A couple of pretty young interns from the *Paris Review* lose no time gushing over him, trying to chat him up. Smiling, he nods at them without interest.

After a few minutes I ask him if I can talk to him in private. I lead him to the bathroom, the only private place.

I mutter, "I was wondering if you might reconsider your decision not to be friends with me."

"No." He rests his hand against the towel rod behind me. "It's too hard. I want more from you," he says.

I look away. I want more, too, of course, but it's impossible.

He leaves the bathroom. I compose myself and exit a minute later. The party is lively, though not yet at its peak. Many more people are still expected.

Neither Peter nor I are in the mood to mingle, so we go to my bedroom-office where Penelope, Jack, and Georgia are gathered. They don't seem to be in much of a mood to socialize either.

Georgia is sitting on the couch, looking bored and grumpy,

her cheek in her hand. Her mien clashes with her festive, bright red lipstick that she only wears on rare and important occasions. Clearly, she expected to have a better time this evening, which is often the case with her and parties.

Earlier, we told her how much we loved her novel. Our praise made her happy for about an hour, and then the effect faded.

The only one of us not here in my bedroom-office is Lily, who's playing the piano in the living room, which may be another reason we're here instead of there. Her grief is audible in her music. You'd think we were at a funeral. The guests don't seem to mind or even notice, but we who are her closest friends can't help being affected by it.

Georgia's cell phone rings. As usual, she answers it on speaker, so we can all hear.

A man's voice says, "Hey, Georgia, is the party still going?"

"Er . . . *yeah*," she says, like it's a dumb question.

"Great! Is there an alternate entrance into your building?"

"Er . . . *no*," she says, like it's a weird question. "The entrance is on Fifteenth Street between Union Square East and Irving Place."

"They're not letting me in."

"Who isn't?"

"The cops."

"Cops?"

"Er . . . *yeah*," he says, like it's a dumb question.

"Why?"

"Er . . . because of what's going on in your lobby, maybe?"

"What's going on?"

"You don't know? One of your doormen is going postal. He has a gun."

We all look at one another, eyes wide.

"The doorman made everyone vacate the lobby, except for the other doormen and staff. So that's why I'm asking if there's like . . . maybe a service entrance in the back or something?"

"Are you crazy? Why would you want to enter a building containing a doorman with a gun?"

With icy indignation, he says, "Because you know very well that I have dreamed of meeting your agent Melodie Jackman for years, if not decades. I've just finished writing my third unpublished novel, and I might be able to pitch it better in person. All I care about is making it past the doorman and to the party."

"Listen to what you're saying," Georgia barks.

"It's easy for you to get on your high horse. You've got it made. This is my chance. I'm not going to let some psycho doorman get in my way."

"My agent isn't coming. She never goes to author parties."

"Ah damn," the guy says and hangs up.

I grab the remote. "I bet it's Adam. Let me put on the doorman channel."

In my building, there's a live security video that is viewable twenty-four hours a day on channel seventy-seven of all residents' TV sets so we can see who enters the building, who leaves, who's at the front desk, etc.

My friends and I stare in horror as the black-and-white image of the lobby appears on my TV screen. At this very moment, the doorman has lined up the other doormen and staff members against the wall. They're standing side by side, facing him. His back is to the camera. He paces in front of his colleagues, holding a young woman in a choke hold and alternately pointing his gun at his colleagues and at her head. Judging from his body language, he seems to be ranting about something.

Just then, he turns his head enough for me to recognize him. "Shit, it *is* Adam," I say.

"How did you know it would be him?" Jack asks.

"Because he's crazy. He insults me all the time."

My friends look at me.

Jack says, "He really insults you? Or are you just being hypersensitive?"

"Why would you ask a question like that, Jack?" Georgia says. "You know very well Barb is *hypo*-sensitive when it comes to herself. I'm sure he really insults her."

"What does he say?" Jack asks me.

"You name it, he's said it," I reply.

"Hardcore insults?" Penelope asks.

"Sometimes."

"Like what?" Jack asks.

I shrug. "Things like 'Marinade of shit and piss' and 'Cocksucking bitch.'"

My friends look shocked. I remain silent, realizing how weird this sounds.

Georgia says, "It's really crazy that you never reported him to the super or anyone."

"Why do you assume I never reported him?" I ask, annoyed.

"Because he wouldn't be in the lobby pointing a gun at people if you had."

"I felt sorry for him. He assured me he insulted only me, no one else."

Georgia frowns. "Oh, that must have been *so* reassuring."

"I thought he was unwell, troubled—not dangerous," I plead. "I was afraid he might get fired if I said anything."

"Oh, yes, and that would have been so *bad*," Georgia says, merciless.

"Thanks for making me feel better," I murmur.

"Well you certainly do feel better than *they* do," she snaps, pointing to the lined-up hostages and arm-choked woman on the screen.

Hardly able to contain my panic, I get up, wiping my moist palms on my pants. "I can't stand to watch this." I begin walking out of the room, feeling horribly guilty for not tattle-taling on the doorman.

"Barb," Peter says, close behind me, softly.

The sound of his voice is comforting. I turn to him.

"Can we talk in private again?" he asks.

"Again?" Georgia says. "Oh, come *on*, we've got a crisis on our hands."

"We have to warn the guests not to leave the apartment," Jack says.

"Peter, you're the anchor. Can you anchor this?" Georgia asks.

"Wait," Jack says, "let me first see if I can get any information from my buddies at the precinct."

After his brief call, he tells Peter what he learned and gives him the go-ahead to inform the guests.

The guests are chatting. Clearly, they haven't yet heard about the lobby situation.

Peter addresses the assembly: "Good evening."

He gets most people's attention.

In his TV anchor voice—authoritative, concerned but calm—he says: "I'm sorry to interrupt this party to bring you some breaking news from elsewhere in the building. Reliable sources have indicated that there is a lone gunman on the loose in the lobby and that a siege situation is ongoing. He's a doorman, and has locked the exit doors and shut down the elevators. Law enforcement officers have surrounded the building. We have been told by authorities that no one should attempt to leave the premises until we receive the all-clear. They assure us there is no need to panic. There are no reports of any injuries. We will keep you abreast of any further developments as they unfold."

A few guests nod their heads politely, and then most of them return to their quiet conversations and aggressive networking. Only a couple of them take out their phones to make calls.

"Wow, you really kept them calm," Georgia remarks.

We retreat to my bedroom-office.

A guest follows us in and asks Georgia, "Do you think that if the crisis gets resolved soon, more guests will be allowed to come up?"

Georgia's face hardens. "Who are you waiting for?"

"You told me your editor, Jen Bloominosky, would be here and that I could show her my manuscript."

"Look here," Georgia says, walking to the TV screen on which the scene downstairs is the same as before. She points to it and says, "Hmm . . . here's a space behind the doorman who's holding his gun against that woman's head. I don't see why the police might not allow a few guests, one at a time, to slink along the wall opposite where the doorman has lined up the other doormen to kill them one by one. I mean, technically there's plenty of room behind him. So I think a few new guests might still show. While you wait, go back to your networking and have a good time."

"Like they did on the *Titanic* as it was sinking?"

"Uh ... right, except we're not sinking. Notwithstanding that analogy, I'm sure your novel's terrific."

Instead of following Georgia's advice to go into the other room, he sits on the couch and watches the lobby scene on the TV.

He is not aware that Jen Bloominosky actually is at the party already. He probably didn't see her because she's always hidden by several people trying to talk to her. Georgia is clearly in no mood to set him straight, which I find amusing yet cruel.

Not all of Georgia's guests are shameless networking self-promoters, but a depressingly large number of them are. Jen Bloominosky is one of the few who are good, kind souls. She is beloved by everyone. And unlike many of the other guests at this party, she doesn't strike me as superficial, but rather as quite genuine—in fact, unnervingly so. Earlier, she came up to me and raved about my living room decor and "breathtaking costumes on the animals." As I was thanking her, I noticed her looking at my face carefully, which caused me to ask, "What?" thinking perhaps I had some dip smeared across my cheek.

She said, "For some reason you don't want people to think you're very pretty, do you?"

Flustered, I tried to respond naturally. "It's very nice of you to say that. You look great too."

"Your hairdo," she said. "Not many women in their twenties would willingly sport short gray frizzy hair."

"I know," I said, smiling. "I like it." I tugged on one of my gray curls fondly.

"You don't fool me. Do you fool a lot of people?"

Rattled, I blinked. I didn't know what to say. Jen Bloominosky is not only an editor but a respected author—clearly an alarmingly observant one. I hoped she wasn't going to scrutinize me more closely and notice how my hands were a bit slender compared to the rest of my arms. I hid my hands behind my back. I closed my mouth, in case she realized that my ugly teeth were fake. I shrunk my head further down into my turtleneck so she wouldn't spot my thin neck.

Making sure to keep my teeth covered by my lips, I replied, "Thank you for the compliments. I really like your shirt. Where did you get it?"

She laughed and said she was going to get a refill (three people swarmed her on her way there).

That was earlier in the evening.

Now my friends and I switch my TV set from the doorman channel to regular channels where there is breaking news coverage of the event. Live aerial footage of the building, surrounding crowds, and police cars are brought to us by helicopters we can see and hear outside my windows. We switch back to the closed-circuit surveillance channel.

Peter again tells me he'd like to talk in private. He whisks me into the same bathroom as before and locks the door.

"Barb, doesn't this put everything in perspective?" he says to me earnestly. "Doesn't the issue of beauty seem trivial when you compare it to what's happening in the lobby? I mean, physical appearance is not a life-and-death problem, right? Can't we get past it?"

The situation with the doorman does make me more vulnerable than ever to Peter. At this moment, there is nothing I'd like more than to sink into his arms and be comforted and loved.

But instead, I say, "If life doesn't feel worth living, that's a sort of death, right? No one has ever genuinely loved Lily romantically. And do you think she seems happy? Some days, like today, she seems so sad I'm afraid she'll kill herself. Yesterday she and Strad broke up because he couldn't love her the way he did when she was beautiful. So when you ask me if the situation in the lobby puts things in perspective, my answer is things were already in perspective. Take a good look at Lily as she sits at her piano and tell me if beauty isn't an issue of life and death."

"Okay, now, let me give you my perspective of what's going on. Hearing about this psycho doorman insulting you every day terrifies me and makes me realize even more than before how much you mean to me. My feelings for you are not about your looks. You're the one hung up on your looks."

"Only because everyone else is."

He nods. "Barb, life is short. Disasters can happen. It's true that you could still meet someone who would fall in love with you before finding out about your beauty. But what if he turns out to be an insufferable ass?"

I realize Peter has a point. I've thought of that possibility myself. But giving in would be against all my principles. If only that didn't matter. There's nothing I would love more than to give in to him right now.

"Would that be better?" he asks.

"No," I say.

"So let me ask you one more time," he says. "Can we have more?"

"I wish we could, but I can't. I'm blocked."

He nods, looking resigned. I doubt he understood that my last comment was a cry for help. But I say nothing more because I can't imagine how anyone could help me.

I leave the bathroom. He stays in there a while longer.

I go to my office, wishing there were some solution, some way out of this cage of principles I've built for myself.

I see that Mike, the guy who was desperate to meet Jen Bloominosky, has now met Jen Bloominosky. He has trapped her in a corner of my office and is slowly pulling his big manuscript out of his bag while she is nodding to him kindly.

My friends are glued to the doorman channel. They tell me that nothing has changed, no one in the lobby's been hurt yet. I'm relieved, but I still don't have the stomach to watch the channel with them, so I look down at the floor.

Georgia comes over to me. "You don't look well. Are you okay?" she asks.

I don't feel like telling her that the horror going on in the lobby is not the only reason I'm not feeling well. So I say, "Yeah, I'm fine."

She strokes my arm. "I'm sorry I made you feel bad before about not reporting the doorman to the super. It's not your fault this siege is happening. Are things okay with Peter?"

Just as I'm trying to formulate an answer, Molly, Georgia's freelance publicist, bursts into the room, hollering at us, "I've got Page Six on the phone! Barb, they want to know if you're involved in any movies right now."

"Uh . . ." I stammer, off guard.

"Molly, will you be sane?" Georgia says.

Molly covers the mouthpiece with her finger and whispers to Georgia, "*You* be sane. Three of my authors, including you, are trapped at this party. And yes, I know that your new novel is great, but that doesn't mean you don't need publicity. You are *only* an author. Your profession will probably be extinct within your lifetime. So stop bustin' my chops. I'm just doing my job, which I do as superbly as you do yours. You should congratulate me on having had the presence of mind to pitch the doorman drama to Page Six while it's still hot. What's more, they're eating it up, which hasn't been the case in a long time."

Georgia grimaces.

Molly goes on: "So when they ask me if our hostess, Barb Colby, who's a member of the Knights of Creation—and remember, *I* came up with that name for you guys—"

"Yes, I could kill you for that, by the way," Georgia says.

Before Molly has a chance to finish talking, Peter bursts in and rushes up to me. He grabs my wig from my head and flings it aside.

Georgia takes a step back, in shock. Jack, Penelope, Molly, Jen Bloominosky, and the guy with the manuscript no longer in his bag, are all staring at Peter and me in amazement.

Before I can react, Peter rips open my extra-large man's shirt. The buttons fly off. He yanks apart my fake-fat jacket underneath. The snap fasteners pop like machine-gun fire. My long blond hair is swarming around my shoulders.

This passionate act of Peter's takes me by surprise. And so does my response to it. I am overcome by a strange sense of relief. My principles—instead of bucking at his disobedience—are paralyzed in the face of such irreverence. I can't muster the will nor the desire to fight him. I remain completely passive.

Jack knocks Peter away from me violently enough that he almost falls. "What the hell are you doing?" he roars at Peter.

Peter hisses an urgent whisper to Jack: "*He's here!* The doorman! In the living room, looking for her. He wants to kill her. The only way to hide her is to change her into what she really is, which is what she never is. If you stop me she'll die!"

I can't believe what I'm hearing. We were watching Adam on the video just a minute ago. I look at the screen. The lobby is now empty. And that's when I remember there's a slight tape delay on the doorman channel.

As for how the doorman ended up inside my apartment, that's harder to fathom. Probably a guest let him in, hoping he was some literary agent or editor.

Georgia scream-whispers at Jack, "Help him, Jack!" And she dives into my closet and grabs some items, crying desperately, "Conceal by revealing!"

My friends are upon me now, like a pack of wolves tearing at me, destroying my painstakingly artificial self—all in an effort to save my real one.

Jack strips me of my fake-fat jacket. Penelope seizes my glasses and chucks them in a corner. Peter unbuttons my pants and begins wrenching them down, both pairs at once—not the most effective method.

Behind me, Jack hooks his arms under my armpits to hold me up while Peter, changing tactics, peels off my huge jeans and then my gel pants. Penelope hides them in two filing cabinets along with my shirt and fat jacket.

I'm in my panties now and Georgia loses no time threading my legs through a black miniskirt—the one I always wear under my disguise when I go to bars for my ritual. She slips my feet into high-heeled pumps I've worn only once, on Halloween.

Georgia sticks her fingers in my mouth, and says, "Spit them out!" She extricates my ugly fake teeth and slams them in my desk drawer.

At Jack, she barks, "Help me with her eyes!"

Jack holds my left eye open while Georgia plucks out my brown contact and flicks it over her shoulder. They do the same with my other eye.

Georgia then grabs my face and rubs her lips against mine, spreading her lipstick onto me and wiping off what smeared around my mouth.

I'm now in my white undershirt, which can pass as a sexy top, so my friends leave it alone.

They are done with me.

Teetering in my pumps, I feel like a decorticated fruit, ready for consumption.

Peter is gazing at me, looking mesmerized, lost in some incapacitating fog of useless admiration. Georgia's publicist, her editor, and the guy with the manuscript no longer in his bag still have not moved, transfixed.

The door flies open. The doorman looms at the threshold,

staring at all of us. "What a bunch of *assholes* in there!" he says, pointing to the living room. "I mean, is my gun invisible? They are so *blasé*. Don't they care about life?"

"Not as much as they care about their careers," Georgia says.

He sneers. "Why does it not surprise me that these are Barb's friends? See, that's why I'm here—to kill the Queen of Jade, presiding over her jaded subjects. Where is she?"

He stays in the doorway keeping an eye on the guests in the living room.

"They're not her friends. They're mine," Georgia says. "They're not even my friends. They're my enemies."

"Why would you have them over if they're your enemies?"

"Grim fascination. Unwholesome addiction."

He scoffs. "Typical."

"With the present state of the book publishing world, you can't blame them for being desperate."

"Where's Barb? I was told she's in here."

He studies us, and his gaze stops on me. "You. Come here."

I don't move.

"You!" he yells, pointing his gun at me and waving me over with his free hand. "Come! Here!"

I am terrified. I walk toward Adam.

There's a slight smile on his face as he ogles me. "Wow. You're spectacular. I would have remembered a knockout like you coming into the building."

I stare back at him, as expressionless as I can manage. My heart is racing.

"That would be naughty, if you snuck past me." He smiles broadly and winks. "Should I spank you?"

I wouldn't want him to recognize my voice, so I say nothing.

"Are you always this stupid or are you just having a blonde moment?" he asks. Then, slowly and loudly, he says, "Do you speak English?"

I shake my head.

"Dumb bimbo," he mutters, looks at the living room, and then at us. "Okay, people, where's Barb?"

No one says anything.

Sticking to his post in the doorway, he scans the room for places where I could be hiding.

"You," he says to me, "open the closet. I'm sure Barb is hiding in there."

I do nothing, at the risk of annoying him—which is still better than infuriating him by revealing I lied about not understanding English.

He repeats his order in mime.

Obeying, I walk to the closet and open it. The inside is visible from where he stands. Thank God my friends didn't throw my fake fat in there.

"Push the clothes out of the way," he says, miming again.

I do as he says. He can see there is no one hiding in the closet.

Then he says to everyone, "I'm going to ask you guys one more time, and if I get no answer I'll shoot one of you randomly. Where is Barb?"

"She went to get some apples," Peter says. Not bad for someone with no imagination.

"I don't like liars," the doorman tells him. "I didn't see her leave the building. And though I did miss this spectacular bimbo when she entered the building, I would never miss Barb.

I don't miss her when she comes, I don't miss her when she goes, I won't miss her when I'll shoot her, and I won't miss her when she's dead."

"She's getting the apples from a neighbor in the building," Peter says.

"What neighbor?"

"She just said a neighbor upstairs."

The doorman flashes another look at the living room. "Come here," he says to Peter.

Peter approaches him.

The doorman tells him, "I only wanted to kill one person: Barb. But if you are lying to me I will kill you, too. Come closer."

Peter obeys.

The doorman presses the barrel of his gun against Peter's heart. "I'm giving you one last chance to tell me the truth. Where is Barb?"

A second passes, and Peter says, "I have told you the truth."

The doorman looks at the rest of us. We nod, except for me, careful not to contradict the impression he has of me as a foreign bimbo.

"Fine, I'll wait for her, then. Hands up, everyone. I want you all in the living room. No touching of cell phones."

We raise our hands and file past him into the living room. The guests are chatting quietly among themselves. They watch us as we join them.

The doorman addresses the whole crowd: "I want everyone's hands up, even the jaded people's."

Everyone's hands go up. At least somewhat up. Some hands don't go up past waist level. A few people are finishing their conversations. I happen to hear the tail end of an exchange between two men standing close to me.

"His last novel sold very well. I'll send you his manuscript."

"No need. I only acquire literary fiction now."

"Ah. Well, I've got some literary authors, too. Here's my card. Could we have lunch some time?"

The doorman stares incredulously at the few people who are still talking. "I have a gun, folks!" he wails. "Are you blind?"

Finally, everyone falls silent with hands at least up to chest level.

While the doorman waits for me to return from getting the imaginary apples, he cuts himself a piece of goat cheese. "Mmm," he says.

To my astonishment, Penelope takes a few steps toward him and says gently, "Excuse me."

"What?" he growls.

"Why do you want to kill Barb?"

"Ah," he says, sounding pleasantly surprised as he puts down the cheese knife. "Thanks for caring. Come a little closer."

Penelope takes another step toward the doorman. They're no more than two feet apart.

Looking deep into Penelope's eyes, he says, loud enough for everyone in the room to hear him clearly: "Barb is a cold inhuman bitch, the most arrogant person I've ever met. The most convinced of her own superiority."

"What makes you think that?"

"You'd never understand," he says, losing interest and turning back to the cheese.

"Yes I would!"

He chuckles, seeming surprised and even charmed by her earnestness. "I insult her all the time. And she never gets offended. It's rude and offensive."

"Sounds like you get easily offended."

He shakes his head. "Not especially. She's just odious. She gets the medal for being least annoyable. And her medal is in this gun. And I can't wait to give it to her."

"But why do you insult her?"

The doorman sits on one of my counter stools. He looks tired. "Because she wasn't offended by my subtle signs of disrespect."

"Why did you give her signs of disrespect?"

"Because she wasn't bothered when I was in a bad mood or slightly rude."

"Wow. So it began small and really escalated."

"Exactly," he says, nodding. "Her ego was incapable of getting miffed by me because she considers people like me so unimportant. That's why I pushed it. She infuriated me."

Penelope is nodding.

Encouraged, he goes on: "Thinking about it makes me very angry. That's why I'm here. To put an end to her. For me, it's a win-win situation. If she's miffed before dying, I'll finally have gotten what I want. If she's still not miffed, that will prove that she's a psychopath and that I shouldn't have taken her behavior personally, which will make me feel better about the whole thing. I'll kill her either way, of course, but right before doing it, I will hold the barrel of my gun against her forehead and I will ask her one simple question: 'Does this bum you out?'"

Penelope says, "I understand. You want to feel that you exist, that you matter, like we all do, but—"

"Exactly! *I* always have the courtesy of being offended when people are not nice to me. I mean, *look at me now!*" he roars, standing up.

Penelope nods. "Of course. But there's something you should know. The reason Barb wasn't miffed is not because she has a huge ego, but rather, no ego. It's not *you* she considered unimportant but herself."

"Oh, *spare* me the *bullshit!*"

"It's true. You were right, you shouldn't have taken it personally, not because she's a psychopath, but because she was traumatized by a terrible event two and a half years ago that left her numb."

The doorman looks like he's about to explode with sarcastic comments, so without a pause, Penelope quickly explains. "Her best friend killed himself out of love for her, and since then she's obliterated herself. Her main concern is to avoid hurting anyone ever again, even indirectly, even accidentally, which is why when you mistreated her, she was concerned about *you*, not about herself. Didn't she express concern for you, for your well-being?"

"Yeah, it was so condescending."

"She never complained to the management about you, did she?"

"I don't know."

"Well, she didn't, otherwise you'd be fired and you know it. Most people would have reported you. And do you know why she didn't?"

"Because she knew I'd retaliate. That's obvious."

Penelope shakes her head. "No. It's because she didn't want

you to lose your job. Understand that I'm not objecting to your desire to kill, per se. What troubles me is that your murderous impulse is based on a misinterpretation of everything she's done. The person you're hunting down doesn't exist. She's an illusion, your delusion. You took the few pieces of her that were visible to you and you put them together into this little grotesque being that you assume is Barb. But I've now handed you the missing pieces, so you can rebuild her into what she really is: a person who has been altered by grief. If you knew the real Barb, you would love her and want to protect her, not kill her."

To my surprise, he looks momentarily moved. But, recovering quickly, he says, "Clever twist, and a very poetic story you've made up, but I know you're lying because you'd be stupid not to, and you don't look stupid."

"I couldn't have made that up to save my life. I'm not very creative. I just like to fix things. Like your misconception of Barb."

"It doesn't matter. I have my heart set on killing her, and plus I think you're lying."

"No, she's telling the truth," Georgia jumps in. "Ever since her best friend killed himself out of love for her, Barb has developed a shell. She's still very caring about the welfare of others, such as yourself or her friends, but not her own. She no longer cares what people think of her. In fact, she now prefers being disliked to being loved too much. This can come off as cold indifference. And someone could, as you have, misinterpret her as being a hard bitch."

I know Georgia means what she says because she's actually said this to me before.

"I don't care what lies you all make up. I'm not going to change my mind," the doorman says.

My stress level is skyrocketing. By now, lots of cell phones are ringing, and so is my landline. No one is allowed to answer their phones, so the room is filled with clashing ring tones accompanied by a gentle tinkling sound as Lily starts unobtrusively playing the piano.

"What's taking her so long?" The doorman turns to Peter. "And why is she getting apples in the first place?"

"They go well with cheese," Peter says.

The doorman cuts himself another piece of goat cheese and says to Lily, "That's very pretty, what you're playing."

"It's called 'Need,'" Lily answers.

"Of all the times I've seen you come in and out of the building, I never imagined you played the piano, and so well," he says.

Penelope continues trying to reason with him. "We think we know people. We think that what we see is all there is. We rarely ask ourselves what goes on behind the curtain. We jump to conclusions. And we take everything very personally."

The doorman suddenly cocks his ear, as though he hears a faint sound. "Do you hear that?" he asks Penelope. "That's the sound of no one caring. You're making me cringe now. If you keep this up, my finger might cringe on the trigger. And, plus, I just realized I have a real problem."

"What problem?" Penelope asks, as Lily keeps playing.

"Well, I know I'm going to prison, I knew that from the start, so that's not the problem. The problem is I forgot to arrange things for when I get out of prison. I mean, in case I ever get out, which of course will depend on whether or not I'll be able to kill Barb."

"What did you forget to arrange?"

"Mainly, I'm out of office supplies, and I forgot to buy more." He now looks very distressed. "I wish I'd made sure my desk was always well-stocked, so then if I did go to prison, at least I'd have everything I needed when I got out. And knowing that would make being in prison so much more bearable."

My bafflement at what he's saying is short-lived because I quickly realize he's being influenced by Lily's music. She must be using that new musical skill she developed recently: the ability to beautify—and create a desire for—things even when they're not there. Clearly, in this case, she chose office supplies.

"Staples is open till ten," Penelope says to him.

"You're kidding!" He looks at his watch. "I'll go to prison even if I don't kill Barb, and I'd love to kill her, but she's taking so long, and I can't face going to prison without a well-stocked desk; that's my priority. Maybe I could get to Staples without getting arrested until after I've bought my stuff."

"You are so wise," one of the guests says. "You should go to Staples right away, before it closes. And if you don't mind, I'll go with you because I'm out of pencils and getting low on thumbtacks."

"You're as bad as I am!" the doorman tells him, while other guests are now also clamoring to go to Staples. "Okay, I'll let you all come with me, but you have to walk in front of me so I can see you."

And the guests in my apartment miraculously depart. Lily

has outdone herself. My urge to follow them to replenish my stock of printing paper almost equals my relief that they're gone. I can tell that my friends are struggling with similar issues as well.

Jen Bloominosky, Georgia's editor, is one of the last to leave. Before exiting, she turns around and says to me, pointing to my body, "I didn't dream the extent of it. But I was onto you, give me credit."

I can't help smiling.

She says, "I wish I could stay and chat about it, but unfortunately I'm in desperate need of file folders."

When all the guests are gone, Jack locks the front door and phones the police downstairs. He alerts them that the doorman and guests are on their way down and headed to Staples, possessed by an irresistible need to buy office supplies.

We melt all over Lily, congratulating her, thanking her, and then we do the same with Peter, thanking him for saving my life. If he hadn't come to the party, I'd probably be dead. I express my gratitude to Penelope and Georgia as well, for their efforts. And of course my friends do some fussing about me—being the one who almost got killed.

We're all in high spirits except for Lily, who seems sadder than ever.

Some of us use the bathrooms, others pour ourselves drinks. When it's my turn to emerge from the bathroom, I'm surprised to see Georgia coming back into my apartment from the outside hall.

"What are you doing?" I ask.

"I was just throwing out some trash," she replies. She pats Lily's arm with concern and says to her, "God, you look even less well than Barb did. You can relax now. The nightmare is over."

"Yours is. Mine never will be." Lily goes back to the piano and resumes her sorrowful playing.

I suddenly feel the need to put my disguise back on. "Excuse me for a minute," I mutter, and head toward my bedroom-office to find it.

"Don't bother," Georgia says. "It's shredded."

I freeze. "What?"

"I sliced it up into a million pieces and threw it down the garbage chute just now." She finally looks at me.

I'm speechless. I feel a rapid headache coming on.

She says, "You don't need it."

All my friends are looking at me now.

"I can make myself another one," I blurt.

"And undo tonight's silver lining?" she says. "That would be a shame. And pointless. My publicist saw you being stripped. Now that she knows what you really look like, you can be sure the whole world knows. The era of the disguise is over. It's no use wearing it anymore. It would just look affected."

"Plus," Penelope says to me, "it's not your beauty that's dangerous, it's your personality. We found that out tonight."

I say to Georgia, "If we ask your publicist nicely not to tell anyone, I'm sure she won't."

Peter is wisely choosing to stay out of the conversation.

I look at Lily, who hasn't yet said anything on the topic. Her feelings on this issue are those I care most about.

Sensing this, she stops playing. "You know my opinion," she

says. "I'm glad Georgia threw out your disguise. I think you should enjoy your beauty. You don't seem to realize how lucky you are. And sometimes I find that inconsiderate. To see you not appreciating something that could have made my life so happy is almost offensive to me."

Even though I realize this might be a selfless attempt to help me overcome my need to hide my appearance, her words come as a shock, which must be visible on my face because she quickly adds, "I'm sorry, I shouldn't have said that. You've been great. I'm just so depressed about Strad."

"You'll get over him," Georgia says.

"I know. What I'll never get over is the world. The importance of the casing." Lily resumes playing her sad but beautiful piece.

"Don't you want to sit with us on the couch?" I ask her.

"No, I just want to play a bit longer," she says.

I have a profile view of her sitting at the piano, and from where I'm standing it looks as though she's wearing gloves. Having never seen her, or anyone, play the piano with gloves on, I approach her to take a closer look.

I stop in my tracks when I realize she's not wearing gloves. Her hands are like nothing I've ever seen, though exactly as she has described them to me. They're as reflective as mirrors.

Filled with horror, I watch the transformation creep up her forearms. I remember full well that she thought this change meant death, and I also remember her telling me she was tempted to give in to it.

"Lily!" I bark.

She doesn't even flinch, as though she hasn't heard me. She continues playing, her expression glazed.

The reflectiveness is spreading over her chest. Her clothing fades away as her skin turns to mirror.

I shake her, but it makes no difference. The metamorphosis descends toward her legs and simultaneously rises up her neck.

I take both her arms and pull them away from the piano keys. She doesn't resist. Nearly her entire body is a reflective surface now, and the effect is crawling up her face like beauty once did. She looks at me and murmurs, "I'm sorry." The transfiguration creeps up to her eyes, making her look as though she's sinking in mirror, drowning in what's around her. I see myself in her. But because she's three-dimensional, I'm grotesquely deformed, like in curved mirrors at amusement parks.

"Lily! Lily!" I yell. I grab her by the shoulders and shake her again, then tap her cheeks. Her gaze, though fixed on mine, is vacant. "Lily, stop that. Come out of it. Fight it, don't let go." And suddenly there's a little crack that appears on Lily's chest, at the level of her heart. And the crack expands like a cobweb.

"What's happening?" I scream, turning to the others. They are gathered around me, looking at Lily's chest.

"Lily, don't," I say, putting my palm over her heart, hoping to stop the web of cracks from growing. But the fissures continue to radiate in an ever-widening circle. It's only a few more seconds before they reach her arms, her thighs, and then crawl up her neck.

I yell to her that she can stop it. I beg her not to let this happen.

The cracks cover her face.

"It's not too late," I tell her, more softly. "There's so much to live for. Everyone loves you."

It's not working.

"I order you to stop."

It does not stop. The cracks continue spreading, dividing each fragment of her into smaller fragments. Her entire being is now cracked in a million places.

I close my eyes. "I can't live if you die."

I sob, my eyes clenched shut. When I open them again, a fragment of her broken reflective surface comes loose and falls at my feet. And then another piece becomes detached and falls. And then a tiny piece of her arm. The holes left behind are dark and empty.

I won't let her come apart. These broken pieces must be held together because they are all there is left of her now. I loop my arms around her. I lift her off the bench to a standing position, and I plaster my body against hers to prevent pieces from falling. I ignore the pain as her sharp fragments cut into my flesh. It doesn't matter. She must be held together. I move my arms against her back to make sure I'm holding onto as much of her broken self as possible. In the process I get more cuts. If I'd still been wearing my disguise, I would have been protected by the padding.

Our friends haven't yet noticed my injuries because my back is to them, and they've barely had a chance to process what's happening.

"Lily, I will help you," I tell her. "We'll all help you. We'll do a better job, this time. Give us another chance. Don't let yourself come apart like this. Fight it! You can still fight it."

To my horror, my friends start pulling me off her. "No!" I scream, resisting them, but I'm weak because I've already lost a lot of blood.

When they see the front of me drenched in blood and with numerous shards of mirrored glass planted in me, they gasp and I hear Peter yell, "Call 911!"

Penelope is standing near us, crying, her hand over her mouth. She's dialing 911 on her cell phone.

I feel faint. My legs give way under me. Jack and Peter gently lay me down on the floor, still restraining me, for I haven't stopped struggling to get back to Lily. They position me away from her. "Let me go!" I turn my head in every direction, looking for her, but I can't see her.

"It's too late," Georgia says, sweeping the hair out of my face, trying to calm me. "It's over."

No. I yank my arm away from them and lift myself up on one elbow, but I get dizzy. Just before losing consciousness, I see, a few feet away, what is left of Lily: a pile of tiny, sparkling pieces.

Chapter Eighteen

When I regain consciousness at the hospital a few hours later—at around six o'clock in the morning—the first two things I'm aware of are a red tube going into my arm and the pain of my wounds. A moment later, far greater pain invades me as the memory of Lily's death comes rushing back.

My failure to keep her together replays in my mind in horrific detail.

I gaze at my arms lying over the covers. Both wrists are bandaged, as well as my left upper arm, and I can see many Band-Aids on the rest of my skin.

I hardly care when the doctor tells me I was lucky the paramedics reached me quickly and began fluid resuscitation as soon as I was in the ambulance. I'm told that if they hadn't, I might not be alive because I'd gone into hemorrhagic shock due to the massive loss of blood. My blood pressure was dangerously low and my heart rate insanely high.

I hardly care when the doctor tells me I arrived at the hospital with over a hundred shards of mirrored glass lodged in me.

And I hardly care when he tells me it took him and his team three hours to remove all the pieces.

But suddenly, I have a question I care deeply about: "Where are the pieces?" I ask, getting agitated.

"It's important that you stay relaxed," he tells me. "You're in the last hour of a four-hour blood transfusion. You suffered a class III hemorrhage and lost 40 percent of your blood, most of it lost through four deep incisions—one on your neck and three on your wrists and arm."

"You're not answering my question. Where are the hundred pieces you removed from my body?"

"Don't worry. We saved them all, per your friends' instructions. We've already given them to Peter Marrick. It must have been a valuable sculpture, eh?"

I sigh with relief, though I have no idea what he's talking about regarding a sculpture.

He comes closer and says, "You were very lucky. You have eighty-five stitches on your body, but you didn't get a single cut on your face." He puts his fingers under my chin and raises my face toward his. "Your face is flawless. It would have been a shame to get it scarred."

I pull away, put off by his bedside manner.

Quickly, he adds, "That's not to say your body is any less perfect. But scars on the body don't matter. They're cool, like tattoos. I'm just saying it's a miracle your face came out unscathed."

There's nothing miraculous about it. I don't have cuts on my face because I wasn't saying goodbye, I was trying to save her. If I'd been saying goodbye to Lily before she died, I would have pressed my cheek against hers, I would have rested my mouth and chin on her shoulder, I would have buried my face in her neck. Instead, I was trying to see how best to hold her, trying to look where best to apply pressure to keep her together. If getting my face disfigured could have saved her, I would not have hesitated.

Tears start running down my cheeks. The doctor wipes one away and says soberly, "I'm sorry. I didn't mean to cause offense."

I burst out laughing and instantly resume crying. A sense of loneliness invades me.

He keeps trying to fix what he thinks made me cry. "Don't worry, you'll hardly have any scars on your body. Most of the cuts were superficial and didn't require stitches." Finally, he wisely decides to change the topic. "Are there any family members you'd like us to contact?"

"No," I say, shaking my head. I don't want my mom's dream vacation in Australia to be ruined by news of my condition. She'd be so distraught, she'd either cut her trip short or at the very least she wouldn't be able to enjoy the rest of it, and I can't bear either option.

"But . . . are any of my friends here?" I ask.

To my relief they are. The doctor lets them in. Georgia rushes to me, looking extremely anxious. Jack and Peter follow. They all look traumatized. Peter holds my hand.

As for Penelope, she's not here. When the doctor leaves and my friends and I are alone, they tell me Penelope is home, trying to piece Lily back together, like she would one of her ugly broken pots. They say she stopped by the hospital earlier and got all the remaining pieces from Peter.

Georgia adds, in an urgent, secretive tone, "Everyone was asking how you got a hundred shards of mirror stuck in you. I had to make up a story. We said you had a large mirror sculpture that you accidentally knocked over and fell on top of as it shattered."

I nod, filled with gloom as I'm visualizing what really happened. After a moment, I ask, "What happened to Lily? What was that?"

Georgia looks at Jack and Peter. Then she replies, "Death by sorrow, we assume. I think the sad music she played each time she felt depressed created a vicious circle she couldn't get out of. Her mood made the music sadder, which in turn made her mood sadder. It's as if her mood and her music became entwined in a dance of despair, reinforcing each other, creating a downward spiral that pulled Lily under."

My throat is clenched so tight I can hardly breathe.

Peter is at my other side. He's caressing my cheek, smiling at me lovingly, wanting me to turn away from Georgia.

The doctors were hoping to let me go home later, but it turns out not to be possible because the transfusion doesn't agree with me. I develop a fever, which I'm told is a febrile non-hemolytic transfusion reaction. They say it's common and won't cause any lasting problems.

The fever goes away by the end of the day, and I'm allowed to leave at four the following afternoon.

PETER, GEORGIA, AND Jack are here to escort me out. We move down the hospital corridor like a funeral procession, our heads bowed, thinking of Lily.

Our plan is to go directly to Penelope's apartment because I want to see Lily's remains.

Before we've even left my hospital floor, I'm being stared at by doctors, nurses, and visitors. They stare at me as we wait for the elevator, then in the elevator, then in the lobby. Not being disguised is even worse than I remembered. And they don't just stare. Some of them whisper to each other while staring. I can't wait to get out of here.

Georgia decides we should sit in the coffee shop in the lobby for tea and a snack, which annoys me because she knows I want to see Lily's pieces right away, and I'm the one who's injured. But Jack's on her side and Peter's neutral, so we go in and get a table.

I refuse all food and drink. While my friends are getting their snacks at the self-service counter, people keep staring at me. It's excruciating. I'm getting agitated, and the stress is causing me to feel my cuts more acutely, as though these strangers' eyes are cutting into me. I won't be able to take this on a daily basis, especially now that Lily is dead from all this crap.

My friends return to the table, unwrapping their snacks and stirring their teas.

"I won't be able to live like this," I state flatly. "I'll have to put my disguise back on. Or attack people looking my way."

"Don't worry, today it's not normal staring," Georgia says. "I'm really sorry, but my stupid publicist secretly used her phone to film you while we were stripping you at the party. You're on most newspapers' front pages today. They've published some photos of you wearing your hideous getup next to some photos of you in all your natural splendor. They seem fascinated by the contrast, and they used headlines like 'Strip or Die' and 'Stripping For Your Life' and 'Psycho Doorman Blinded By Beauty.' You're being referred to as 'The Woman Who Was Stripped of Her Ugliness to Save Her Life.' The video of your stripping has been online since yesterday morning. They keep showing it on TV, too."

After several seconds of shocked silence, I say, "That sucks. Why didn't you tell me right away?"

"We were afraid you wouldn't leave your hospital room if you knew."

"So you figured you'd prolong my suffering by making me sit here to be gawked at by everyone? Did you want to torture me?'

"No, we wanted to prepare you. The paparazzi are outside, waiting for you to come out. They're being kept out by security. We couldn't let you walk out without warning you, right?"

"Right," I mutter.

"Don't worry," Georgia says, "the crazy staring will pass. Until then, it'll be rough because people are going berserk over this story. They find your story inspiring, for some reason. There's even imitation going on. I heard on the news that earlier today there was a fashion show in which male models pounced on female models on the runway and stripped them of their dowdy, unflattering clothes, to reveal their chic couture outfits underneath."

"It's true," Peter says. "And a wedding took place today in which the bride walked down the aisle wearing a big ugly sack or tent and a bunch of her friends stripped her, uncovering her beautiful wedding gown."

Jack says, "A buddy of mine was at a strip club last night and said some of the strippers were doing it, too, taking off big hideous outfits to reveal their sexy little selves underneath."

"You see what I mean?" Georgia says to me. "But mostly the media wants to know why such a beauty as yourself would hide her looks for years. That's what they want to ask you."

"I don't want to talk about it," I say.

"That's fine. You can leave it up to the men."

"What men?"

"The men you did your ritual on, at bars. They're coming out of the woodwork, offering their theories, their gibberish, not always flattering to you, by the way—obviously, because their pride was wounded. They describe how you misrepresented yourself. One guy said it's as bad as dishonesty the other way around, like when he meets women online who pretend they're better-looking than they are by showing him photos of themselves younger, thinner, or photos of other women."

Clearly, I can never put my disguise back on. Too many people would know it's just a disguise. And it would excite them. And their excitement would make my life more miserable than simply enduring my appearance.

"Do we want to get out of this hospital the straightforward way or do we want to sneak out?" Georgia asks.

"Sneak out, obviously," I say.

"I think it would be a mistake."

"Why?"

"If you're elusive they'll never leave you alone. If you're accessible they'll get bored faster."

"Okay, the straightforward way, then," I say.

I'm holding on to Peter's arm as we exit the hospital through the main entrance. Georgia wasn't kidding. There are TV news crews and a throng of photographers shoving one another, shouting things at me, like—

"Barb, show us your cuts! Your stitches!"

"Do you hate men, Barb?"

"Why didn't you go into modeling or acting? You could have made a fortune!"

"Barb, you're gorgeous!"

"Smile, Barb! Show us your teeth!"

"Got anything to say to TMZ?"

I fight my urge to turn away or run. It's challenging, because I feel as though I'm in a pool of sharks. And yet that's exactly what one's supposed to do in a pool of sharks: move calmly, don't panic, don't go berserk trying to escape.

Despite my efforts to remain accessible per Georgia's advice—at least visually if not verbally—their excitement is growing. They seem energized by my lack of resistance.

Trying to control the edge of hysteria in my voice, I say in Georgia's ear, "They're not getting bored like you said."

A paparazzo shouts, "She spoke! What did she say? Barb, say that again, we didn't hear you!"

Georgia's face reaches up to my ear and replies: "Yes, they are. This is them, bored. If you had fled, you would have seen true madness."

Peter's driver is double parked, waiting for us. As we're about to get in the car, several of the paparazzi behind me shout, "Over your shoulder, Barb!" I look behind me to see what they're talking about. They just wanted to get another shot.

We're followed by a few news vehicles.

When we arrive at Penelope's building, we hurry inside.

In her apartment, we stand around Lily's feet, which Penelope has succeeded in putting back together. On the coffee table is a portion of her face, which Penelope has also put back together like a separate piece of a puzzle. It's heart-wrenching. Every part of Lily has retained its horrible mirror-like reflectiveness. Next to the excerpt of her face is her reassembled hand, and part of her other one. Penelope says the extremities are the easiest, whereas the larger, less detailed planes such as the thighs and back will be more difficult—like sections of clear blue skies, or virgin snow, in puzzles.

I give Penelope a hug and a kiss of gratitude for her touching but pointless efforts to put Lily back together.

After our visit, Peter takes me to my apartment. He helps me get into bed. He lies next to me, dressed. I cry and he caresses my face. It all seems so inevitable. Lily, dead of sadness, me, here, loved for a worthless reason by an otherwise wonderful man. It's all so predetermined and inescapable.

AT NINE THE next morning, the ringing of my cell phone wakes me. I don't usually sleep this late, but my injuries have exhausted me and I took some painkillers in the middle of the night.

I answer my phone. It's my mom, calling from Australia, sounding excited.

The first thing out of her mouth is: "That video is the most beautiful thing I've ever seen! I was at a bar a few hours ago and saw you on the TV getting stripped! I've been partying ever since, waiting until it was late enough to call you. I want to thank your crazy doorman. I'm sorry you got injured by all those pieces of glass, but sweetie, it was *worth* it!"

"I needed a four-hour transfusion. If I'd been wearing my disguise, I would have been protected from those shards and I wouldn't have lost 40 percent of my blood."

"Oh, honey, I'm sorry. But I still think it was worth it."

Hurt, I say, "If it hadn't been for my disguise and the chance it gave me to hide by taking it off, I probably would be dead, shot by the doorman."

"If it hadn't been for your disguise, perhaps he wouldn't have wanted to shoot you in the first place."

"You don't understand my doorman. He wanted to kill me because of my personality, not because of how I looked. I was too calm for his taste. He hated me for never getting offended by his insults. He found it belittling. His desire to kill me had nothing to do with my appearance."

"So you think."

I huff. "I'll have some scars on my body," I say, thinking at least she'll care about that, since it has to do with beauty.

"Who cares! Bodily scars are nothing compared to how hideous you looked. I hope you're *never* going to put back on that disgusting fat. I have my beautiful daughter back!" she screams.

Not wanting her vacation shortened on my account, I talk her out of jumping on the next plane to care for me. I tell her my friends have been helping me plenty.

AND THEY HAVE been, especially Peter, who is devoted to me. During the next few days, he stays with me, nurses me. He leaves me only to go to the station to anchor the news and comes right back to take care of me. He is endlessly attentive and affectionate. I tell all my clients that I need extra time to complete the various projects I'm working on. Everyone is, of course, very accommodating.

I can tell by the way Peter looks at me that he's affected by my real appearance. I've noticed this every day since he ripped off my disguise. Yet, he makes no pass at me, which is just as well because if he did, I know I would rebuff him. Despite my attraction to him, I would reject him because I refuse to let beauty win. Especially now that Lily has been destroyed by it.

When I go out, people's stares get on my nerves.

I screen my calls. I ignore the many messages I get every day from journalists asking me to grant them interviews and to explain why for years I squashed my beauty under a load of hideousness and why I did my bar ritual.

Why should I grant interviews? Only to become even more recognized, even more stared at? I wouldn't have minded explaining myself, or expressing my harsh opinion of beauty, but the cost is too great.

Plus, Georgia does something much more powerful to further my cause against beauty worship. She turns Lily into a legend. She doesn't mean to. She means only to honor Lily's memory by writing an in-depth article for the *New York Times* about her life.

Surprisingly, at the bottom of the article, in a separate section entitled "What Happened to Lily?" Georgia doesn't shy away from describing Lily's end—the true version. Given its supernatural nature, everyone takes this finale to be an imaginative and metaphorical account of Lily's breakdown and alarming disappearance. They believe Lily got depressed and "fell to pieces" after her breakup with Strad. They believe the split "shattered" her and that then she decided to vanish, leave town. For a while or maybe forever.

Correcting this misconception would be unwise of us, we feel, particularly as her parents have already recruited the police's help in trying to locate her, and any insistence on our parts that Lily broke to pieces literally, not metaphorically, will only make us seem like lunatics, deserving of being more thoroughly investigated in connection with her disappearance—an investigation we would not welcome for fear it might uncover the fact that there does happen to be, coincidentally, a killer among us.

But that's not the only reason we don't want people to know Lily is in real pieces. We're afraid Penelope will go insane if those pieces are taken from her. She's already demented, spending her entire days trying to put Lily back together.

Georgia knows her article is powerful, but she didn't expect fashion magazine editors to be so stunned by Lily's tragic story as to discuss it among themselves and decide to turn Lily's ugliness into the new beauty.

These editors are smart, realistic women and men. They know that radically redefining modern beauty is not going to happen overnight.

But they're wrong.

It does.

Virtually.

Here's what happens. First, Georgia's article stirs up a vigorous debate in the media about beauty. Two days after her article appears, Ellen DeGeneres announces she is going to devote a show to the topic of the unfortunate importance of physical beauty in our world. She invites the editors-in-chief of the top four monthly fashion magazines, as well as the head of *Women's Wear Daily*. She wants them to defend themselves on her show after they've read the *Times* article—not an easy task, she predicts.

Far from defending themselves, the magazine editors agree with Ellen. This makes for a surprising show. One of them, the editor-in-chief of *Elle* magazine, confesses she's been made sick by Georgia's article. She says she wishes she could do something about it.

The show ends with a plea from Ellen for Lily to come back, wherever she is. Everyone is distraught over her disappearance.

The next day, *Women's Wear Daily* introduces the new ideal face: Lily's face. They cover the story incessantly, with front-page updates and news about models who are being discovered all over the world and signed before they even create a portfolio.

The monthly beauty magazines redo their cover shots and cover stories; they whip up new feature articles based on the new beauty; and they quickly reshoot, in studio, either twelve, twenty-four or—in *Elle*'s case—forty-eight pages, out of sixty fashion pages, for their next issues, using models who are ugly in ways that resemble Lily as much as possible.

It's a holistic, industry-wide embrace, a coordinated effort. Even nightly newscasters offer regular updates, particularly Peter Marrick.

We're sad that Lily is not alive to enjoy her new beauty.

Several top fashion designers in London, Paris, New York,

and Tokyo announce that they, too, are supporting this new beauty ideal and replacing all the models in their upcoming runway shows.

Not everyone's reasons for joining the trend are noble. A few are mercenary.

Three high-ranking plastic surgeons report that there's been a dramatic decrease in business. They say women are having second thoughts about getting rid of flaws that are now highly prized. When the three surgeons are asked if they are disappointed in this turn in fashion, two of them—possibly insincerely—say no. The third one, however, says yes he is disappointed but expects that women will start booking appointments to get flaws (now considered "improvements") incorporated into their faces and bodies. He adds, "As long as women are dissatisfied with how they look, I'm satisfied. I don't care what form their dissatisfaction takes, provided it requires me to fix it."

This comment fans the flames, causing more articles to come out condemning the fact that the basic underpinning of the fashion, beauty, and cosmetics industries is women's dissatisfaction with themselves. I think that people getting this glimpse into the dark side of beauty has enabled them to see pulchritude for what it is: something as disgusting as it sounds—putrefaction; rot; another one of life's necessary lunacies.

Of course, not everyone hears about the new beauty, especially people who don't keep up with fashion. That's why I still get catcalls and come-ons from non-metrosexual men who are behind the times. I'm allergic to them, but I have to be patient, take it one day at a time.

No longer ladylike or meticulously groomed, Penelope lives in sweat clothes and her hair is disheveled. She used to be the only one among us to wear makeup on a regular basis, and even though I think she's much more attractive without it, we all know its absence is a bad sign about her mental state.

She's been rebuilding Lily for weeks with little progress, yet she's showing no signs of letting up. Quite the opposite. Her focus is sharpening and her determination is acquiring a certain savagery.

Not once since Lily broke has Penelope met us anywhere other than at her apartment, and her reluctance to let us visit increases each week. And she's cranky, which I know is understandable given that as soon as she makes any progress, Lily falls apart again.

In her desperate desire to bring Lily back to life, Penelope at first tries to rebuild her in the exact position she died in—standing up—but she quickly realizes it's impossible. So she tries rebuilding her friend lying down. Penelope believes that horizontally the task will no longer be impossible—merely horrendously difficult.

Even though Penelope does start making some progress, Lily still keeps collapsing. But Penelope continues working on Lily with as much passion and single-mindedness as Lily did when working on her musical pieces. Day after day, with infinite delicacy, Penelope balances Lily's pieces on top of one another. No matter how careful she is, however, there always comes a time when she is not careful enough, when her hand shakes a little too much, when the mere fact of being human makes it impossible for her to place every single fragment with the exact degree of gentleness necessary at the precise angle required. She's killing herself trying to attain perfection in all her gestures.

And we don't stop her.

We don't have the energy.

Lily's death has left us weak and despondent.

Plus, we know it would be useless to try to stop her. Penelope would continue. And the truth is, we want her to continue because even though our minds know that her enterprise is hopeless, our hearts can't stop hoping—stupidly and relentlessly.

Jack is the last one to see Penelope.

That was three days ago. He said she looked bad—haggard and pale—and that she'd lost weight. In the middle of her living room floor was Lily, close to being fully recomposed. But the same problem kept happening. Each time she was almost back together, she'd crumble.

Jack was upset to discover that there was no food in Penelope's fridge or cabinets. He bought her groceries and made her promise to eat.

His account was so disturbing that each of us made concerted efforts to see her after that. But we failed; she was no longer receiving visitors, saying she needed to work on Lily without distractions.

Thankfully, we don't have to endure the situation much longer. Everything changes dramatically one evening when Jack's phone rings while we're gathered at my place, brooding over Lily's recomposition and Penelope's decomposition.

Peter is not with us. As my cuts have been fading, so has his presence from my life. I still see him once or twice a week, but

I sense his visits will grow farther apart. He's been withdrawing because he feels that nothing has changed between us, that I'm still blocked, that we have no future beyond a friendship. And I can't say I disagree. Lily's ugliness as a new beauty trend has in no way touched the core of the beauty worship problem. Just because beauty's been redefined doesn't mean it has lost its importance. And I'm resigned to being stuck for as long as beauty rules—which I expect to be forever.

This night, Jack almost doesn't pick up his ringing phone. At the last minute he checks the caller ID. "It's Penelope," he says, and eagerly answers it.

He listens for a few seconds and then snaps the phone shut.

"What did she say?" Georgia asks.

"It was her number, but it wasn't Penelope," he answers, in shock. "It was Lily. She said 'Help us.' And then the line went dead."

We rush to the elevator, out the building, hop in a cab, and reach Penelope's apartment in under ten minutes.

It takes us another ten minutes to persuade the doorman and the super to open Penelope's door with the spare key they have.

We find Penelope and Lily unconscious on the living room floor. We call 911, and while we wait for the ambulance to arrive, we're able to find a pulse on each of our friends. We can't believe Lily is alive again, and not only alive but not reflective.

The superintendent, who is hovering over us, seems perplexed as to why Penelope's unconscious state terrifies us while Lily's delights us.

The ambulance squad arrives within minutes and Lily regains consciousness on the way to the hospital but Penelope doesn't. The doctors say she's dehydrated and malnourished. Her vital signs are weak.

Much of the ecstasy we feel over Lily's resurrection is dampened by our worry for Penelope.

NOW THAT WE'VE got Lily back and that Penelope possibly sacrificed her life to reassemble her, I want to place Lily on a shelf with a big sign that reads: "Fragile. If you break her you will pay."

When word gets out that Lily is back and alive, journalists start calling her incessantly, asking for interviews. She doesn't give a single one, being in no mood to talk about herself when the friend who brought her back to life is in the hospital in a coma.

In an effort to distract her from her crushing feelings of guilt, we show Lily how much the world of fashion has changed during the past few weeks. We want her to see that, at least for now, she's beautiful in this world. But Lily doesn't care. She doesn't care about the many fashion magazines that use models who resemble her. She doesn't care that on the streets, many women who, until last month, would have been considered unattractive are now carrying themselves with more confidence and self-appreciation. She doesn't care that her physical appearance is now desired.

And not only does she not care, she doesn't believe it. She doesn't feel beautiful. How can she, after years of being ignored, dismissed, avoided, insulted—insulted like she was by that man at the bar who ended up murdered. The damage to her self-esteem was far too great for her to feel beautiful now. As though all it would take would be for the whole world to find her beautiful.

Lily is swamped by adoring fans and by men who want to date her. But she's not interested in men who see the beauty in her ugliness only now that everyone else does.

She is contacted by old schoolmates and acquaintances who never showed much interest in her before. Those are the worst. Extricating herself from having to meet up, catch up, or hook up is so awkward that she changes her phone number and becomes a recluse within a week of coming back to life. This, of course, only increases her mystique and feeds the frenzy.

She also hires a bodyguard (at our insistence), after Jack points out that she might be a tempting target for kidnappers, now that Georgia's article has revealed the extent of Lily's powers and her ability to beautify—and create a desire for—not only objects but people, and not only a desire for those objects and people who are present, but also for those who are not.

It doesn't take long for her fans, acquaintances, and old schoolmates to start approaching me and Georgia and Jack to try to get to Lily. We tell them she doesn't want to talk to anybody. There is one old schoolmate who is not only persistent but evasive—a particularly annoying combination. He says his name is Derek Pearce. He has contacted all three of us multiple times but won't tell us why he wants to reach Lily beyond saying it's important.

We give Lily everyone's messages. She's not in the mood to call back anyone, including Derek Pearce.

Lily's only regular daily outing is to visit the hospital where Penelope is languishing on life support, and play for her on her portable synthesizer. She composes music that she hopes will awaken Penelope from her coma. In vain. She keeps lamenting that her skills are nowhere near capable of achieving such a feat. She can tell she's not even close.

ONE RAINY AFTERNOON, after eleven days in the hospital, Penelope comes out of her coma. According to Lily, it has nothing to do with her music because nothing she composed had that kind of power.

Penelope simply awakes on her own—as comatose patients sometimes do. We are euphoric and relieved.

Physically, she looks okay except for several purple patches on her arms, legs, and torso where the doctors have been injecting her twice a day with a blood thinner.

She's released from the hospital the next day with instructions to get physical therapy three to five days a week until her strength returns.

MY MOM CALLS and says, "You haven't put your fat suit back on, have you?"

"Not yet," I reply, to torture her.

"Seriously, Barb, please don't wear your disguise to protect yourself from ending up like me. I know you think your father loved me for my beauty and had affairs when it faded. But it wasn't as simple as that. I mean, yes he did become increasingly attracted to younger, more beautiful women as I aged, but that wasn't our only problem. We also grew apart, we had different interests. In a lot of ways we simply weren't compatible. I like not having to cater to a man anymore. And who knows, I may still meet another special man someday, but in the meantime I'm content, and often even happy—definitely happier than I

was with your father at the end. I like my solitary life. I'm having a good time traveling. I have good friends. Don't deny yourself happiness while you're young. Ending up like me is not the
worst thing that could happen to you."

AFTER BEING TAKEN care of by her mother for two days, Penelope
is able to walk a little. Lily picks her up and brings her to my
apartment so we can celebrate her recovery and—most importantly—thank her again for her phenomenal feat of bringing
Lily back to life.

When Penelope walks through my door, I'm taken aback by
how weak and sickly she still looks. We are the opposite. We're
exuberant, bouncing off the walls. We settle her on the couch,
prop her up with pillows and blankets, and call her our hero, our
miracle worker.

We shower her with attention, hugs, and gifts. Georgia models a long purple angora scarf she bought for her.

Our only sorrow is that Peter isn't here to share our
happiness.

In an effort to amuse us, Jack goes to the bookcase to demon-
strate how attractive the bookends he just bought for Penelope
will look with books between them. "Oh, God," he says, laughing at something he sees tucked at the back of a high shelf. He
grabs the object and faces us. He's holding the ugly ceramic box
Penelope gave me months ago to thank me for having lunch
with her parents.

Jack says, "Isn't it amazing that the person who made this
sorry-looking box is the same genius who put Lily's million
pieces back together?"

My friends laugh—even Penelope, who seems to be enjoying the teasing.

"It is astounding," Georgia says, reaching for the box.

Jack hands it to her.

Studying the box, opening and closing it, Georgia says, "Wow, Penelope, you've come a long way, baby. Though the metal clasp is nice. Have you thought of going into metalsmithing?"

Penelope chuckles. "I've told you before, the clasp is the one thing I can't take credit for. I'm not the type to take credit for other people's work. The clasp was made by a very talented girl who I always buy my clasps from." The effort to speak seems to tire Penelope quickly.

Then, in all innocence, Georgia makes a comment without realizing its implication until the words are out of her mouth and can never be taken back: "It's unusual, the design of this clasp. I like how it's encrusted with a stone, kind of like the clasp on that mirror-knife . . ." She puts down the box.

As though wishing she could distract us and herself from what she just said, Georgia turns to the window and asks, "Is it supposed to rain today?"

But it's too late. Lily picks up the box and looks at the clasp. Her gaze meets Penelope's. She puts down the box, not saying anything, but she seems deeply affected.

I'm staring at Penelope. Could it be? Could it be that Penelope is the killer among us?

Jack rolls his magazine into a tight tube. He uses it to turn the box around as he would use a stick to inspect a vile carcass. Once the clasp is facing him and he's had a good look at it, he rests his elbows on his knees and buries his face in his hands without glancing at Penelope.

"Yes, I'm the one who wanted to kill Strad," Penelope says, blushing fiercely. "I'm the one who made the preparations, who sent the gifts with the hidden blades. I had those gifts custom-made by the same woman at school who makes the clasps for my boxes. It didn't occur to me you'd recognize the clasp. I'm the one who arranged the phone calls to lure Strad away from the dinner. I did do all that. But when it came down to actually killing him, I couldn't go through with it."

Georgia immediately voices what I'm thinking but am too stunned to articulate: "You couldn't go through with it?" she exclaims. "We made it *impossible* for anyone to kill Strad that evening. Don't make it sound like you had any choice in the matter. You *did* kill the guy from the bar, after all. You were able to go through with *that*, when no one was stopping you."

"No," Penelope says, shaking her head, "I'm not the one who killed the man from the bar, even though I told Gabriel I was. What happened was, I saw in the paper that the guy had been murdered. I have to admit it made me happy. It seemed as though justice had swooped down and for once done something right in the world, performed this beautiful act, discreetly. My only quibble was: the wrong man had been murdered. If *only* it could have been Strad. The article made me realize I could kill him myself."

"You're crazy," Jack says.

"Ever since I was kept in that coffin for three days, I've had a lust for vengeance. I never talked about it and never acted on it, but I can't stand seeing bad guys get away with stuff, especially if a friend of mine is being hurt."

"You're psychologically broken, like one of your pots," Jack says. "You try to make yourself appear whole and sane, but you're not."

Penelope goes on. "I knew that killing Strad would probably ruin my life, probably get me arrested, possibly even killed. But I felt I had nothing to lose, that I was a total failure, lacking any talent, so why not sacrifice myself by doing something noble and selfless? My own life was worthless—I'd be putting it to good use. I felt that if Strad were dead, Lily's life would be saved, or at least her happiness would be saved, which, in my opinion, amounts to almost the same thing."

"You're a lunatic," Jack says.

Teeth clenched, Georgia says, "Shut up, Jack. We know. Let her finish."

Penelope continues: "I wasn't very comfortable with the idea of killing someone, even though I was determined to try. I had an easier time accepting the idea if I put time parameters on it and pushed it far into the future, so I could get used to it. I decided that if Lily was still miserable over Strad in two years, I would attempt to kill him between the hours of eight p.m. and midnight, on one particular day, and I picked the day randomly, October 27th, which was a little over two years away."

Lily says, "If it's really true that you didn't kill that guy from the bar, why would you tell Gabriel that you did?"

"I'm getting to that," Penelope says, gathering her thoughts and her strength before continuing. "Gabriel kept talking of killing himself. I desperately wanted to tell you guys of his frame of mind so that you could help me help him, but he'd made me promise not to tell. I did all I could to be comforting, caring, everything one's supposed to be. It made no difference. So finally, one day, out of frustration, I decided to reveal to him my plan to kill Strad. I hoped it would freak him out and make him want to stay alive to stop me. He didn't believe me at all, of course, which was something I'd expected, so I showed him the article about the first man's murder and claimed I was the one who'd killed him and that now I was going to do the same thing to Strad. That cinched it. He believed me then. But it wasn't enough to make him want to live."

We ask her a few more questions, but finally take pity on her. She looks exhausted. I fetch her a glass of water.

She says, "Barb, there's something you need to know. Gabriel saw a psychiatrist who told him he was clinically depressed and that all signs pointed to the likelihood that it was biological, not due to external circumstances such as his unrequited love for you. But Gabriel refused to take antidepressants. He thought it was just his love for you that was ruining his life. The shrink told him that was very unlikely, that even if you had loved him back he probably would still have been depressed and would simply have assumed the reason for his depression was some other frustration in his life. I believe the shrink. I'm convinced Gabriel had a mood disorder and couldn't have been happy for any length of time unless treated."

I feel my throat clenching with emotion.

Georgia comes over and squeezes my shoulder affectionately. "See, you shouldn't have thought his suicide was your fault," she says.

Lily and Jack chime in, expressing their support of this view. I nod, blinking back tears.

A FEW DAYS later, Lily calls and asks if she can stop by because she wants to give me something.

When she arrives, she hands me a CD and says, "I hesitated for a long time . . . but finally I made this music for you. It'll work only for you. It's not something that most people should have. But in your case, maybe it'll help."

"What is it?" I ask.

"You seem unable to tolerate the blindness which we—as human beings—all have." She pauses. "This music will enable you to know people's true feelings. It'll allow you to see into their hearts. Use it sparingly. Use it on Peter. Next time you're alone with him, play this piece. Then you'll know how he truly feels about you. And you'll know what path to take."

TWO DAYS LATER, Peter and I are in my living room, sitting on my couch, chatting. I cherish his dwindling visits.

The time has come. I get up and go to my stereo.

My heart pounding, I open the unlabeled CD case Lily gave me. I put the disk in the player. I stare at the Play button, my finger hovering over it. I wonder what the music will sound like, and what it'll reveal.

And that's when something incredible happens: I realize I already know—not what it will sound like, but what it will reveal. For the first time, something in me unblocks and I feel it, I know it—his love for me and the nature of it. And I realize I've known it all along, on some deep level, but just hadn't known how to recognize it. It took being on the verge of discovering the truth to perceive it was already in me.

"What are you doing?" Peter inquires.

I turn toward him.

"Are you going to play a CD?" he asks.

"I don't think so."

I go back to the couch and sit next to him, close. He's following my every move and puts down his glass. I lean toward him and we kiss for the first time. He seems hardly to believe it. He responds passionately.

I give myself to him, abandoning all reservations, all doubts. Perhaps tomorrow, I will have doubts again. But not now. If tomorrow I doubt, I can press Play.

BUT THE NEXT day, I don't press Play. And the day after that, I don't press Play.

ON THE FOURTH day, I get a visitor. It's Derek Pearce, Lily's old, persistent schoolmate. He's here because when he phoned me yesterday asking me yet again for her number, and I asked him yet again why he needed to reach her, he said, "Please don't ask me to tell you."

I replied, "Then please don't ask me for her phone number."

As I was about to hang up, he said, "Wait. Okay, I'll tell you. But I can't just blurt it out over the phone; it's too awkward. Could I meet you to make my case in person? Five minutes is all I need. I'd be so grateful."

I caved in.

When he arrives, I realize right away that I've seen him

before. Two things make him memorable. He's strikingly handsome. And he played in the same recital as Lily a couple of years ago and was in fact the performer whose music Strad had admired so much, describing it as "music that beautifies the world"—those fateful words that led Lily to her path of unimaginable musical powers.

When Derek tells me that his very important reason for wanting to see Lily is "I like her very much," I'm annoyed to no end that this ridiculously good-looking guy, who I'm sure didn't give her the time of day back in school, is now seeking her out.

Feeling protective of her, I'm getting ready to dismiss him.

"The fact is," he adds, "I would like to ask her to have dinner with me, to see if we might hit it off."

"Why now? Why didn't you ask her to dinner when you were in school?"

"Because I was in a serious relationship then. It only just ended recently."

"How convenient. If you date her now, you'll have all the perks of her fame, which I'm sure will be very useful to you."

He looks aghast. "The timing is a coincidence. If I'd been single back in school, I would have asked her to dinner then. Even though I hardly knew her, I found her extremely appealing. I feel like an idiot explaining myself to you." He huffs and looks down at the floor. "I always had it in the back of my mind that if I was ever single again, she was the one person I would want to get to know better."

I've been far too disenchanted too many times to believe a word he's saying. So I reply, "I'm sorry. We're not allowed to give her number to anyone, including old friends. Strict instructions. No exceptions."

After a moment of stunned silence, he nods sadly and takes out a piece of paper on which he scribbles his name and phone number. He puts it on my ottoman cube and says, "Please give her this and tell her I'd be very happy to hear from her if she wants to call me."

"I sure will!" I snap. "But don't hold your breath. I've already given her your number all those other times you've given it to me, and she's not calling anyone."

"Okay, I understand." He thanks me for the meeting and heads for the door.

As he's about to leave, I say, "Wait."

He turns around.

I go to my stereo and press Play—not so much to test Derek as to witness his worthlessness. I need to be thorough for Lily's sake and for my own peace of mind.

As soon as the music starts, I blink, taken aback. Like a strong gust of wind from a suddenly opened door, the truth hurls itself at me. I see such honesty and power in his soul, such genuine love for Lily in his heart, I can hardly believe it. His feelings for her are not only real, they are old, just as he claimed. They are not yet very deep, because he hardly knows her, but they are pure.

"That's a beautiful piece," he says. "I've never heard it before, though it's obviously by Lily. Her music is unmistakable. I could listen to it all the time."

I nod, too moved to speak. Finally, I manage to say, "Her number. Are you ready?"

He flips open his notebook, surprised, and I give him Lily's number.

"Thank you so much," he says. "I really appreciate it."

I nod.

He heads back to the door.

Suddenly, I know what will happen. His beauty will blind Lily, just as it blinded me when he first arrived a few minutes ago. She'll see nothing else about him—not his decency, not his gentleness, not his goodness. She'll assume his interest in her can only be corrupt. And she'll dismiss him without giving him a chance.

"Wait," I say again, softly.

He turns and looks at me.

"When you call her, don't tell her who you are. Just say I gave you her number."

He doesn't respond.

I go to the far end of my living room. "Let me also give you this." I unhook from the wall my most darkly beautiful, mysterious mask.

I bring it to him. "Wear it when you're with her. At least the first few times."

He takes the mask and looks at it, perplexed. "Why don't you want her to see me?"

I smile. "On the contrary. I do."

THE END

Acknowledgments

I would like to thank my brilliant editor, Jill Bialosky, and my extraordinary agent, Melanie Jackson, for their advice, support, and enthusiasm.

For their encouragement, thoughtfulness, and, in some cases, help with special expertise, I am grateful to Sondra Peterson, Daniel Filipacchi, Katherine J. Chen, Rebecca Schultz, Martine Bellen, Allegra Huston, Louise Brockett, Angie Shih, Jennifer Cohen, Shelley Griffin, Kathleen Patrick Bosman, Bruce Champagne, Régis Pagniez, the team at Norton, and, everlastingly, to Richard Hine.